BEAUTY & THE BEAST

GEORGIA LE CARRE

ACKNOWLEDGEMENTS

Much love and many thanks to:

Elizabeth Burns
Nichola Rhead
Brittany Urbaniak
Kirstine Moran
Tracy Gray

Beauty & The Beast

Copyright © 2020 by Georgia Le Carre

ISBN: 978-1-910575-77-2

CHAPTER 1

LUCA

https://www.youtube.com/watch?v=8AHCfZTRGiI
-Hurt-

*J*t was a beautiful winter night, but I hardly noticed it. I had no time for things like that anymore.

Lately, I'd even lost interest in women. Sure, I slept with them, but I kept it as anonymous as possible. They were bodies I pumped into and discarded in hotel rooms after I'd satisfied my needs. Every one of them was picked for her beauty and nothing more. Sometimes when they began to talk I had to bite back the desire to tell them to shut the fuck up.

Sometimes I looked in the mirror and I couldn't recognize the cold, heartless monster I saw. His eyes were like morgues filled with the frozen bodies of all the men he'd put to death.

I had become my father.

He was a great dad to my brother and I, but you couldn't run a business like ours and be anything else. It was a ruthless business. You had to be prepared at all times to kill or be killed.

From where I was sitting in the summerhouse, I could hear the sounds of the party floating from the big house. It was a boring gathering of low-lives and their broads. I didn't even know why I came. This had stopped being my scene a long time ago. After this cigarette, I planned on leaving through a garden gate I'd noticed on my way out here.

I put out the cigarette under my heel, and as I lifted my head I saw a woman in a white, short dress heading towards the summerhouse. It was a crisp cold night and she wore no coat. Something about the way she moved made me watch her. Even in the near darkness I could tell she was very young. Early twenties, perhaps. Her hair was blonde and she had incredible legs. Long and shapely. As she opened the door of the summerhouse I caught a glimpse of her mouth. It was the sexiest thing I'd ever seen.

My cock stirred. It wanted to be in that mouth.

She closed the door and leaned against it. Quickly, she pulled a phone out of her purse.

"Mariam," she said urgently. "Is Dad okay?"

She listened to the reply and almost sagged with relief.

"Thank God. It was just a false alarm, then."

From the light of her phone I could make out her head nodding to whatever was being said to her.

"Me? I'm fine. Of course, I'm fine. Is it okay if I come around to see him tomorrow?"

There was quiet as she listened, then she said, "Yes, five o'clock is fine. Please tell him I love him very much."

She ended the call suddenly, just as a small, choking sob escaped out of her. She pressed her hand to her mouth as if to stop more from coming out. With great interest I watched her take deep breaths to calm herself down.

"It's going to be okay," she whispered to herself. "Everything is going to be just fine."

From far away a man's voice called out and she froze. Her whole body went still. The man's voice came closer. From my position by the window I could see him coming towards us. It was too dark to make him out properly, but I thought I recognized his voice.

"Skye," he called.

She opened the door and went out. "I'm here."

"What are you doing there?" he asked.

"Nothing. Just wanted to take a break from the noise."

"Come back to the party, baby. I'm missing you."

She didn't answer.

They started walking towards the house together. He had his arm around her waist. Her hands hung limply at her sides. As I watched he let his hand drop down to her ass, caress it, then grabbed it roughly, greedily. She did nothing.

Inside me something came alive. Like a reptile that had been slumbering for many, many years. It opened its eyes, scented prey nearby, and began to move its cold-blooded body towards the warm, breathing thing. It remembered it had not eaten for a long time. And it was hungry. Very, very hungry.

I uncoiled myself from the rattan chair I was sitting on and sauntered towards the party.

I was in no hurry.

I knew exactly who the man was and exactly how to handle a man like him.

CHAPTER 2

SKYE

https://www.youtube.com/watch?v=RrxePKps87k
-Red Right Hand-

I could feel his dirty hand grabbing my butt, kneading it as if it was dough. God, how I hated him.

A long night lay ahead of me. Judging from the way his top lip kept sticking to his teeth he had obviously snorted a lot of coke in the toilets, and whenever he did that he wanted to go all night.

A shudder went through me when I thought about his sweaty body on top of me. I was so desperate to invent an excuse, and for an insane second I even contemplated breaking my ankle on the steps leading up to the house. The pain would be worth it. But knowing him he would callously ask in that grating way of his, 'your pussy is not broken, is it baby?'

"Come on," he urged as he pulled me up the steps of the house. "I want you to blow me off in the toilet."

I forced myself not to jerk away from him in revulsion. I pushed down the blind rage I felt inside and answered him as calmly as I could. "Can we wait until we get back to your house, Salvatore? I have a headache. I need to take a couple of tablets now, but I'll be good to go in an hour."

He stopped and looked at me, a sly expression on his face. "You seem to be getting a lot of headaches these days."

I took a step away from him and his hand fell off my body. "I guess I worry about my father too much. I think he might need more tests done again."

His eyes narrowed. "Are you asking for more money?"

I shook my head. "No, I'm just telling you why I'm worried."

"Good. Because I have no intention of giving more when I haven't even been paid back for what I gave the last time."

That made my dam of fury burst. "Actually, you have. Our agreement was for one month and you've dragged it out to more than two now. When is this arrangement going to be over, Salvatore?"

"I never said the arrangement was for one month. I said, it usually takes a month for me to get bored of a woman. You assumed it would take a month for me to get bored with you. I'm not bored with you yet."

I swallowed the bile that rose up my throat at his words.

He had tricked me into becoming his sexual slave indefinitely, and I knew it was my fault. I should have got a contract drawn up, put something down on paper, but I was so desperate to get the $120,000 for my father's treatment.

When the owner of the Italian restaurant where I worked said he didn't have the kind of money I was asking to loan from him, I had asked him to help me locate a loan shark. He told me a loan shark would be sheer madness since I would never be able to pay back the loan in time. He suggested asking his friend Salvatore who sometimes gave out loans and was kinder about the repayment time frame.

Salvatore, it turned out, had a different payback method in mind. He wanted me to be his mistress for one month. In fact, he reckoned, most probably he would need me for even less time than that, since he was easily bored and liked to change women more often than he changed his shirts.

I didn't even have to think about it. I agreed immediately. My father's life hung on the balance and nothing was more important than saving him. And because my boss had said Salvatore was a friend it never crossed my mind that Salvatore would cheat me.

I could almost bear it during the first month, when I could count the days when it would be over, but now that the end was no longer in sight, I actually felt physically ill at the thought of going to bed with him. Especially, as I had begun to notice recently that his sexual demands were slowly but surely taking a nasty twist. The other day he shocked me by talking about branding me with a hot iron, or getting his name tattooed on both my breasts.

The freezing cold night air was making goosebumps rise on my arms and I folded them around my waist and tried to keep my voice level. "When do you expect to get bored, Salvatore?"

He smiled that sly smile again and let his hand sweep down in front of my body. "I don't know. I mean what man can be bored with all this beauty? Because you are one smoking hot beauty, Skye baby."

My hands clenched. "You have to give me a date, Salvatore. I can't go on like this forever."

He chuckled. "You know what's wrong with you? You're too uptight. You need a drink."

"Please, Salvatore," I begged, my voice breaking. "I just can't go on like this-"

"Hey… what's all this about? I'm good to you, no? I bring you to nice parties. I don't beat you up. I buy you expensive dresses. Hell, I treat you like a queen."

I gritted my teeth. "I know you're a good man, and I know you treat me well, really well, but our arrangement was for one month, and it's two months and five days now. I need it to end."

He shrugged. "Why?"

"Because I want to be free again," I cried passionately.

He threw his hands in the air in a gesture of incomprehension. "You are free."

"But I'm not, am I? I have to come to your house whenever you call me, which is almost every night."

"How is that a bad thing? You enjoy the sex. I make you come." His voice was slippery.

I felt like I was hitting my head on a brick wall. My head was already a bloody pulp and there he was so confident and sure of his right to use me until the day he got bored. I had tried everything. Flattery, anger (which had backfired spectacularly), reluctance (which he enjoyed tremendously), coldness (also a turn-on for him). The only thing I hadn't tried yet was brutal honestly.

I looked him in the eye. "I don't enjoy sex with you. I've never come with you."

His eyes changed. Became black with fury. For the first time, I saw that I'd got him where it hurt, but he recovered quickly.

"You know what I thought when I first saw you. I thought that's a mouth that's been made to suck cock. You're a whore, Skye baby. Just a whore. I didn't go looking for you. You came to me and offered yourself for money. And now that you've had the money you're trying to worm your way out of it. Well, we have a deal. I get to use you until I'm bored. I'm not bored. So what do you want to do? But before you reply, think carefully, because I already told you once what happens to people who renege on their promises to me. The people they love most get hurt."

I dropped my head in defeat. I felt cold inside. No matter what I said or did, we always ended up at this impasse. I wanted to run away. I wanted to stick a knife in his miserable heart. I didn't know what to do. A little voice inside me said, 'Just stick it out, Skye. He will get bored. The more passion you show him the more he will want to keep you. Be cold. Be passionless.'

"I helped you when no one else would. A bit of gratitude would be nice."

I knew it was going to be a very long night. I was going to be punished for my honesty. This time I had wounded him and he was not going to let me get away with it. I needed to numb the pain that was coming. I raised my head.

"Yes, I will have that drink," I said slowly. My voice sounded hollow, as empty as I felt inside.

"Good. Have a few. It might cure that headache of yours because tonight I am going to make you enjoy sex with me. I am not going to stop until you come."

He slid open the French doors and I stepped into the warmth of the house. As he closed the doors I began to walk quickly towards the main living room where the party was in full swing. The sounds of their laughter washed over me and I felt like a caged animal. I arrived at the entrance to the large room and my gaze moved desperately around in search of a drink. A big, stiff drink that would make me feel numb and prepare me for the ordeal that stretched before me.

I didn't find that drink I was looking for.

Instead, my gaze collided with that of a tall man with raven hair. His eyes were so light they shocked me. For a few seconds, I couldn't move. Frozen, I stared into those icy gray depths. It was like looking into the eyes of a predator. No pity. No sense of right or wrong. No emotion. Nothing but razor sharp focus.

I recognized him. I'd read and heard about him. Who hadn't? But I'd never seen him in person before. Inside me something was happening. The only way I could describe it would be like watching one of those time-lapse videos of a seed rooting, then growing into a plant that opens into a gorgeous flower.

I knew what Salvatore was by looking into his eyes. He was a slimy, small-minded, dime-a-dozen crook, pretending to be a big-time mobster. When I looked into this man's eyes I knew exactly what he was.

A beast with a heart of stone.

CHAPTER 3

LUCA

https://www.youtube.com/watch?v=EPo5wWmKEaI
-Give Me Everything Tonight-

*U*nder the bright lights of the chandelier her blonde hair shimmered. She was far more beautiful than I had imagined. An angel made for sin.

I stared at her until our eyes met. I knew the effect I had on women when I looked at them the way I was looking at her, and like a little deer in headlights she froze with shock.

I felt it then. The strong urge to open those long, long legs and fuck her until she screamed. Yes, once would not be enough with this one.

Satisfied with my decision to have her, I let my gaze slide away from her and to the man coming up behind her. Ah yes, I remembered him clearly now. As he arrived next to her, he said something to her which she didn't respond to. I started walking towards the happy couple. When I stood in front of them he looked up, saw me, and nearly jumped out of his skin.

"Don Messana!" he blurted out, his eyes bulging with surprise.

"Salvatore," I acknowledged quietly.

His astonishment was almost comical. "You know who I am?"

"I never forget a face or a name. You were pointed out to me at Garibaldi's funeral five years ago. You used to do some work for him, didn't you?"

His whole face lit up. "Yes, yes, that is completely correct. But this is totally amazing. I never knew you were even aware of my existence. It makes me very happy. Very happy indeed to know that Don Messana knows me. If there is anyway at all I can be of service to you, please, please, let me know and I will be more than happy to do it."

I allowed one corner of my lips to drift upwards. "Hmm... perhaps there is something you can do for me."

He beamed happily. "That is wonderful. Just wonderful. I would love to help you in any way I can."

Garibaldi was right, he was pretty pathetic. "Will you join me for a drink?"

"Of course. Of course," he cried eagerly. "That would be absolutely marvelous."

"Good. Let's have it in Soleiman's study. I believe he keeps his best whiskey there."

"Oh yes." He turned to the woman. "Wait here for me, Skye. I'll be back when I'm finished with the Don."

I didn't look at her, but from my peripheral vision I knew her reply had been a wooden nod.

"Let her come," I said softly.

"Oh no, she will be bored with men's talk," he said quickly.

I turned to her and let her have the full force of my gaze. "Will you?"

"I... I... yes, I mean... no," she said in confusion.

I let my eyes gaze away from her mouth and returned it to the joker in front of me. "There you go. She won't be bored."

He forced a smile. "Of course, Skye can come with us."

"This way." I turned and led the way towards Soleiman's study. I knew he wouldn't mind if I used it, or even finished his rare whiskey. I opened the door and switched on the lights. One wall of the very large room was lined with shelves that were filled with leather-bound books. The books went all the way up to the ceiling. There was a big antique desk in front of the window and a nest of black leather sofas in one corner.

I waved my hand towards the sofas as I walked towards the mini-bar. "Take a seat."

I poured out three generous measures of Soleiman's best whiskey into some crystal tumblers and carried them towards the sofas. Salvatore immediately jumped up, as if sitting while I was standing was a direct affront to me.

"Sit," I said. His eagerness to please was beginning to grate.

14

And he dropped back down to the sofa. I handed a glass to Skye. Deliberately I let our fingers touch. She jerked back as if I had burned her, her eyes flying upwards to meet mine. Hers were wide and surprised and her cheeks were pink with color. So, we were on the same page.

"Thank you," she whispered, dropping her gaze hurriedly.

I put Salvatore's glass on the coffee table and lowered myself onto the sofa opposite him. I raised my glass. "To good times."

"To good times," both Skye and he echoed.

I leaned back and took a sip.

"Whoa! This is great whiskey," Salvatore opinioned.

It was at that point I decided I couldn't bear another second of his company. "I want your woman," I said bluntly.

Skye gasped with shock, and Salvatore choked on his whiskey.

"Sorry," he spluttered.

"You heard me." My voice was cold.

For a second he seemed totally bewildered. He looked at me, then at Skye, then back at me. He opened his mouth, closed it, and opened it again like a tiny-brained fish. Then he swallowed so hard, his Adam's apple bobbed. Sweat began to bead his forehead.

I waited.

The silence in the room became so deep I could hear the woman breathing. Fast and shallow. Like a little creature that had been running for a very long time from a predator and finally, at the cliff edge, when running was no longer an option, turned around to confront its enemy. It knew it was doomed, but it was not going to give up. It was going to fight to the death.

I never looked at her. I kept my eyes on Salvatore. He didn't look at the woman either. Instead he looked down at his clasped hands. I stared at him curiously as he fought a lost battle. He didn't want to give the woman up, but the lure of working for me was too much.

"Of course. It will be an honor," he mumbled finally.

"You have made a wise decision. Someone will contact you in the morning with an... opportunity."

"Thank you. Thank you so much. I will look forward to his visit and proposal."

"You may go now."

He shot to his feet. "Have a good night, Don Messana."

I nodded. "I will."

At my words, his whole face turned red. I had not thought it possible, but he must care for the woman. As he turned and started towards the door I shifted my attention to the woman. Her face was as white as a sheet and that delectable mouth was trembling.

Fury or fear. I didn't know and didn't care.

CHAPTER 4

SKYE

https://www.youtube.com/watch?v=DUT5rEU6pqM

"I'm not a whore," I said, but I was in such a state of surreal disbelief my voice came out in an unrecognizable hoarse whisper. Never in my life had I been passed from one man to another like this. With me present but having had no say in the decision. As if I was without consequence. Or even a thing.

"I know you're not," he said quietly. "But as you clearly detest him, and you need money to pay for your father's medical bills I'd have thought you'd jump at the chance to kill two birds with one stone."

I leaned forward, my eyes wide with shock and disbelief. "How do you know I need money for my father?"

He shrugged casually. "I was enjoying a cigarette in the summerhouse when you came in and made your phone call."

"Oh." I was too astonished to think properly. I shook my head to clear it. He was inside that summerhouse at the bottom of the garden. I had gone there for just one moment of refuge and he was there. He had seen me when I thought I was alone, and let my heartbreak show. I felt violated. I took a deep breath. "So," my voice was trembling with fury. "I have no choice. I'm just supposed to come with you tonight and be your mistress instead of his."

"No," he said calmly, "you have choices. If you don't come with me tonight, Salvatore will understandably, and judging by his reluctance to let you go, quickly lay claim on you again."

The spectacular anger I felt towards him because he had coldly watched me at my most vulnerable and decided to take advantage of it collapsed into a shapeless lump. I couldn't hold back the shudder of revulsion at the prospect of going back to Salvatore.

"You will be compensated financially," he added softly.

"What is the matter with all of you?" I exploded bitterly. "Can none of you find a woman without having to buy her?"

He smiled, if that could even be called a smile. It was a humorless twist of his lips. "Buying women is my preference. It keeps the transaction smooth and unemotional. Both parties understand exactly what is on offer."

"That is horrible," I gasped in disgust.

He was utterly and totally unmoved by my condemnation. "Here's the deal. Take it or leave it. I will pay for all of your father's medical bills until he is given a clean bill of health. In return you will be my mistress for a month."

Oh, not that again. I was not going to be cheated with that one-month bargain again. "Where have I heard that crock of crap before?" I asked sarcastically.

He frowned.

The action made him look so forbidding, I felt a frisson of fear run up my spine, but I was too far gone to stop. There was a month and five days' worth of rage inside me. "You take advantage of women who are desperate for money with your offers of 'I want your body for a month' and then you just keep on moving the goalposts. A month becomes two and three and—"

I stopped suddenly at the cold fury that filled his eyes.

His voice was deceptively calm, silky even. "If we are going to get on, Skye, then you must remember one thing. Never put me in the same category as that hustler you were with. Yes, you are beautiful, but no more than some others I have had. I can assure you I will not require you for more than a month. As a matter of fact, you will have a written contract of our agreement."

I stilled. "A written contract."

He nodded. "You will also have to sign an NDA that prevents you from ever revealing to anyone, anywhere, anything about me, our relationship, or what you see or hear in my household during the time you are in my employ."

In his employ. Wow! No bells or whistles there. He was hiring me for sex. A body to slake his lust. He sure knew how to make someone feel really small and insignificant. But in a way it was better. When Salvatore used to call me baby, I wanted to throw boiling water in his face. I was not his baby.

He didn't care about how I felt. He was using my body against my will.

I dropped my head and tried my best to clear the fog in my brain. What were my choices? Let Salvatore swoop down on me again. Ugh... I'd rather die.

I raised my head and looked into those dangerous eyes watching me. Set against the charcoal eyelashes the irises were so light they looked like a wolf's eyes. The grainy long-lens photos I'd seen of him in magazines did not do him any justice. For a few seconds, I stared into those amazing eyes, intrigued by how beautiful they really were. Not beautiful like a wonderful tropical sunset, or a perfectly formed flower, but beautiful like a highly-colored poisonous snake.

Then my gaze dropped to the white scar running down his left cheek. Were the rumors true? Was it from a tiger's claws? Probably not. He was so elusive most people didn't even know what he looked like. My fingers itched to run down the raised, shiny skin, but of course, I did no such thing.

His nose was proud and aristocratic. Reminiscent of those marble statues from ancient Rome with their perfectly flared nostrils. I let my gaze move lower down his face. If not for his mouth, his face would have been unbearably cruel. His mouth alone made him human. The lips, full and sensuous, especially the bottom one. I could almost imagine how soft it would be if I went over and kissed him. Obviously, I had no intention of doing anything of the sort.

My gaze travelled down to that strong jaw. So perfectly masculine it should have belonged on a photo-shopped magazine spread. I let my eyes follow that smooth line down to the golden-brown column of his throat. Thick, raven hair grazed the crisp white collar of his shirt.

I followed the broad shoulder of his flawlessly cut suit jacket down his arms all the way to his hands. One big hand lay lightly curled and relaxed on his thigh and the other was cradling his drink. My eyes moved on from the powerful muscles showing under the stretched material of his pants upwards. To the bulge between his legs.

For a second I stopped and stared. Inside me, I tried to arouse the instinctive revulsion I'd felt the first time Salvatore had touched me, but there was nothing. I was quite numb. I let my eyes rise up the belt, up the shirt, and back to those merciless eyes.

"What's it to be?" he asked.

"You will pay my father's medical bills until he is completely better?"

"Yes."

"Even if it costs hundreds of thousands of dollars?"

"Yes."

"I will have that in writing?"

"Of course."

I felt my whole body go limp with relief. Would my father finally be cured?

"Are you on the pill?"

"Yes, I am, but we have to use condoms."

He shook his head. "You will have to undergo some tests. Once the results come back if you are clean we will not use them."

"What if you are the one with the STD? Will you take the tests too?"

His lips twisted. "I've kept myself disease free and you'll just have to take my word for it."

Even though he'd refused to take the test, the fact that he needed me to take one before he would sleep with me meant he was extremely careful about his sexual health. It all just sounded too good to be true. Why would a man like him pay that much just to have a woman like me? Especially, as he'd said, he'd had other more beautiful women than me. There had to be a catch and I suddenly thought I knew what it would be.

Everything about him gave the promise of ruthless brutality. Once when he looked down the sooty thickness of his lashes against his cheek seemed to soften the severity of face, almost giving the illusion that perhaps he wasn't dangerous. However, when he looked up again and stared straight at me, the light, almost translucent grey of his eyes was piercing enough to make a shiver run through me.

I swallowed hard. "Will I have to do anything kinky?"

He shook his head. "You won't have to do anything you don't want to."

"I don't want to sleep with you," I couldn't help shooting back.

His watchful expression didn't change at all. "Are you sure about that, Skye?"

I felt heat rush up my face as I lied to him. "Yes."

One eyebrow rose sardonically. "Prove it."

"W-what?" I stammered in shock.

"Come here and prove it," he taunted softly.

CHAPTER 5

SKYE

https://www.youtube.com/watch?v=SwYN7mTi6HM
-Go Ahed And Jump-

*H*e remained still, but his pupils grew. Hypnotized, I stared into their bottomless depths. Looking into them was like nothing I'd ever experienced. Then without warning, the atmosphere in the room changed. The air became thick and charged. My skin tingled with electricity. Something began to slither inside my belly. A need. It was irresistible. It wanted me to go over and... oh God, mate with him. To my shock I became wet for him.

At that moment nothing else existed, but my clawing need for that cold, calculating monster.

I wanted to tell him to fuck off, or stand and tell him to keep his damn money... but I couldn't move, couldn't think, couldn't even breathe. The breath had been sucked out of my body. I could only stare in utter shock.

"I'll let this one pass, but no more lies," he murmured.

I felt my hands clench, but I nodded automatically, dumbly. What the hell just happened?

"Are you ready to go?"

I nodded again, but I did not rise. I was not sure my legs were strong enough. I reached for the glass of whiskey, and downed the bronze liquid in one go. Whiskey was not my thing, but the fire running down my throat was welcome. It reached my stomach and radiated heat into my confused, stunned cells. I put the glass back down and found him watching me. There was cold amusement in his eyes.

"You don't like whiskey," he observed.

I frowned. "Why do you say that?"

"Just an instinct."

I touched my hair self-consciously and something shifted in those startlingly light eyes. He reached out and I froze. Then his warm hand was curling around my upper arm. He turned it slightly so the soft inner side of my arm was exposed. I glanced down at my arm to see what he was looking at and saw the four bluish marks Salvatore had left when he grabbed me hard the night before. He had not been truly rough. I just bruised easily. There were more on my hips, and inner thighs where he had been truly rough.

Our eyes met. Neither of us spoke, then he let go of my arm, leaned back, and regarded me calmly.

"Take your phone out and text me your full name and address."

"Why?"

"My solicitor will need the information to draw up the necessary contracts."

"Oh, okay."

He continued staring at me.

"You want me to do it right now?"

"Yeah."

Great. That was all that was missing from my life. A man of few words. I fumbled with my purse, opened the flap, and fished out my phone. He called out his number and I texted him my last name and address.

"What should I call you?" I asked.

"Luca," he said simply.

When his phone pinged from inside his jacket pocket, he rose.

"Let's go. I've got a long night ahead of me."

I stood and together we walked to the door. There was at least a foot between us, but I could feel the power and energy emanating from his lean, but tightly muscled body.

He pulled the door open and held it for me. I walked through and we travelled silently through the long corridor towards the party. As we got closer the sounds of music and people began to filter into the corridor. As we arrived at the entrance of the main room I saw many heads turning to look at us. First, they looked at the Don, then at me, then back to him.

I couldn't help it. My gaze looked for the man in the electric blue suit. Salvatore was standing by a pillar. There was a drink in his hand and he was staring at me with a strange expression in his face. It was clear he was not happy.

I thought about how happy he had been that he had managed to snag an invitation to this party. How he had boasted it would be filled with rich and powerful people. That he was rising on the ladder of success to be even considered good enough to be invited.

Well, he got his wish. He was now going to be offered an opportunity of a lifetime.

I felt Luca's hand touch the small of my back. It was only a light touch, but it was full of possession. I saw the flash of jealousy that crossed Salvatore's face before he concealed it. He must have thought he'd keep me for a long, long time and now I had been snatched away from him by a bigger predator. I felt a great relief wash over me. Without the Don's intervention tonight God only knew how long he would have held me trapped in his ownership. Silently, I sent a prayer to God.

Please God, protect me. Don't let it be that I jumped from the frying pan into the fire.

Keeping my face expressionless, I turned my eyes away from Salvatore, and looked towards the arch that led to the foyer of the house. I never wanted to see him again.

CHAPTER 6

SKYE

*A*s we reached the arch, a man whom Salvatore had introduced as the host, approached us. He glanced at me, and showed a microsecond of surprise to see me leaving with Don Luca, before his face was wreathed in a big smile as he gave his whole attention to the Don.

"You are leaving so soon?"

"I stayed far longer than I intended," Luca replied.

"I hope you enjoyed yourself."

"Far more than I thought I would," he replied cryptically.

The host laughed. "I am happy to hear that. Perhaps you will come again soon."

"I will see you on Thursday at the office."

"Of course. Have a good night."

"The same to you," Luca said formally, then his hand was guiding me towards the front door where a man was standing guard.

"Do you have a coat?" Luca asked me.

"Yes," I said and walked over to the hat check girl. I gave her my ticket and she came back with my aged green coat. Before I could take it from her and slip into it, Luca had taken it and was helping me into it. His warm fingers brushed my neck and I shivered.

The doorman nodded at us politely and opened the door.

A gust of cold wind blew into us as we stepped out into the night.

When we started to descend the steps, a man got out of the long black limo that was parked directly in front of us, and nodded politely at Luca. He was obviously Luca's chauffeur. Salvatore had parked his car further down on the driveway, but it seemed as if Luca Messana had been given the honor of being able to park his mode of transport right in front of the entrance.

"Home, Cullinan," Luca said shortly.

Cullinan, the chauffeur, was a thin man in his fifties or maybe even in his sixties. He had a stoic, distant expression on his face as he came around to hold open the door for me. Brand new, luxurious black leather waited for me inside.

For a moment I hesitated.

There would be no going back after this. I turned and looked at Luca. In the light from the overhead lamp, he looked almost sinister, the scar on his face, glowing livid, and yet that heat, that unnameable thing between us, sizzled in the cold air. He was not Salvatore. I never felt this with him.

This cold, heartless man had zero feelings for me beyond wanting me as a temporary toy to discard as soon as he was bored. But for me it was already different. Different than I had felt for any man I had ever come across before. I felt a cold finger of fear run up my spine. Some instinct told me to run away. Now. While there was still time. For this man would break me and I would never be the same again.

Then, an image of my father flashed into my head. Bald from the chemo and looking older than his years, his pale hands laying limply at his sides, but smiling bravely at me. I had known he wanted to say something to me, so I had bent my head towards his bloodless lips. "Don't worry about me. I'm just going where I belong, with your mother," he had whispered in my ear so my stepmother, who was standing by the door wouldn't hear.

"No, Daddy. It's not time for you to go. Mama can wait a little longer for you. Don't leave me now," I had whispered in his ear, my voice choked, and tears welling up in my eyes. At that moment, I had decided I would do everything in my power to keep him on this earth.

And I had. And not a single regret either.

I would do it all again for you, Dad. All of it. Even those unbearably long nights with Salvatore when I felt battered and bruised because he had tried and tried but couldn't come because he was too damn high.

It was easy to slip into the car and listen to the door seal my fate with a quiet click.

Seconds later, Luca entered the plush space. I turned to glance at him. In the dim of the interior, he seemed even more aloof and forbidding. The driver took his place and the car started. Almost immediately, I noticed the two cars that rode with us. One in front and the other behind.

"Can you amuse yourself for the next hour?" Luca asked.

"Of course," I replied woodenly.

He opened his laptop, and I turned my head and stared out of the window. I stared at the scenery and watched buildings become houses and houses become trees and countryside. Then finally, we arrived at a big set of black gates. Black lion statues sat on the pillars of the gates.

Of course, this was his house. Torrington Hall was one of the most famous houses in Boston. Once it had stood in England. Then a billionaire fell in love with it and decided to import it to the states. Every block of limestone, decorated tile, oak panel, and marble slab in it had been meticulously taken apart and put back together again in a vast estate he had purchased in the countryside. It had made the news two years prior when the billionaire who owned it sold it for sixty-two million to an opaque off-shore company.

Very bizarrely, I had once been so fascinated by it, I had even dreamed I was living in it. In my dream, I was Beauty from *Beauty and the Beast* and I was in its grand, tall-ceilinged dining room. I was sitting alone at a long dining table set for two. The room was lit by the many candles inside the many chandeliers and the great candelabras positioned around the room. I was dressed in a long white dress and my hair was done up in an old-fashioned style. It was as if I had gone back in time to a different century.

I knew I was waiting for Beast.

I could already hear his heavy steps thundering through the house, making even the floor quake with fear. In my dream, I felt no fear. Calmly, I stood and turned towards the entrance of the beautiful room. As the Beast's footsteps came nearer even the huge double doors started to shake.

Just as the golden handle turned, I suddenly woke up.

CHAPTER 7

SKYE

*A*nd now... here I was.

It was too surreal to believe I was at the house of my dreams until the limo rounded the unforgettable and massive fountain of a group of lions shooting water from their mouths, and stopped in front of its limestone steps.

My hands trembled slightly as the driver got out of his seat and came over to my side to pull the door open. His face was still and expressionless and his eyes did not meet mine. And yet I could feel the judgment in his body. I was there for his master's entertainment. Just a slut.

A wintry night breeze had picked up when I stepped down from the vehicle, I felt the cold rattle my bones. My old coat didn't have any pockets that I could hide my hands in so I held my hands behind my back, and followed Luca silently, in awe of my surroundings and the colossal wealth, beyond anything I could comprehend, that was necessary to own such a place.

The stunning mansion and its environs were generously lit. Rays of light shone from the buried lamps scattered amongst the surrounding shrubbery and dense trees. As we climbed the steps, I noticed the massive lion-head knocker. There were two lamps on either side of the great doors, and I noted that there was no switch for a bell, and decided that it was reasonable since only those granted access through its gates would be able to arrive before this door.

In seconds, the door was pulled open revealing a uniformed woman with a healthy amount of white in her dark chignon. She had a round face and a motherly figure, but her sharp gaze on me through round rimmed glasses was discomforting. She stepped aside so that we could come in.

"Melania, this is Skye. She will be staying for a month. Settle her in the Oyster room," Luca said.

"Yes, Sir," she replied immediately with a deeply respectful nod.

Without another word or glance at me Luca took his leave, and I was left standing in the midst of a gigantic foyer with a woman who very obviously disapproved of me.

"Follow me," she said coldly, and started walking away quickly.

My throat tightened with emotion because some small piece of me secretly knew and recognized that was what I had become, but I swallowed my feelings of despair. So what, if she and the driver thought I was a whore. Their condemnation changed nothing. They knew nothing of my circumstances. I was doing this for my father and nothing anyone said or did could change my mind or make me feel as if I was doing something wrong.

I caught up with her quickly and followed her ramrod straight back through wide hallways dotted with marble statues and walls decorated with huge chilling dark art until she opened a door and we reached a different section of the house. A much poorer section with plain walls and poorly lit, narrow corridors. It was also much colder here. We went up a wooden staircase and walked through another corridor so badly lit that my shoes caught on the edge of a strip of carpet.

At my gasp, she stopped and turned around to glare at me.

"Sorry," I whispered. I was no shrinking violet, but the things that had happened that night, meeting Luca, this intimidating house, her stern disapproval had all made me feel unsure of myself.

She turned around and continued on her way. Suddenly, she stopped and opened another door, and to my surprise we were back in the majestic part of the house. Halfway down the wide corridor full of doors, she turned the handle of one of the doors, and opened it.

I followed her into an absolutely stunning room and looked around me in awe. At the exquisite wallpaper, the wonderful huge bed full of snowy white pillows, the fairytale lead windows, the gorgeous velvet curtains. It was an almost magical room. When I was young, living in my tiny home, I would read fairy tales about princesses and always imagine rooms like these.

"This will be your room," she announced robotically.

I turned to look at her unsmiling face and it dawned on me then, she had deliberately taken me through the servants' quarters to demonstrate how lowly my position was.

"This way," she said, and proceeded towards a pink marble bathroom. There was a claw feet bath on a pedestal. I was so in love with it I could hardly pay attention to her as she explained how the shower and bath worked.

"The dressing room is through there," she said pointing to a door. Then she turned around and started walking back towards the room.

I followed her.

In the middle of the room she stopped and turned around to face me. She pointed towards a bell on the wall by the bed. "There's the service bell if you need anything. Press it and someone will come to you, or if you just have a query, you can pick up the phone and dial 9. You can have breakfast brought up to you here, or you can have it in the sun room. If you require a full cooked breakfast, please give us half-an-hour notice. Dinner is served at eight. Attire is formal. If you require nothing else, I bid you goodnight."

"I require nothing else," I said.

She nodded and withdrew from the room.

When the door closed the tension in my body snapped. I walked over to the bed and sat down on it. My finger stroked the rich damask bedspread. It felt cool and silky under my skin. It felt real. And yet... in a state of disbelief, I looked around me. Was this really happening to me? It felt like a dream. Utterly unreal. I stood and walked to the romantic windows.

My window faced the front of the house. Below I could see the lion fountain, and follow the line of lamps that lit the driveway, but most of the estate's grounds were shrouded by the darkness of the night. I turned my face towards the sky and found it full of twinkling stars.

Even though it was freezing outside, I opened a window and leaned out to look at them. For a second, I felt as if I was a charmed Princess in a fairytale. And just for that fleeting moment I forgot I was a bought woman. Then the enchanted air was shattered by the thunderous engine of a high-end sports car. Headlights appeared at the end of the driveway and instinctively, I pulled back, and stood hidden behind the curtain.

A canary yellow Lamborghini screamed to a stop in front of the stone steps. The driver's door floated up and rap music blared out. A balding, portly man, hopped out. He was wearing a blue shirt, and had his sweater slung flamboyantly around his shoulders the way men from the Mediterranean sometimes did. In his hand, he carried a large envelope. Nimbly, he ran up the stone steps and disappeared from my view.

Frigid winter wind blew into the room I was in, but I didn't move an inch.

I couldn't see her face, there was a young woman in the car, a redhead with very pale hands. I watched her change the channels of the stereo. She pulled down the visor mirror and applied lipstick. Then she examined her nails. Afterwards she pulled a small tube of cream from her purse and creamed her hands.

The man reappeared. The car door floated up once more. Pop music blared out. He got in and the car roared off. I realized the room was now freezing cold and I was shivering. I closed the window and went to sit on the bed and wait. There was a steel claw tightly furled around my heart.

I didn't have long to wait.

CHAPTER 8

LUCA

I pushed open the door to her room. The room was cold and the only illumination was the lamp by her bedside. Still wearing the same white dress she'd worn to the party, she perched on the edge of the bed. In yellow glow from the lamp, her blonde hair shimmered like spun gold. She seemed ethereal, almost unreal. I felt as if I'd snared an unsuspecting angel into my lair of sin.

I shut the door and leaned against it.

We stared at each other and I could feel the lust spreading through my veins. I couldn't remember the last time I'd felt this pure, visceral, uncontrollable lust for a woman. I was intrigued by the effect she had on me. I understood that it was not just her beauty. There was something about her… something I couldn't put my finger on. From the first moment I'd noticed her walking towards the summerhouse, even before I had seen her face properly, my attention had been arrested.

Yes, I wanted to listen to her scream as I brought her past the brink of sanity, her body quaking and shuddering at the storm of pleasure engulfing her, but it was more than that. I was already falling into the trap Salvatore had fallen into. I wanted to keep her, make her mine for a long, long time. I pulled back the thought. That was moth to flame stuff. No, she was here for a month and not a day longer, and whatever this 'fascination' was had to be completely and totally purged by then.

I straightened from the door and walked over to her. Stopping a couple of feet away from her I held out the thin sheaf of papers in my hand. She took them from me wordlessly and glanced at it.

"Ah, the contract… and NDA. So quickly," she murmured.

"Yes, I had my solicitor draw it up as we drove here. It's pretty standard stuff."

"Do you have a pen?" Her voice was small, defeated.

It made me angry. I didn't want her to be small and defeated. I wanted her to be wild and strong. "Don't you want to read it first?"

"Not really."

I frowned. "Haven't you learned anything from your dealings with Salvatore? Read the contract. It's only a page long. You can go through the NDA tomorrow."

"Okay," she said.

I brought my pen out of my pocket and handed it to her. Then I headed over to the velvet armchair that directly faced the bed and settled into it.

Silence descended upon the room as she went through the contract.

There wasn't a time in my past when I would have sat down to watch someone read a contract. I'd have been bored to tears, but I couldn't stop watching her. It seemed as if she wasn't quite reading the thing. Just letting random words jump out at her. She exhaled softly and lowered the documents to her lap. Then she uncapped my fountain pen and began to sign, date, and enter her address into all the places that required it.

A quiet excitement buzzed through my veins. Now she was mine.

When she was done, she placed the signed papers on the bed next to her and raised her eyes towards me.

"Let your hair loose," I said.

She lifted her arms to undo the pins that held up her hair and I saw again the ugly bruises the two-bit hustler had left on her skin. It made me angry. I examined the emotion curiously. Strange, anger was not an emotion I associated with women. Actually, other than the deep feelings I had for my mother, I never felt anything for the female species. Other than lust, of course.

Shiny blonde hair fell in a cascade down her shoulders and back. Her beauty took my breath away.

"Good. Now, strip," I ordered.

Her blue-eyed gaze collided with mine, and what I saw in them sent a powerful kick to my libido. I was used to timidity, flirtatiousness, eagerness to please, sometimes even fear in the women I took to bed, but never outright defiance and smoldering hate.

"Changed your mind, Skye?" I taunted, when I knew she had done nothing of the sort. She was so desperate to save her father and get out of Salvatore's clutches she would have sold herself to Shylock himself.

She didn't say a word. She didn't look away from me, and she didn't stand either when she hooked a hand under the thick strap of her white dress and let it slip off one shoulder. She was trying to make the strip as unsexy as possible. She had no idea. There was nothing she could have done to make this less sexy. The other strap followed, a couple of buttons at her side were unhooked, and the material slid down her torso.

She was wearing a nippleless lacy black bra. I knew instantly she would be wearing matching crotchless panties, and that the hustler had forced this unimaginative paraphernalia of a sexual slave on her. I let my eyes travel over her pink nipples and creamy skin and felt my dick hot and hard against my stomach.

She had to do a slight shimmy to get the dress off her hips and down to her knees. Then the dress slid down her legs and pooled at her feet. I saw more blue-black bruises on her hip which pissed me off. She sat in her matching slut's bra and panties and stared at me as though she was hoping I wouldn't ask her to go any further than this.

As if that were possible.

I always got my money's worth.

"Open your thighs. Wide," I commanded.

She pressed her lips together, looked away from me, and spread her legs. And I saw what I had stolen away from her captor. Both her inner thighs had ugly bruises, but inside the crotchless panties her pussy was young, freshly shaven, and sweetly pink. It looked like a fruit that had just been cut open to reveal the juicy insides. My mouth began to water.

"Take off the bra." I could hear the sexual tension in my voice. I was holding myself tightly in check. I wanted her on my face and rocking that pretty pussy into my mouth.

She reached behind her and pulled away the offensive garment. Her full, gorgeous breasts popped into view.

I stared at the erect mounds. The pale pink buds were flat and unaroused. I liked that. It aroused the hunter in me. I'd never had any woman so unaffected in my presence before.

Suddenly, she lifted her face to mine. There, exactly how I liked her. Defiance, hatred, and something else swirling between us. I could already feel her neat little pussy stretched tightly around my cock.

CHAPTER 9

SKYE

*I*t took everything I had to keep staring into the raw hunger in his piercing eyes. Thanks to the ridiculous panties Salvatore insisted I always wear I was basically naked. And my legs were open like a whore's, but I wouldn't give him the satisfaction of knowing how exposed, humiliated and vulnerable I felt at being treated like a piece of meat.

I stared at him defiantly until something strange happened, the feelings of shame and humiliation dissipated and were replaced by something else. Something that had never happened with Salvatore. I was becoming wildly aroused. The throbbing between my legs was becoming an unbearable ache. Even though I tried to damp it down, thick liquid started to ooze out of my sex. I wanted to clench my thighs together to hide the wetness, but I knew if I did I would only be calling attention to my own shameful lust.

Thank God, the room was lit by just the bedside lamp behind and to the left of me, and maybe, just maybe those translucent wolf's eyes could not see what was happening in the shadows between my legs.

He stood and I froze. I thought he was going to approach me, but he sauntered over to a bank of switches on the wall and turned one on.

"Damn you," I swore under my breath as I squinted in the harsh light that poured down on me. My only refuge was gone.

As my eyes adjusted I realized the light only illuminated the area I was sitting in. The rest of the room was still in the shadows. I could barely make him out anymore as he returned to the armchair and lowered himself lazily into it.

"Play with yourself, Skye. Make yourself come." It was a command, but it was strangely seductive.

I drew a sharp breath of shock. No one had ever asked me to masturbate while they sat in the shadows and watched. I didn't want to do it. The thought of letting myself go and climaxing in front of a fully clothed stranger made me shudder. But as if on autopilot my hand moved towards my sex to comply with that silky command. The willingness of my body to obey him, even against my will made me realize I had sold myself to the devil himself.

Gently, my fingers circled my clit.

"Finger fuck yourself," he called out from the darkness. There was something new and cruel in his voice. He didn't want softness. He wanted to keep it callous and unemotional. He wanted me to behave like a prostitute.

My teeth sank into my bottom lip to keep it from trembling, but I complied. I pushed two fingers into myself. The rough entry made a squelching sound, and an involuntary sound escaped from him.

That was the moment everything changed.

That was the moment I knew. I was not a pitiful creature he had bought. One who could be made to open her legs and treated like a whore. I had the same power Delilah had over the mighty Samson. One day I could get him to cut his hair.

And he knew it too.

I licked my lips and with my other hand I touched my nipple. I let my thumb flick at the swollen peak. In the shadows, I saw him stiffen. Moaning softly, I pinched my nipple and increased the speed of my fingers. I couldn't climax in this way, but this was not for me. This was to bring him to his knees.

Falling back on the bed I raised my legs in the air and slowly opened them into a big V. I stretched my legs as far as they would go, until they were almost touching the bed. Now he could see all of me. The slutty panties would even give him a view of my butthole. As I could no longer see his reactions I carried on fucking myself, I knew I had to be careful not to make my show last too long. I didn't want to bore him.

With a groan, I arched my back sensuously, clenched my body, and started to shake as I went into my big orgasm act. I'd gotten very good at it with Salvatore. It was a necessary evil. Sometimes it would cut the time he pumped into me by less than half.

When I finished my performance, I lay on the bed panting, my legs collapsed on the bed on either side of me. I knew his eyes were focused on me. I could feel them watching me. I didn't know what came next, but I imagined he would come over and have sex with me. It shouldn't have, but the thought of being under his strong, lean body excited me. Made my sex tingle.

For a few seconds there was silence in the room, then I heard the sound of clapping.

CHAPTER 10

LUCA

https://www.youtube.com/watch?v=1w7OgIMMRc4
-Sweet Child O' Mine-

I stopped clapping as she raised herself on one elbow to squint into the darkness. There was something arrestingly beautiful about the pose she had unconsciously adopted. It had been quite fascinating to watch the routine she'd put on, but this, this unrehearsed response was what I had bought.

Her face was a myriad of fleeting emotions, all of which I could guess. I dealt with criminals on a daily basis, for me this woman was an open book, all her feelings displayed clearly on her face.

"Do it all again, but this time for real," I said.

"W-what?" she breathed, her eyes large with shock or dread.

"Scoot up to the pillows. Lay against them. Open your legs, and start all over again," I explained in a bored voice.

At first, she didn't react, then she flopped back on the bed, and stared up at the ceiling. I supposed she was weighing her options. My cock was hot and heavy, but I was in no hurry. She had *no* options. Minutes passed while she ran through the possibilities open to her.

Then she did something authentic. Something that made me lean forward with interest.

She ripped the vulgar panties off her body and flung it away. There was genuine passion in that action. She detested them as much as I did. All of my attention narrowed in on that moment. Without even a glance in my direction she crawled towards the pillows. I watched her pussy with the greed of a fucking caveman. She positioned herself so I could see her face clearly. It was full of fury and insubordination.

She hated my guts. And that was exactly how I wanted it.

"Open your legs more," I commanded.

She spread her legs further apart.

"That's better," I murmured approvingly. Now I could see every part of her.

"Fuck you," she lashed out.

I stilled and so did she.

I stared at her and she stared back... I could see the fear in her eyes, but her mouth was tight and her gaze hard. She was refusing to take the words back or even apologize. She stared at me as though she hated me with every fiber of her being, and was not afraid to let me know it. And I loved it. A woman who stood up to me. Well, well.

Suddenly, I was desperate to be inside her, but I didn't want her to know just how much I wanted her. And even more than the urge to fuck her senseless was my need not to let her win this first round.

"Only one of us is getting fucked tonight and it won't be me. Now carry on," I said softly.

She swallowed. It was a mixture of relief and fury. Then she grabbed her mound roughly and my breath caught in my throat at the sudden and violently sensual move. I was more aroused than I ever thought I could be as I watched her face. I couldn't believe such a girl had been with that slime, Salvatore. But the ugly blots on her hips and the insides of her thighs never let me forget. I hated that he had made them. I wanted them to be my bruises. Marks I'd made.

Her thumb began to massage the area around her engorged clit.

I could see now that she was also becoming aroused. Despite how hard she tried to fight it, the muscles of her lower stomach were beginning to softly contract, her eyes were becoming glazed.

My skin prickled with excitement as she slipped her middle finger between the slit and began to stroke along the length of it. I felt my cock double in size.

She couldn't hold back her moan, it was low, almost a sigh, and of a completely different timbre from the ones she had entertained me with earlier. Despite how soft it was the sound floated over to me. Her neck arched, exposing the long whiteness of it. Then she slipped her soaked finger inside her little pussy, and my entire pelvis went numb.

She ground her hips upon that finger, her eyes now barely open, before allowing another finger to join the show.

"Three fingers!" I rasped, my voice hoarse and strained, foreign even to my own ears.

She responded intuitively and immediately to the command. A third finger joined the ones that were already inside her and then her back arched. She pushed gently in and out of her at first, and then her speed increased.

In almost the blink of an eye she went from a languid and slow rhythm to fast and almost brutal thrusts as she finger-fucked herself. My mouth dried as I watched her hips respond eagerly to the onslaught, pumping uninhibitedly to the rhythm of her fingers until her moans broke through.

I gripped the arms of the chair as she fucked herself to the edge of her orgasm, her body jerking and seizing at the torrent of pleasure that was wrecking through her.

Then her fingers slipped out of her. Juices dripped out of her as she continued the brutal strokes on the swollen flesh around her clit. I was so hard now that I was close to bursting.

A whimper escaped from her throat. With her eyes closed, she brought her slick fingers to her lips... and slipped them into her mouth. I could no longer sit still as she sucked her fingers greedily, then returned them back inside her, only to take them back to her mouth. And again, hungrily suck at her own juices.

The desire to know her taste was beyond anything I'd ever experienced. Without realizing it, I was on my feet. Barely aware of my actions I walked over to the bed. Before I knew it, I was climbing on the bed.

Her eyes flew open when the mattress caved with my weight, but before she could have the chance to even register anything, my hands had grabbed her thighs, and my face was buried between her legs.

"No!" I heard her harsh protest, but nothing was going to stop me. I had already had a taste of her and she was heaven. My mouth closed around her clit and sucked deeply.

"*Fuck*," she cried out at the contact, her hands landing on my head trying to pull my head away. Then her fingers clawed in my hair and she writhed at my relentless and hard pressure. When my lips moved down to her opening to lap up her juices with my tongue like a starving man, her back arched off the bed.

"Let me go," she cried, and something about her tone told me she was already at the edge. Touching her clit would end this and I didn't want it to end. Not yet. So I dug my tongue into her little hole and licked it out.

Her hands gripped the sheets as I slipped my fingers inside her. She struggled to stay coherent as I curved my fingers and stroked her insides, but once I increased the pace of my fingers, mercilessly fingering her until I found the cadence that was just hard and fast enough to completely unravel her, she began to moan and beg me to stop. I remained inside of her, finding a sensitive spot and coaxing it till her eyes began to roll into the back of her head.

"Stop," she cried out but I refused, even when her nails began to dig into the skin of my arms.

Instead of stopping, the pad of my left thumb joined in coaxing the pleasure from her clit.

SHE EXPLODED ONTO MY HANDS, her orgasm gushing out in a heated, steady stream and her scream ringing out across the silent room. I pulled my soaked fingers away and gave in to the mad craving for her taste.

My mouth covered her sex, lapping and sucking till every ounce of her release was drawn out of her. Then I raised my head and looked down at her. She lay against the pillows, her golden hair spread out behind her. A slight sheen of perspiration despite the cool room shimmered across her forehead and glued strands of her hair to the sides of her face. Her skin was flushed and her bottom lip was swollen from her biting down on it. Her body was still quivering gently from the aftermath of her climax.

She was astoundingly beautiful.

And I wanted to fuck her so badly that I felt the craving in the pit of my stomach. But I had already done something I had never done before. I had allowed myself to lose control. She had won this round. I turned back and saw the contract lying on the bed. I grabbed it and put it under her body. Then I looked down at her again.

There. That put everything into perspective. I had bought her. And I had thirty fucking days to get rid of this... this itch.

Not tonight, because tonight was about me proving to myself that I could still walk away, but after tonight, her poor pussy was going to get well and truly fucked. Day and night. Until I was so bored of her I couldn't even bear to be in the same room.

I pulled away and got off the bed, and without a backward glance, walked away.

CHAPTER 11

SKYE

I didn't know when I fell asleep, but when my eyes opened, I was in a darkened strange room.

In a flash, I shot up to a sitting position, every cell in my body tense, my eyes darting wildly around the room in alarm, but as my surroundings registered, as the armchair where he had sat, came into view, the memory of last night came back.

Oh God!

I flopped back on the bed and closed my eyes. The way I had behaved last night. I cringed with the memory of me ravenously sucking my own juices off my fingers. That was totally, completely, and utterly not me. I was actually extremely conservative and unadventurous in bed. I didn't like giving blowjobs, no back-door, no threesomes, no BDSM, not even light spanking. Once, when Salvatore lost his temper, he told the truth of what he really thought of me and called me frigid.

I had no idea what had come over me last night, but I was unrecognizable to myself. I *wanted* him inside me, and desperately. Unbidden the reel of the best orgasm I had ever had in my life began to play in my head. That orgasm was so strong, so overwhelming, it felt as if it had pulled my soul out of my body. Even now my body began to crave the same kind of release again.

I pulled my thoughts around sharply. Beyond the discovery that such orgasms existed even for me, my situation was hardly anything to celebrate.

I had sold myself to another man, and I was now the prisoner and sexual plaything to a cold, ruthless beast of a man. I thought of his translucent eyes again. How icy they were. Even when his mouth was on my sex and he was looking up into my face.

Other things fluttered into my head. Things I didn't want to think about. Like that powerful, irresistible attraction I felt for him. It was almost as if he had some strange dark power over me. I had felt it the moment our eyes met. Almost as if I belonged to him. Of course, it was no such thing. Nobody belonged to a man like that. And he couldn't have made it clearer. I was just a sex object to him. If nothing else his abrupt exit last night was the clearest declaration of that fact.

I reached for my phone and looked at the time. It was actually already half-past seven, but the thick curtains had kept the light out of the room. It was too early to call my dad, but I promised to go see him later, and I had to somehow arrange the visit with Luca's staff. I got off the bed and naked, padded over to one of the windows. I pulled the curtains open, and gasped. It had snowed during the night and the grounds were covered in a blanket of white.

I had never seen anything so beautiful in my life.

Wow! How lucky anybody who lived like this was. For a long time, I let my eyes drink in the special peace and quiet that came from centuries old trees standing in the soft snow.

Eventually, I headed to the gorgeous bathroom. To my surprise the marble floor was not cold on my bare feet. I had never experienced underfloor heating before and I relished in such delicious luxury.

I got into the glass cubicle and turned the shower on.

The powerful cascade washed over my body, and I basked in its soothing warmth. I squirted some body wash onto my hands, but I felt almost hesitant to touch myself.

It reminded me too much of last night and him… the cold, pitiless gaze in his eyes, the quiet steel of his voice, and the pure magic of his lips and hands. Deliberately, I forced his image out of my head and swiftly washed myself.

After my shower, I slipped into a thick bathrobe that had been neatly folded on a blue and white armchair. I used the hairdryer and finger dried my hair. It didn't look too bad. Then I brushed my teeth using one of the travel packs that had been laid out neatly next to the basin.

There was nothing for me to change into so I put on my white mini again. I wondered if I should run over to my apartment to get some clothes, but I remembered one of the conditions of the contract I signed was all necessary provisions for my wellbeing within the stipulated period of thirty days including shelter, meals, residence, and attire was to be provided by only him.

As I was getting into my shoes my phone began to ring. It was Katie, my best friend. She had seen me through some bad times, that was for sure.

"Skye," Katie's airy voice came through, and boy was I happy to hear it. "Where are you?"

I remembered the first time she asked me this question. When I had first hooked up with Salvatore. She had asked me where I was and I couldn't answer. Only after she had threatened to go to the police and report me as missing, had I finally spilled the truth.

At first I had begged her not to interfere in my life, but Katie was like a terrier. She never gave up. In the end, it was a great relief to tell her, and although difficult to admit even to myself what I had done, I had needed someone to cry my heart out to. Someone who didn't judge me.

Breaking down to her had given me the strength to go through the last two months with my mind intact. But right now, I wasn't' ready to tell her about Luca. I didn't have it right in my mind.

"Katie, can we talk in a couple of hours?"

Her tone was immediately wary. "Where the hell are you? He hasn't released you yet, has he?"

I let out a heavy sigh. I didn't want to have this conversation just yet.

"Katie, please. Can I call you back?"

"No, you cannot, Skye Morrison. I swear I will go to the police," she yelled into the receiver. "Right this moment. And don't you dare think that I'm kidding."

"Oh, Katie!" I muttered. "Why are you so dramatic?"

"Dramatic? Me?" she screeched. "Are you even aware what kind of dangerous position you are in?"

I took a deep breath, but before I could say anything she launched into a tirade.

"I can't stop you and don't blame you for making risky decisions for your father's sake," she said. "But you promised not to keep me in the dark. That bastard is dangerous, Skye, and you promised to always let me know what's going on. Did he extend the prison sentence again?"

"No," I replied quietly. "I... uh... got into a different deal."

She went silent for a few seconds. "What do you mean?" she breathed.

My voice was smaller than I wanted it to be, but I couldn't help it. "With another man. Um... he is going to pay for everything, Katie. All of Dad's medical bills. Until Dad is completely better."

"Skye!"

"Please don't make me feel worse than I already do."

"Then why did you freaking agree to something like that again?"

Tears burned my eyes. I couldn't speak. I knew everybody else thought I was a whore, but I couldn't bear it if Katie began to think that too.

"I'm sorry," she apologized in a creaky voice, and I knew she was trying to hold back from crying too. "I just... I want you safe and free again."

"I want that for me too," I mumbled. "But I just couldn't pass up this opportunity to have Dad made completely better. If I hadn't taken this deal all those times with Salvatore it would have been for nothing. Do you understand me?"

"No, I can't understand you, Skye. And if your dad knew he wouldn't understand why you would agree to be the mistress of another slime ball either."

"He's not a slime ball…" I glanced at the crumpled sheaf of papers sitting on the bedside table. "And I have a signed legal contract this time. Thirty days and not a day more."

"What about Salvatore then?" She had to spit his name out. She was that furious and disgusted by him.

"He agreed to walk away."

"What?"

"The man who offered me this deal last night is Luca Messana."

"No!" she exploded so loudly, I had to hold the phone away from my ear. "My God. You better be kidding me?"

"I'm not," I said quietly.

I could hear a rustling sound. I guessed she was sitting down.

"God, I feel almost dizzy," she said faintly. "How?"

"He saw me at the party and decided he wanted me."

"Just like that?" she said in disbelief.

I sighed. "Just like that. When you are insanely rich, you can buy people for your amusement."

"Are you okay?" she breathed.

"Of course, I am. I'd tell you if I wasn't."

"No, you wouldn't. You'd go to hell and back for your father without a single word of complaint."

My smile was sad because she was absolutely right. "Things are a little better this time around though."

"How so?"

I sighed and took a seat on the bed, my eyes fixed on a faraway spot outside the window.

"He's…" I hesitated. All the words in my head seemed too simple and inadequate to describe his appearance, or the dark and magnetic power that extruded from his eyes, his face, his body. In the morning light he almost seemed unreal. Like a dream or a nightmare. Perhaps the shadows had played tricks on my mind and when I saw him in the starkness of daylight, he would look like an ordinary human being.

"He's what?" Katie nudged impatiently.

But as if on cue, there was a knock on my door. My heart fluttered inside my rib cage at the sound, and I turned around to look at the door.

"I've gotta go. There's someone at the door," I whispered into the phone. "I'll call you later."

"Please keep me updated, Skye," Katie said urgently. "I need to know that you're fine at all times. And maybe send me an address?"

"Later babe," I said and ended the call.

I pulled open the door and found a uniformed young maid standing politely outside. Her hazel eyes were friendly, and her chestnut brown hair combed away from her face, and secured with pins.

"Good morning, Miss," she said with a small smile. "I'm Mary Jane. Breakfast is ready. Would you like to come down for some or I can bring a tray up for you?"

"First of all, can you please call me Skye from now on," I said.

Her eyes widened, then she grinned. "For sure, I can do that."

"Second, I'm not an invalid so no trays for me."

Her grin got wider. "Then please come this way, Skye."

CHAPTER 12

SKYE

reakfast was served in a massive orangery. It was at least three times the size of my apartment. The lofty glass roof allowed the winter sunlight to flood the room. It was full of plants, flowers, and vines creeping along the walls. Despite it being a winter wonderland outside, the heat emanating from the floors created a toasty atmosphere inside that glass hall.

Mary Jane led me to a long banqueting table, where there was an impressive, almost wasteful display of dishes on it. I had only seen this kind of spread offered by five-star hotels or in luxury cruise liners. Not that I had been in any, only photos in magazines. I stared at the assortment of pastries and bread, fruit, doomed dishes of cooked food standing on electric warmers, jams, honey, and different cereals in tall glass containers, but these, I only glanced at. What truly held my attention was the view from the glass walls.

"The Chef can also make an omelet or cook some eggs for you in any way you want if you prefer," Mary Jane said softly next to me, but I couldn't take my eyes away from the scenery. Beyond the glass was the panoramic view of the other side of the house. It was a picturesque, endless tapestry of rolling, meticulously cared for lawns and hedges. In the distance another massive fountain stood. It was simply too beautiful to put into words.

I pulled my attention back to Mary Jane. "I'm sorry," I apologized. "But this place is just incredible. It's so massive and so beautiful."

"Yes, it is. The grounds stretch across 1065 acres, and the house was recently voted in *House and Country* magazine as the most beautiful home in Boston."

"I'm not surprised," I murmured.

"So… would you like some eggs?" she repeated, handing a plate to me.

I looked at the lavish selection again and actually felt overwhelmed by the available options. Who was going to eat all this food? The house seemed empty. Or was this perhaps just the way of life here?

"There's so much food here. Is it always like this?" I asked, waving an arm.

She shook her head.

"You mean the Chef went to all this trouble for me?" I asked, shocked.

"Ah, it's no trouble," she replied. "We rarely have anyone stay anyway. Actually, we've only ever had one visitor stay the weekend."

"I'm not much of a breakfast person so I won't be able to eat even a fraction of all this food."

She smiled, a warm friendly smile. "Don't worry. There are many mouths to finish whatever you can't eat. Plus, our Anton couldn't help but go overboard. He thought the boss was staying for breakfast, something he never does."

"Oh," I said as I picked up a slice of bread.

"Here, let me toast that for you," Mary Jane offered. Using a pair of tongs, she took the slice off me and popped it on a rolling toaster. I watched the bread disappear into the machine and pondered whether to glean more information from her about Luca. I couldn't see a reason not to.

"The boss doesn't usually stay for breakfast?" I queried casually.

"Nah. To be honest, I've never seen him, and I've been working here for almost two years. Sometimes I even wonder if he is just a mirage. He comes in at the oddest hours and leaves just as inconspicuously. Madam Mitterand, the housekeeper, is the one who personally attends to him. Besides her no one else has any access to him apart from his many bodyguards, of course."

"So you've never seen him?"

"Nope. Madam never allows any of us to attend to him." She looked at me curiously. "Did you see him last night?"

I nodded.

"Really? Last night? So you're—"

She stopped just in time, but we both knew what she had been about to say. All of the staff would eventually realize I was here to service their boss. My stomach clenched at the thought, but I squared my shoulders and straightened my spine. It didn't matter what any of them thought. All that mattered was my father recovered. I'd take being labeled a whore a million times over than to have him unable to undergo his treatments because my pride was greater than my love.

"I'm sorry for badgering you," she apologized.

"You're not badgering me. I'm glad to have someone to talk to." I knew she had meant no harm and I smiled.

She grabbed a small bowl. "Do you want some fruit? What about juice?"

"Um... sure," I said.

My toast appeared perfectly golden brown as I reached for it. I grabbed a small jar of strawberry jam and a pat of butter that had fashioned into a flower and started walking towards the table.

I took my seat and began to eat.

Soon Mary Jane came over and placed the fruit bowl and a glass of orange juice on the table.

"It must take the gardeners hours to keep these plants so healthy looking," I commented.

"This is nothing. Wait till you see the greenhouse. It's so much bigger than this, and they grow all kinds of vegetables there. Even fruit."

My heart jumped at the information. "There's a greenhouse here?"

"Yes," she nodded. "South of the estate. You have to cross the bridge over the lake to get to it."

"The greenhouse," I zeroed in. "Are there only food plants there? What about flowers?"

"Hmm." She lifted her gaze to think. "I'm not really sure about that. The gardener is in charge of it, and I think he focuses more on growing vegetables than flowers. The boss prefers his food be home grown. Do you like flowers?"

"I love them," I replied. "I've always wanted the chance to grow them, but it's just never happened. Never had the space or the time." I shrugged. "I live in a small apartment."

Curiosity about my situation and how I had come to be in this house glittered in her eyes, but she knew better than to go there. "Well, the greenhouse is massive so I'm sure John, he's the head gardener, won't mind if you want to grow a few flowers there."

"That would be wonderful," I replied in a heartfelt tone, feeling a spark of excitement that I hadn't felt in so long.

If I was able to get access to the greenhouse then perhaps I would be able to pass my time there, tending to some flowers. Nothing else would make me happier.

"I'll leave you to it," Mary Jane said and turned around to leave, but I quickly stopped her.

"Can I go after breakfast? To see the gardener?"

"Not today," she replied. "I think Madam said you're having a meeting with a stylist immediately after breakfast."

"I am?" I asked.

"Yes, Madam said you came without luggage last night."

"Oh, okay," I said.

"Is there anything else you need?"

I shook my head.

"All right. If you need anything, just press that button," she said pointing at a little device that looked like a computer mouse.

I nodded. "I will, thanks."

"Great. Now, I guess I better go do some actual work. Catch you later, Skye."

"Catch you later," I echoed as she walked away.

I felt hollow after her departure, but I pushed the feeling aside, and focused on my surroundings. Everything was so clean and beautiful that I couldn't help feeling a little envious at how little Luca seemed to appreciate his good fortune. I couldn't even imagine owning all this amazing beauty and only coming here to sleep at night and disappear before anyone else awakened.

It occurred to me then even though there was so much wealth and luxury around, it all seemed empty and barren. The irony of life was staggering to me, and once again, Luca came into mind. I wondered why he chose to live this way. Without any real companionship, children, or warmth. His behavior deliberately discouraged anyone from getting close to him.

After I'd finished my breakfast, I decided to wander a bit around the house. After all I was supposed to be living here for a month. However just as I reached the doorway, I met the housekeeper coming in from the corridor.

"Please remain here," she told me coldly. "Miss Anna Franklin will be arriving soon."

Instinctively, I took a step back and she made as if to turn around and leave, but I stopped her.

"Madam Mitterand," I called.

"Yes," she replied with a frown.

"I just wanted to inform you that I have an appointment at five so I'll be calling for an Uber."

Her frown deepened. "I don't have any instructions to let you leave the house."

"Please, I have to go. I have to see my father. He is sick." My voice broke at the last word because sick didn't explain how poorly my father was.

She stood as still as a stone. At first, I thought she was completely unmoved by my plight, but then she asked, "Do you have to be at your appointment at five or do you have to leave the house at five?"

"I have to be there at five," I said, my voice full of hope.

"I will ask Steven to wait for you at the entrance at four o'clock. Do not be late."

"Thank you so much. I really appreciate it."

Madam was unsmiling. "He will take you to your destination. He will wait for you. And he will bring you back when you are done."

"Thank you."

She nodded formally then walked away.

CHAPTER 13

SKYE

*M*iss Anna Franklin was a tall glass of sophistication and sunshine with her burnt auburn bob, sprinkling of freckles, and wonderfully manicured nails, painted in the palest rose. She had a bright smile for me the moment she appeared and I smiled back gratefully.

I couldn't help but instantly appreciate her appearance. She had paired a tweed blazer, a heavy, eggplant colored coat slung casually across her shoulders, black trousers, and leather boots. She was carrying a massive dark red purse which exactly matched some of the thread in her tweed blazer.

I gulped down what was left of my orange juice and immediately rose to receive her.

"Skye," she greeted. "It's a pleasure to meet you."

I accepted the hand she held out. "Nice to meet you too."

"I'm sorry I'm late. The traffic was murder. I swear I could have got here faster if I'd walked," she declared dramatically.

She put her big red bag on the floor and took a seat next to me. At that moment, Madam appeared at the doorway, unsmiling and distant. "Can I get anybody anything to eat or drink?"

"God, no. I'm stuffed. I had a whole apple for breakfast," Anna said seriously.

I suppressed a laugh and decided then I really liked Anna Franklin. "I'm fine too," I murmured and Madam retreated, her body stiff and disapproving.

"Well, she's a whole bag of fun, isn't she?" Anna commented as she opened her bag.

"She could have a heart of gold," I said with a smile.

"If she did it would have melted by now with all that acid."

I giggled.

"Right, let's get down to business and see what we can do for you," she said, pulling out a thick leather bound diary/planner.

She uncapped a slim pen, opened what looked like an assessment form and proceeded to ask me to describe my personal style.

I stared blankly at her. "Um, what do you mean?"

She shrugged prettily. "What kind of outfits are you most drawn to? How do you want to look?"

I was a little perplexed at the complication of it all. "I don't necessarily need outfits. I just need a few basics to tide me over for the next few weeks."

She paused. "I don't know your circumstances, Skye, but let me put all my cards on the table so you know where I am coming from. I am the best stylist in Boston if not the whole world. People come from all over the world to use my services. They pay a shedload of money because I am really good at what I do. I can turn a frog into a prince. I was hired to make you look like a million dollars, and by the time I'm finished with you, you will look like a million dollars or my name is not Anna Franklin."

"Okay."

She smiled. "Good, we'll begin with colors. What are your favorites?"

"Uh, black?"

Her smile widened. "Mine too. What about fabric?"

"Silk." I didn't own any items in silk, but I'd always loved the feel of it.

She noted it down. "Any others?"

"Actually, I will need underwear, thick socks, something to sleep in, and also walking shoes. All I have is what I am wearing," I confessed.

I saw quick speculation flash across her eyes and was pretty sure that she had guessed exactly what was going on, but she nodded, and said, "No problem. We'll get you a whole working wardrobe." Then she pressed on with her questions. Thirty minutes later, she closed her dark red bag, waved a cheery wave, and hurried away. Her plan was to be back at one that afternoon with the first batch of clothes.

Once she left I had nothing to do but wander around the stunning house. I could hardly believe how beautiful and luxurious everything was. It was like being in a dream. Everywhere I looked was beauty and cleanliness. When I looked out of the tall windows I saw more beauty, pristine snow on painstakingly precise hedges and flat grounds that seemed to go on forever. I would have loved to have gone for a walk, but it would have been impossible in the high heels I had on let alone most likely freezing cold too. It was nearly time for lunch and I had still not finished exploring the house.

I was on my way back to the conservatory when I saw Mary Jane coming towards me. "There you are," she called cheerfully. "A doctor is here to see you."

I felt my stomach clench, but I smiled. "Oh good."

She smiled back. "After you have seen your doctor, you can have lunch."

"That's good because I'm hungry."

"Would you like to eat in the orangery, the blue room, or the dining room?"

"The orangery will be fine," I said quietly.

We dropped into an easy conversation about the house until we got to a small room that looked exactly like a doctor's exam room. I turned to Mary Jane. "There's an exam room in this house."

"Yes, but nobody's used it before."

At that moment a man in a white coat walked in from a connecting door. He had a swarthy complexion and dark, shifty eyes. He looked coldly at Mary Jane. "You can leave now."

She disappeared like smoke and he turned to me. "This won't take long," he said, opening his bag. I had been dreading a physical exam, but all he did was draw some blood. He asked me if I was on the pill and I nodded. He asked me for the brand and noted it down. After that he nodded formally and told me I could leave.

The relief of not being poked and prodded was so great I almost skipped towards the orangery. I knew I had no diseases. In my whole life I'd never had sex without a condom. Mary Jane was waiting for me.

"That was quick," she commented.

"Which is always a good thing."

She laughed and gave me a choice between lasagna, pan fried chicken breast with rocket salad, and lightly smoked salmon with wild rice. I chose the salmon and it turned out to be the best thing I'd ever tasted. Whoever the Chef was he was astonishingly good.

The rice was delicate with a faint whiff of some spice I could not recognize, and the creamy yellow sauce that came with it was to die for. Dessert was a slice of cherry pie, not made in the way American pies are, but open with a thin flaky crust. It reminded me of a piece of pastry I'd once bought from a French patisserie.

Anna Franklin must have arrived while I was eating, because just as I finished she was at the doorway and had prepared everything in another room for me. "Are you ready to try out some clothes?"

I nodded and rose.

"I am pretty sure everything will fit perfectly, but there might be one or two things that you simply don't like and we can take those away," she said, as she led me to the music room where there were three racks of clothes and a long mirror on wheels. A dark-haired, pale girl, in jeans and a turtleneck sweater, smiled at me.

"This is Elizabeth, my assistant," Anna introduced.

"Hi," I greeted.

"It's lovely to meet you, Miss," she replied formally.

"What would you like to begin with?" Anna asked, waving towards the racks. On the racks were sequins, silk, and tweeds. Dresses, coats and skirts.

"Um, the underwear."

"Of course," she said and made a gesture with her hands towards one of the racks. The assistant jumped to her command. I grabbed a lacy white bra and panty set and both women turned away politely as I got out of my slutty bra and into my new underwear. It was obviously very expensive, because the fit was amazing, but the material felt soft and silky.

"Ready," I said and both women turned around to face me.

"Great, let's start with this dress," Anna said, as she reached for a blood red, silk dress with a plunging neckline.

I stepped carefully into it and the assistant zipped me up. It was so expertly cut it flowed over my body like a second skin. I stepped into the red shoes Anna's assistant laid out in front of me. It had a modest slit that came to about halfway up my right thigh. If it had been blue or green I would have felt like a mermaid.

Anna clapped her hands together with satisfaction. "Wow! I knew the moment I saw it that it would be perfect for you. You look fantastic."

Her assistant wheeled the mirror towards me and I saw my reflection.

For some seconds I couldn't help staring in astonishment at *me* in *that* dress. I looked... regal and beautiful, like a Princess in a fairy tale. And yet, I was not regal or a princess in a fairy tale.

I was...

When I was growing up I had always been given the role of the fairy or the Princess in school plays and even as far back as two months ago I had felt unsoiled and unblemished, but now I no longer knew what I was.

When Katie had first found out about my arrangement with Salvatore, she had asked me how I was going to survive the psychological impact of selling myself for money?

My response had been simple. "By not thinking. If I don't think about it, I'll get through it. And besides, there's really nothing to think about. It's just one man, for one month. For my father's life, it's worth it. It's truly not that big of a deal."

Then it had become two months, and now it had become two men. Suddenly a panic arose on my insides and I couldn't stand the dress on me. This was not who I was. I immediately began to take it off.

"Hey," Anna called, her eyes filled with surprise. "Don't you like it?"

"It's beautiful. I'm just not sure about the color," I mumbled as I pulled the zip down.

"Okay, no problem. But red is always a good color for blondes."

"Yes, I'm sure, but um… maybe… um… something black."

"All right we'll try something black, but I'm not taking that red dress back. It was made for you. One day you will realize that."

I nodded numbly.

Anna and her assistant stayed for nearly two hours. At the end of it I had more clothes than I had at home. I kept saying I didn't need that many, but Anna just kept reminding me that she had been hired to dress me for a month and she had to earn her keep. They had also brought velvet covered boxes of jewelry. I stared at my reflection in a daze as they fussed about with my appearance.

Finally, they left. For a while I stared bemused at the shoes, the jewelry, and two racks of designer clothes that was now all mine. I was the girl who shopped at Target. Once this month was up I wouldn't even know where to wear these fine clothes.

Then I snapped out of my stupor and quickly changed into a pair of jeans, a t-shirt, and a thick sweater. I pulled on knee-length, flat-heeled, black boots, and shrugged into a gorgeously soft cream coat.

It was nearly time to visit my dad.

CHAPTER 14

SKYE

A dark green BMW waited for me at the bottom of the entrance steps. The engine was running and a man with black hair and a very hard face was sitting in the driver's seat. When he saw me appear at the top of the steps he jumped out of the car and held the passenger door open for me. He made no greeting and his face was unsmiling. But I was used to it by now. Except for Mary Jane it seemed to be the popular expression across the staff I'd met so far. She was a much needed dose of fresh air in that house.

After I got into the car, he closed the door, and got in himself. To my surprise I noticed that my father's address was already keyed into the GPS system inside the car, which meant Luca must have given it. I didn't want to think about how Luca knew it. Without a word to me the sullen driver put the car in motion, and we were on the way to my father's home in Beacon Hill.

I turned my head towards the window and thought about my father. Two years ago he beat colon cancer and was declared to be cancer free. Five months ago I was devastated when I found out it had come back, and the doctors needed to remove the metastasized cancer in his left lung.

I had exhausted all my savings with treatments and surgery with his first bout of the disease. Everything was gone. The bank turned me down on the spot. I even contacted a loan shark who laughed at my naivety when I told him I was a waitress and would pay with my wages. And then my boss told me about Salvatore. He gave me the money for the initial treatment, but he had already made it clear there would be no more for further testing and treatments.

Then Luca walked into my life…

My gaze lowered to my fidgety hands and upon pulling them apart, I regretted not stopping by my apartment and dressing in my own clothes. My father probably would not notice my lavish clothes, but my stepmother might.

I couldn't bring myself to completely lie to either of them so I prayed the issue would not come up. With a sigh I leaned my head against the cold window. What did it honestly take for one to get out of poverty so that their life didn't keep getting chipped away day after day? No doubt that was a question millions of people across the world asked each day, and they too had never found the answer.

Trees and empty landscapes became suburbs, and they melted into the city scenery. The car turned into the poorer areas, and finally we arrived at our destination.

"Could you park and wait here for me, please," I said, when we were about two houses away from my father's bungalow.

The driver frowned, but he did as I asked.

I debated leaving the coat in the car, but that would be even more suspicious. Snow crunched under my new black boots as I approached the red scuffed door I had grown up seeing. I walked up the old wooden steps and rang the bell.

A few minutes later, Laura, my stepmother answered the call. I always liked Laura. Sometimes I pitied her, because she was such a good woman, and she didn't deserve being married to a man who was still in love with his dead wife. But she had hung in there, steadfast, loyal, and never once wavering in her love or devotion to my dad. She was wearing her apron and had a carrot in hand and was still finishing a sentence to someone, most probably my dad as she had opened the door.

"Hi," I greeted. Already, I felt a little sad, because the first whiff from inside the house was the stale smell of medicine and illness. The difference between the living conditions of my family and that of Luca's couldn't be starker.

"Oh, wonderful. You just caught Diana in time. She was just leaving, but now you can both say hello to each other."

My heart sank at her words. Diana was Laura's daughter and my stepsister, and we simply didn't get along. Growing up together and sharing a room in a tiny house had been difficult to say the least. Diana was four years older than me and I was desperate to please her, even be like her, but no matter what I did I always managed to irritate and annoy her. I must have been ten when I finally stopped trying and simply avoided her as much as I could. The strange thing is we both pretended to be friends in front of our respective parents. It was almost an unspoken agreement.

I plastered a smile on my face. "That's good."

Diana already had her coat on and was standing in the middle of the small living room. Her eyes narrowed when she saw me.

"You two girls sit down and have a little chat. I'll go put the kettle on. It's nearly time for your dad to take his pills."

"Where did you get that coat from?" Diana demanded, as soon as Laura disappeared into the kitchen.

"A friend gave it to me," I said casually. Calling Luca a friend was a bit of a stretch, but what the hell. I didn't owe Diana any explanations. She certainly didn't furnish me with the details of her life.

"A friend? What kind of friend?" she asked incredulously.

I looked at her curiously. "What's up with you? You're never interested in anything that happens in my life."

Her head jerked forward. "Are you aware the coat you're wearing was featured on the front cover of *Vogue* last month?"

"What?"

"Yes, it costs twelve thousand dollars," she whispered fiercely.

I blinked in shock. Of course, I knew it was expensive, but I had no idea it was worth six months of my wages at the restaurant.

"So… who gave it to you?"

I could hear children playing in the snow, shouting, carefree. In the kitchen, I could hear Laura talking lovingly with my father. Here in the living room the air was thick and poisonous.

"My boyfriend," I said quietly.

There were twin spots of color on her cheeks as she walked up to me. She stood directly in front of me. Her eyes glittered strangely. And I realized then that she was jealous of me. She always had been. Maybe even from that first day Dad and Laura had introduced her to me. She was ten and I was six, and when my father and her mother had left the room, she had told me my blonde hair was ugly, and I should dye it a different color. Maybe brown or black. I was so young and clueless I had actually believed her and grieved that my hair was not brown like hers.

Now I looked into the jealousy pouring from her eyes and said, "My boyfriend is Luca Messana."

She gasped with shock. "I don't believe you." She dropped her voice again to a whisper. "You think I don't know what you've been up to. I know exactly how you paid for your father's medical bills. You're a whore, Skye. Nothing but a cheap whore. You can wear the most expensive coat in the world and it won't change that little fact."

Without waiting for an answer from me, she stalked out of the house. I turned towards the window and watched her walk away, her movements were stiff and full of fury.

"Has she gone without saying goodbye?" Laura asked in surprise as she came into the room.

I turned to look at her. "Yeah, I think she had to go somewhere."

"Oh, she never mentioned it, but that's okay. I'll see her tomorrow," she said cheerfully.

"How's Dad doing?"

"Come and see for yourself," she invited.

I took my coat off and slung it over the sofa.

"That's a lovely coat," Laura said admiringly. "I've never seen you in it. Is it new?"

"Yes, it's new. A friend gave it to me."

"I'm glad. You're a good person, Skye. And you deserve good things."

I looked into her eyes and all I could see was sincerity. Unlike her daughter, it appeared as if she believed my story about borrowing money from my boss to pay for all my father's bills. Well, I was about to stretch her credulity even more when I came up with the story that I was going to borrow even more money soon.

"Thank you for being here for Dad, Laura."

She shrugged. "There's no other place in the world I would rather be."

Her words were simple, but powerful because they shone with truth. In that tiny house that smelled of medicine and sickness, she shone like an angel. She was truly heroic and I admired her.

"You're a hero, Laura, and one day I hope to become like you," I said softly.

"You've already done far more than I could do for your dad," she replied softly, sadly.

And suddenly I knew that she knew what I had done to get the money for Dad, but there was no condemnation there. Only sadness that we had both been brought to this level, by a medical system that was the cause of two out of three bankruptcies in America. There was no more to say and we walked quietly down the dark narrow corridor towards the kitchen. The sounds from the television grew louder.

Dad was in a wheelchair, which immensely surprised me. Although his grey and thinning head was facing the television, the slight slant of his neck told me that he was probably asleep. It seemed like just a while ago, I'd heard Laura speaking to him, but this quick knockout was nothing new to me. He had always been able to fall asleep at the drop of a hat, and I had always been like that too until I took on the responsibility of his hospital bills.

I gently tugged Laura back out into the corridor. "Why is he in a wheelchair?" I whispered.

"He slipped," she replied with a sigh.

My heart slammed into the walls of my chest. "What? When? Why didn't you tell me?"

"What's it to you?" my father's weak but annoyed voice rang out across the kitchen.

Laura nudged me with her fingers, and smiled. "Go on. You haven't been around for a week, and he's missed you. So much."

"What the hell are you whispering about behind my back, woman?" he called out again.

Laura rolled her eyes. "You called me a piranha last night," Laura shot back at him. "Why the hell wouldn't I whisper behind your back today?" Then she gave me a gentle push into the kitchen.

"Hey big guy," I said as I rounded the wheelchair and came face to face with him. I definitely wasn't ready to see how much weight he had lost in just a week. He looked frail, the disease was quickly sucking the life out of him and I felt despair inside me if we were ever going to beat this. The feeling made me choke up.

He watched me, ever able to read what was going on inside me. "You're going to choke up at seeing me when you've abandoned me for a week?"

"I didn't abandon you!" I said quietly. "I've been busy. You know I would never do that on purpose."

He was quiet for a while with me refusing to meet his gaze. "I know that," he said finally. "And that's why I've been so worried."

"Oh, Dad," I whispered as the dam in my chest broke.

I turned away and a quiet stream of pain ran down my face. He waited till I was back under control and his silence allowed me to attain that state faster than if he or Laura had fussed over me. I wiped my eyes with my hands and turned back to face him.

He held out his hand to me and I hurried over, knelt down in front of him and, desperately clutched his bony hand. The skin on his palms had become as soft as a woman's. He regarded me closely.

"You've lost weight," he said.

"So have you," I replied.

"I have cancer, what's your excuse?"

I smiled, it was wobbly, but it was a smile. "I've been worried sick out of my mind about you having cancer."

"Then why didn't you come see me? And don't give me that cock and bull story about being too busy. I'm fighting for my life and I know you. Nothing would have kept you away unless..."

He gazed at me, hoping he would see something in my eyes, but I kept my eyes blank.

"Unless it's to do with me. To do with getting more money for me. Is that it? Are you trying to raise more money for me?"

I let a smile spread on to my face. "Yes, I was and good news. I've found someone who is prepared to help." I hoped with all my heart that it would stop there.

He frowned and shook his head. "You're lying to me about something. You haven't done something illegal, have you?"

I groaned. "Of course not."

"If you don't tell me the truth right now I'm not going to use any more of the money," he threatened.

"Dad!"

"I'm not joking with you."

"I'm not lying to you, Dad. I'm really not. I didn't steal, or kill, or commit any crimes for it. I would never do that. I got lucky and found someone to lend me the money."

He stared into my eyes for a while longer. "Who is this generous soul?"

"If you get better soon, I'll introduce you. How about that?"

He nodded slowly.

"How did you fall?" I asked.

"I didn't fall," he replied with a snort. "I just slightly slipped when I was getting out of the shower and twisted my ankle. So I'm stuck to this damn thing till I heal."

The phone in the living room started ringing, and Laura jumped up from the chair she was sitting on, and went to answer it.

I leaned forward and encased my father in a gentle hug. I could smell the sickness inside him and it brought fresh tears to my eyes. I never wanted to pull away from him. I wished I could take the sickness inside my own body and fight it myself, but I couldn't.

"There, there," he said softly. "Don't cry, little Skye. It's all going to be alright."

"Just fight, Dad. Fight hard for me. I still need you. If you die, I'll be all alone in the world. Don't let the disease win," I sobbed.

"I'm fighting it, honey. I'm fighting it as hard as I can."

I could hear Laura's footsteps in the corridor so I kissed him on the cheek and straightened.

"Why did you call Laura a piranha?"

"Because she's vicious," he said, but I could tell from his tone that he didn't mean it and had just been lashing out. "She hasn't shut up about the fall yet, constantly insisting for me to call on her help at all times."

"You need to be nicer to her, Dad."

"I know," he said, just as Laura walked into the kitchen.

"Who was it?" Dad asked.

"The hospital," she replied, but something in her tone made me look at her.

"What is it?" I asked worriedly.

She looked at me in a daze. "They're sending an ambulance to take your father in. Apparently, it's all arranged. A team of specialists are going to examine him and they are going to undertake the treatment for him immediately. I asked them who was going to pay for everything, but they said all the expenses would be covered by an insurance company. Do you know what's going on, Skye?"

"Yes, it must have been my friend who arranged it all. He said he was going to help, but I didn't expect him to be so swift."

"Who is this man?" Dad asked.

I turned to him. "He is that man I told you about earlier who said he would help. Get better soon and you can meet him and thank him yourself for his help."

Both Dad and Laura seemed struck dumb and I knew Luca's driver was waiting two houses down.

"I have to go now, but I'll call tomorrow and be back in a couple of days."

"You're leaving already?" he asked, immensely disappointed. "Why don't you stay here for a few days?"

"Soon, Dad," I said and lowered my face to place one last kiss on his forehead. "Very soon."

CHAPTER 15

LUCA

*I*t was late evening when I arrived back in Boston.

I wasn't feeling good. Blood had been shed today. I didn't do wet work, but I might as well have. It was to my orders my men maimed and murdered. Out there somewhere in the burning depths of hell there was another stain on my wall of sin. Sometimes I dreamed of that wall. I dreamt I was washing it. Meticulously, washing, but as soon as I finished the ugly stain returned.

But it was not that, that bothered me now.

It was a feeling inside my body. A feeling that there must be something better than this. The wealth, the power, the control, the respect, the never-ending parade of women, the dignity of my position, all of it felt like nothing. Dust in my mouth. There was no happiness in my heart.

I was numb.

At times like this I wished I could become as blasé as my father about the dog-eat-dog world we lived in. "What are you crying about? He'd kill you in a heartbeat if the shoe was on the other foot," he used to say when I was a lot younger, when he was a tiger and I was only a cub. Now he was toothless and I was the capo del capo of our world.

As Cullinan and I drove home through the familiar roads out of the city, the girl came into my mind.

Instantly, I felt my cock twitch with anticipation. The doctor had given her the all clear. Yes, it would be good to sink myself into her heat. Make the heavy feeling go away. I suspected it would only be a temporary release, but even that fleeting moment without the weight of this dread would be welcome. I glanced at my watch. It was much later than I'd expected to be back for dinner, but if she had obeyed the instructions I'd left with Melania, she should be waiting in the dining room for me.

As soon as the car stopped, I ran up the stairs. As usual one of my men had already been alerted and he stood at the front door, ready to open it for me. I went into the house and headed straight for the dining room. At first glance I thought she had disobeyed me and not waited for me, but then I realized she was there.

I stopped at the entrance and stared at the scene before me. This was my dining room, but I almost couldn't recognize it. The girl. It was the girl. She changed everything.

In the candlelit room, she was seated at the far end of the long dining table, but her fair head was resting on the white tablecloth, and she was busily scribbling onto a small pad with a pencil. She was so deeply engrossed in whatever she was doing she seemed to be totally unaware of my presence.

To my surprise, I found myself curious about the notes she was making, which perversely, annoyed me. Because I wanted to know, I decided to deliberately deprive myself of the knowledge.

I strolled towards my seat, and the movement caught her attention. She immediately jumped to her feet.

My gaze moved down the diamond studded choker around her neck to the silky red dress. How strange. Any other woman would have looked—depending on the size of her tits —slutty or sexy in that dress, but she looked like a slice of heaven, pure, unsullied, and strangely fragile. As if I would stain her purity if I let my sinful hands touch her.

My gaze moved upwards.

I was mesmerized at the magical way the warm glow of the candlelight made her skin glow and illuminated her hair. Her eyes were wide and uncertain. I walked up to her and I touched her mouth. It was the thing that first caught my eye when I saw her in Soleiman's living room.

Her skin was soft and silky... and covered in a layer of red lipstick. I picked up a white napkin laying on the table and wiped the lipstick off. All the while she simply stood there, like a doll. Like my doll. I could do anything with her. I had bought her. I had left a slight stain on the skin around her lips, which I liked. It made her look less pure, but I might have been too rough in my efforts to erase the lipstick, because her lips now looked swollen.

As if she had been sucking on my cock for hours.

Her tongue, pink and small, came out to lick the swollen flesh, and my hands itched to throw her on the table and take her right there and then, but I forced myself not to give in to the need. I wanted to prove to myself I was stronger than any cravings my body had. It was only sex. I *could* resist her. She was just a woman. All women were just pretty playthings. Never would I trust one again. I would fuck her after dinner and not before.

I moved towards the head of the table and sat down.

"Come and sit next to me," I invited but even to my own ears, my voice sounded cold and indifferent in the silence of the room.

She obeyed. I liked her walk. Not like a model high stepping her way down a catwalk, but fluid and unconsciously sensuous. It was what caught my eye the first time I saw her walking towards the summerhouse.

"Thank you for all the arrangements you made for my father," she said, as she lowered herself into the chair next to me.

I had no interest in her gratitude. I hadn't done it to please her. It was my end of the bargain. In fact, I had no interest in her father's health or her life outside of our arrangement.

Melania appeared in the doorway. "Good evening, Sir. Would you care for an aperitif before dinner?"

"No, bring in the food," I replied, not taking my eyes off Skye.

Melania backed away and Skye turned back to me. I reached out and touched her hair. "Is this real?"

Eyes enormous, she nodded. The room became so silent I could almost hear her heartbeat. I let my finger run down her throat, over the choker, to the point where her pulse fluttered like a trapped bird. I rested my finger on that spot, and felt the blood inside her flowing swiftly, frantically.

It reminded me of watching a female lion pretending to be in heat and mating with a marauding lion for days because she was trying to tire the male lion and keep it from finding her cubs hidden not far away in the bushes. I was that marauding beast, and like him, I didn't care why she was here. It was enough to know that the lion eventually got tired of the lioness. He walked away in the opposite direction of her cubs. She got what she wanted and he got what he wanted. It was a HEA, African plains style.

At that moment Melania returned with three of her staff carrying baskets of bread, a bottle of wine and plates of food. It felt strange to see the others, but then again I never ate here or knew how many staff it took to run this place.

"Seared scallops with parsnip cream and spicy shrimp tapas," she announced as the girls placed our plates of starters in front of us, and poured wine into our glasses. All the while I never took my eyes away from Skye's, and as if hypnotized, she couldn't pull her gaze away from mine.

The need to possess her was so strong, again I wanted to sweep the food, wine, and bread off the table, and mate with her for days. Until I could put her away from me and walk away in the opposite direction of her and her troubled life.

Pulling my hand away from her warm skin, I picked up my glass of wine and took a sip. As I released her gaze I felt her expel her breath in a rush of relief. The wine felt cool on my tongue. Later, I would taste her on my tongue.

CHAPTER 16

SKYE

*J*f I had hoped for an uneventful dinner I would have been very disappointed. He had come so quietly he had startled me out of my own dream world, and now I found it hard to find my equilibrium.

To start with I was already in a complicated mood. On one hand, I was ecstatically happy to know my father was finally going to get the best care possible, but on the other, I felt like a cat on a hot tin roof about my own situation. Being with Luca was nothing like it had been with Salvatore. With the other I was in full control of my feelings and the way my body responded. The only emotions I ever experienced were either shame or disgust, both of which I could handle.

With Luca, I was like dry tinder. One touch and I went up in flames.

Even just now, when he touched my throat, the desire to have his tongue on me again, and to know what his cock inside me would feel like, was so strong I felt heat radiate out of my core. It made my skin feel extra sensitive and I could feel my skin begin to flush.

Luca highly intrigued, attracted, and confused me.

He was so mesmerizing and all I wanted to do was keep on staring at him, but I forced my gaze to drop to my plate. Away from his wolf's eyes and the scar running down his cheek that his dark evening stubble made more visible. It made him sinfully gorgeous.

What the hell was the matter with me? I stared at my food. It looked more like a piece of modern art than a plate of food. But I could still feel myself free-falling down an unknown abyss, where there was only darkness and those eyes, those translucent eyes watching me fall. Jesus, I really had to get a hold of myself. Before I did something really stupid... like fall in love with him.

I was already acting in ways I never normally would dream of.

Like wearing this red dress tonight. Why had I done it? Did I want him to see me as someone regal and sophisticated and not some woman he had acquired from a two-bit hustler? But how could I possibly want him when he had made it so damn clear all he wanted from me was sex? When he had shown not one ounce of affection. In fact, if I was truly honest with myself he treated me more like a prostitute than Salvatore had ever done. Salvatore had always wrapped it up with indulgence, endearments, presents, and looks of adoration.

I picked up my knife and fork and cut into a golden scallop. I put a tiny dollop of the parsnip cream on it, and slipped it into my mouth. It melted luxuriously on my tongue, and was truly the most delicious thing I'd ever eaten. If I had been with anyone else I would have made a long 'mmmm' sound of appreciation, rolled my eyes, and enthusiastically commented on how delicious it was, but with him I was like a frozen statue.

I stole a glance at him and saw no appreciation at all for the delicious food. He appeared to eat his food in the same way I would eat a slice of toast. As if it was not special at all.

Reaching for my glass of wine, I lifted it to my lips and took a sip, and without me realizing it my eyes had found his scar. Something about it drew me. From the first moment I had seen it, I had wanted to run my fingers along the mangled line.

He must have felt my gaze, because he turned suddenly and caught me staring at it. I quickly returned my eyes to my meal, but it was too late. I had fully incited his attention.

His eyes remained on me as I put my glass down and tried to stab a spicy prawn as casually as I could and bring it to my lips. Self-consciously I chewed on the flesh and swallowed, but the heavy silence that filled the space between us made me feel like I was swallowing a tasteless stone. I couldn't take it anymore. I cleared my throat.

"Did you have a good day?" Great, my voice worked. A bit strained but it sounded clear and calm enough.

"Please do not engage in small talk with me," he said quietly and carried on eating.

My eyes widened with astonishment. He actually intended to have this whole meal in complete silence. The message couldn't be clearer: in his opinion nothing I said could be of value and talking to me would be a bore.

Well, I also had a message of mine to send. I allowed my fork to clatter to the plate and it rang loudly in the silence, but I didn't care. That was the point. Shame my heavy chair made no sound on the plush rug as I scraped it backwards, and rose to my feet.

"In that case, there is no point in me sitting here," I told him, my voice shaking with emotion. "If you need me later on, you know where to find me."

A part of me expected him to be rough with me, to grab my hand and pull me back down, but instead he watched me, his light eyes utterly unreadable.

I turned around to walk away and he didn't stop me. My knees were trembling, in anticipation of retribution.

"Come back and sit down," his quiet voice cut across the room.

I froze mid-step. Slowly, I turned back around to face him. My lips parted slightly with a response but nothing came out. My blood was roaring in my ear. With a mix of anger and fear churning in my chest I tried again. "What for? It's clear I have no value for you other than sex. I will wait for you in bed."

A smile appeared on his lips, but it was brief and mocking. "Is bed the only place you have sex in?"

My mind had gone blank. I swallowed and tried to think of a suitable retort, but there was nothing in my head.

His gaze bored into mine as he leaned into his chair, and the confidence emanating from him felt like a punch to the gut because once again he had succeeded in making me feel gauche and naïve. He picked up a small device on the table and pressed one of the buttons on it. Then his hand went to the buckle of his belt as he said, "Come here."

I felt my eyes open wide with shock. "The staff…" I whispered in horror. "Any one of them could come in and see us…"

"I've activated the Do Not Disturb sign," he said with a careless shrug, as he rose to his feet and started walking towards me.

My heart jumped into my throat and a lie came to my lips. "I need to use the bathroom first."

He stopped and looked at me with those unreadable eyes. "No lies, Skye. Remember?"

I stared at him like a deer caught in headlights. "Sorry," I whispered.

He continued his approach and suddenly, without warning, I felt terror seize me. A deep-seated fear that had me on the edge of sprinting. Not because I didn't want him to touch me, but because I wanted him to… desperately. I already knew he possessed the ability to bring to life something in me I'd never suspected lay buried inside me.

I tried to stand my ground, but my legs took on a life of their own. They began to retreat until my back hit the wide double doors, and there was nowhere else to escape.

CHAPTER 17

SKYE

https://www.youtube.com/watch?v=rfSN_lJ7cuw
-When I need You-

*H*is eyes never left mine, and I stared hypnotized into those truly strange and exciting eyes. I was trembling and my heart was pounding so hard in my chest my blood roared in my ears. I remained frozen even when his hand touched my cheek. It felt like hot coals on my skin. I inhaled deeply and breathed in his scent. It was unbelievable the effect this man had on me.

I tried my hardest to act unaffected but failed miserably when he curled his hand till his knuckles replaced his palm and brushed them gently across my cheeks. I could feel the flush spread across my face like a burn.

Then his hand reached my bottom lip and his gaze dropped to the quivering flesh. Using the smooth pad of his thumb he pulled my bottom lip down, let it go, then watched it bounce back into place with a curious expression on his face. The only way I could describe the look in his eyes was the way a cat plays with a mouse. Pawing it; throwing it in the air and letting it run; catching it again with quick reflexes; letting it run…

Slowly, his gaze returned to mine. *Kiss me*, my heart pleaded, but I was still sane enough not to say it aloud. My hands clenched into fists by my side. I was aching with the gnawing need to grab him and kiss that sensuous mouth, or to push him very far away from me.

He lowered his head and I immediately clenched my eyes shut and waited for the moment his mouth would touch mine. At that moment, it felt as though only a taste of him would feed the vicious need in my belly. But his lips did not connect with mine, instead he lay them on the exposed swell of my breast.

It was such a simple act: his lips on my skin, but it shot such a bolt of pleasure through me that it tore a gasp from my lips. My bones weakened into jelly, and unable to trust my knees to keep me upright, I gripped his bulging biceps.

Then, like an animal he licked me. And I gasped at the bolt that ran through my body. It felt like a bolt of electricity. My entire groin went numb.

As I stood there in shock, he straightened and began to caress my breast through the fabric of my dress. His thumb stroked the traitorous hardened peak in the middle. There was simply no hiding my desire for him when it was that blatantly obvious. When he took away his hand a cry of complaint almost escaped me.

Those piercing grays were full of knowing as he slipped his hand into the slit of my dress. I stared into his eyes entranced. With one swift motion, he ripped the material all the way up to my hips.

My head shot down to see the destruction of the beautiful dress. It was the most beautiful thing I had ever worn in my life and he had destroyed it without a second thought. A wave of sadness engulfed me. The metaphor between me and that dress couldn't be clearer. I was that dress. Something he had paid so much for and yet was of so little value to him, so disposal.

"Open your legs," he commanded.

Blindly I obeyed.

One of his hard hands slipped around my hips to stroke the taut flesh of my butt, while the other boldly grabbed my sex in an imitation of what I had done to myself last night.

The stimulating surge was too much and I visibly jerked at the direct assault. I was already soaked and ready, so his long fingers were immediately able to push away the lacy thong and slide between the wet folds into me. Then he began to thrust them in and out of me at a leisurely pace, and I began to squirm like a worm.

At the same time that he angled his body to band an arm around my waist, he leaned forward, and whispered something into my ear. However, all of that was lost when suddenly, and unexpectedly, he increased his thrusts to such a brutal pace I actually felt dizzy.

My upper body struggled away from him while my lower body pushed into him as he finger-fucked me to within an inch of my life. I had never been used in this way before. It was obscene. It was nasty. It was also breathtakingly delicious and wildly exciting. I wanted to call out his name. I needed to… otherwise it seemed I would lose my mind. I wanted my brain to connect the man to the ferocious pleasure my body was experiencing. But I didn't. I didn't want to give him the satisfaction of knowing even this uncaring, indifferent, callous treatment of my body was pure heaven.

The whole time his eyes watched me. Sweat beaded across my forehead from the effort it took not to let him see how affected I was. Then my back started to arch. And there was no more hiding.

Still, he held me in place and drilled into me until I spilled onto his hands with an excruciating cry. My vision was blurred from the orgasm, my hands were clawed onto his jacket. The floor was wet with my juices. It was embarrassing.

I hated that I was like this… that he could reduce me to this, so I buried my face into the crook of his neck and pounded my fist against his chest.

It was probably a very bad idea to assault him in this way, but I didn't care. How dare he? How dare he treat me like this? Just because he was a sophisticate who knew exactly how a woman's body worked didn't mean he had to make me feel so cheap and dirty.

He remained still while I beat at him. I knew my efforts were puny and useless.

When I was spent, he grabbed my wrists and peeled me away from him. With a firm grip he held them over my head. Then ripped my flimsy thong from my hips and flung the scrap of fabric away. It fell on the floor with a whisper of defeat.

My chest was still heaving as I struggled to catch my breath.

I *hated him*, I decided as I watched his eyes darken. He unzipped his pants, and before he could pull out his cock I shut my eyes and turned my face away.

"Look at me!" he growled.

The quiet threat in his tone frightened me and I swiveled my head around.

He had his cock out, and it was the most massive, thickest, most aggressive looking cock I had ever seen. Throbbing veins snaked along the smooth skin. Something strange happened inside me. The hate was replaced by liquid desire. It flowed into every crevice and cell inside me.

I wanted that angry, untamed cock deep inside. Deeper than any man had gone before. I felt close to combusting and needed my release. Afterwards, I could run away and hide, but now...

My hips jerked shamelessly forward with the strength of the need clawing inside me. Gripping the base of his cock he pushed it along the slit of my sex to spread my slickness all over the shaft. With his gaze boring into mine, he bent his knees, positioned the thick head of his rock-hard cock at my entrance, and rammed it into me in one vicious thrust.

I hissed.

He was so big for a second I'd felt as if I'd been split open. Then my head fell backwards as I relished the unfamiliar sensation of being that stretched. He thought he had hurt me and stilled, but he didn't know I had welcomed the sweet pain. I wanted it this way. The way beasts did it. Wild, and without apologies. Without pretending anything.

Pinned to the door, I ground my hips on him, the soaked, engorged bud of my clit rubbing desperately along his skin.

"Don't stop," I urged, unable to take the torment any longer.

"Beg for it," he growled.

"Fuck me, Luca. Please fuck me," I snarled back.

I'd lost control. I didn't care about anything else except the need to feel the delicious friction of him moving inside me. My hands went to his ass and I fought to pull him even further into me, but his body was like sculptured granite. I couldn't move him even an inch. I couldn't stop my cry of frustration.

"Please, Luca, please," I pleaded. I felt nearly half-mad with desire.

He stared down into my desperate eyes. Hard lust and satisfaction were mixed in his. Then he started to withdraw out of me. Without thinking I slipped my fingers into his hair and pulled hard, trying to draw him towards me. He didn't seem to feel it.

His large hands cradled my hips. Then his knees lowered a little more, and he finally gave me what I wanted. He slammed into me. Hard. With that one thrust, he hit a spot inside of me that no one had ever reached, and I felt a pleasure I'd known before start radiating out. I was filled to bursting and had never felt more complete. Even the pain from the thickness of his length was inconsequential as I reveled in the ecstasy of being so completely possessed by him.

When he buried his face in the crook of my neck, I sank my teeth into his shoulder. He didn't flinch. His fingers dug into my ass and I ground my groin on his. It felt amazing. He gripped the back of my thighs and lifted my feet clear off the ground, forcing my arms around his neck and my feet to curl around his waist.

He fucked me ruthlessly, uncontrollably. The room filled with sounds of our smacking flesh and the animal grunts that came out of my own mouth. The grating of his flesh against my inner walls, and the heat that engulfed me from the tips of my toes to the crown of my head made the world tilt around me. I crushed myself to his body as I felt my spirit lift just an inch further out of my body.

"Wow," I gasped.

I never wanted this to end. I never wanted to come out of this state where it was for certain that I had transcended into a different plane. He positioned me against the wall and began thrusting with a relaxed rhythm.

I was perfectly content with this new pace. Tortured but at the same time willing to drag this out for as long as was possible. He took his time and it was delicious. I felt myself hover on the edge of the abyss. "I'm going to come," I choked out.

Immediately, he increased his pace to a crazed tempo. My cries rang out across the room as he slammed over and over into me. I pushed onto him, wanting the roughness. We had both gone mad, and my pussy suffered for it. My inner walls felt bruised with the force of his fucking.

And then I climaxed. Harder and more intensely than I'd ever had in my entire life.

Tears stung my eyes and rolled down my face and I didn't even give a fuck. I screamed into his shoulder as the orgasm took over. I couldn't recognize myself as the restraint that I had promised I would hold on to, was ripped from me. In that crazy moment I felt the burst of his hot seed inside me, and I was completely undone.

I started pounding my hips against his, desperate to milk out every ounce of pleasure left between us. It was as though nothing else beyond that mattered. All I could think of was drawing out the orgasm, needing my spirit to continue to transcend till the point of no return.

His hand smacked painfully into the side of my ass and the sharp strike drew out another burst of sensation. I was shaking as I held onto him, unwilling to be apart. Unwilling to face what he had done to me.

Sex with Salvatore had been a revolting experience, and even before that it had been no big deal. I could take it or leave it. To be honest, I got more pleasure from my vibrator than any man I had been with.

Now I knew what all the fuss was about.

I could have never imagined it could feel this way. That something that felt this amazing could even exist. I kept pumping my hips into him, until my body couldn't make any more movements, but I didn't stop shaking. It was impossible he was also as unraveled as I was, but it was as though we had become melded into one devastatingly satiated being.

Then I felt him start to pull away and I clung on. Before I could be pushed off him like a dog I let go, loosening my legs from around him. But I couldn't stay up. My knees were like jelly. All the strength had been drained from my body. I felt myself collapse slowly to the floor.

He stepped away from me.

I was slumped on the floor and leaning weakly against the door. I felt exposed and vulnerable, chaffed and bruised, but I looked up at him defiantly. Fuck him. I refused to feel shame.

He stared down at me expressionlessly as he tucked his dick back into his pants, and zipped up the fabric.

Then he opened the door I was now leaning against, and he walked away. I could do nothing but listen to the sound of his polished shoes on the hard floors, until they faded away.

I dropped my head into my hands. How could it be that the best sex I would probably ever have in my life would come from a man that I would no doubt come to loathe like no other.

I wished I would never have to see him again, but I was well aware my body was already counting the seconds until I would.

CHAPTER 18

LUCA

I'd wanted to stay with her. And hold her.

The startling need had crackled through my chest.

So I'd forced myself to walk away. Now I stood in the middle of my study staring out of the window almost in a daze. My breathing was still uneven, my heart racing, and my body thrumming with the afterglow pleasure and heat. What the fuck just happened?

I'd fucked so many women in my life, all as beautiful and some even more beautiful than her, but none of those encounters even vaguely resembled what had just happened. For fucks sake I had unraveled like a dropped old movie reel. It was the closest thing to a miracle I'd ever experienced in years.

What was it about her? Why did she have this effect on me? She was just a dumb broad. Dumb enough to get entangled with a fool like Salvatore and a monster like me. But from the first moment I'd laid eyes on her, something inside of me had stirred to life. And I had wanted to see what it was.

Now I knew. Now I fucking knew.

I had to get rid of the turbulence inside me. With a shuddering sigh, my gaze went over to the tray with a bottle of aged whiskey and a single crystal glass on the low table next to the fireplace. Every night it was put out for me. Some nights I came and drank it, others I didn't. I went over and poured myself a generous measure of the golden liquor.

Then I collapsed onto the sofa and leaned back into the comfortable leather. The fire crackled. I took a sip, watched the dancing fire before me, but saw only her... in that red dress. I'd been with heiresses who would not have been able to pull off the regality she brought to that dress. I thought of the shocked expression on her face when I ripped the dress. She loved that dress. Someone like her would never have been able to afford a dress like that.

Without warning I experienced a twinge of regret. It was so rare I studied it as it appeared in my head and moved to somewhere in the region of my heart. I didn't like the feeling. I shouldn't have destroyed the dress. It was not right. When she left in twenty-nine days I wanted her to take it with her. I pulled my phone out of my jacket and sent a message to my PA.

The first red dress tore. Get another.

It was brief and without context, but Gemma had been picked for and was paid a huge sum of money for her astonishing resourcefulness. I'd bet my last dollar she'd have the exact dress for me by the end of tomorrow.

I took another sip of the liquid and relished the burn as it slid down my throat. I forced my mind to concentrate on a project I was taking on in Sicily, but I simply couldn't stop thinking about her. Even though I pretended to myself she was little better than a whore. I had paid for her body after all, I knew deep down that she was no whore. What she had done for her father was the highest form of love. She had sacrificed herself for him. It was a rare and precious thing. In my life, I only ever met people who put themselves first. The best for me and the rest for thee.

I chucked the contents of the whisky down my throat. I felt vaguely irritated with myself. What the fuck was I doing making excuses for her? If I carried on in this way I was going to become totally infatuated with her. And never again was I going down the road where I trusted or cared about a woman. My phone rang. It was my brother Angelo.

"Yeah," I said.

"Whoa, what's up with you?"

"Nothing," I muttered.

"If I didn't know you better, I'd say it was a woman that got you all tangled up and—."

"It's late," I interrupted coldly. "I was at Brighton Beach all day and I'm tired."

"Hmm…" He sounded unconvinced. "Anyway, it's all set up. Come over tomorrow."

"Good."

"Right then. I'll see you tomorrow."

"Angelo?"

"Yeah?"

"Well done," I said sincerely.

"Thanks, Luca." I could hear the pride in his voice. Praise from me was hard to come by.

I ended the call and rose to my feet. All I could think of was of her lying in her bed upstairs. My body was throbbing. There were only twenty-nine days left and I was going to have my fill of her. I would get tired of her. I always did. Even the most delicious thing will become a bore if you have it every single day, often more than once, for twenty-nine days.

When I arrived at her room I did not knock. I simply turned the handle and walked in. Her red dress was on the middle of the floor in a heap. She'd probably just let it fall off her. There was a lacy bra not far away from the dress.

My gaze moved away the discarded garments to the shut door that led to the bathroom. I imagined she was taking a shower or a bath. Probably washing away the semen. Even while I was watching her I had seen my seed dripping out of her.

I considered heading into the bathroom and fucking her in there, but the inviting bed had a higher strength to its call. I wanted to explore all sorts of positions there with her. My hands went to the buttons of my shirt while I kicked off my shoes.

I shrugged out of my shirt and just as I was pulling the strap of my belt out of the buckle, I heard the door to the bathroom open. I didn't turn around to look at her even though I was well aware that she was startled at my presence.

"What are you doing here?" she gasped.

I almost smiled at her bravado. "Isn't it obvious?"

"I'm tired," she whispered. "Don't I have the right to be tired?"

"You don't."

I let myself glance at her... and I couldn't look away. She was wrapped in a white towel and her hair was wet and hanging in clumps down her pale glistening shoulders. Her eyelashes were still damp, her ocean blue eyes were enormous and filled with child-like innocence, and her face was scrubbed clean of all make up.

She looked fragile, vulnerable... and too young. Way too young for me. I felt as if I was robbing the cradle. I hated seeing her like this. I wanted her to be just a slut with a great mouth that I bought at a party, and it infuriated me that at every turn she managed to get the better of me. She was twenty-fucking-three, I wasn't robbing the cradle, and I *did* buy her. I sat down on the edge of the bed and glared at her.

"Get on your knees," I ordered. "And suck me off."

Defiance flared in her eyes, but she fought it down and came forward. She stood in front of me, her chin tilted proudly. You can use my body, but you will never break me, it said.

"Take off the towel," I commanded.

She pulled the fabric from her body and the towel pooled around her. My eyes devoured her body hungrily. As I ran down her body, I saw new bruises around her wrist, and knew instantly I had made them earlier when I grabbed and held her by her wrists. I reached forward and took her unresisting hand in mine. I stroked the bruise with my thumb and looked up at her. "Does it hurt?"

She shook her head silently. There was something sad and pitiful about her tonight. And I didn't like it. I thought back to how violently she had trembled earlier in the evening and how she had clung to me almost refusing to let go and the challenge to once again lower her to that state burned in my chest.

I let my other hand move to the bruises between her thighs and she flinched automatically. "Do these hurt?"

She shook her head again.

I wanted to lean forward and lick her little pussy, but I didn't give in to the temptation. With my shoe, I kicked her towel away.

"Get to work," I said, spreading my legs further apart and resting my palms on the bed.

Her knees hit the floor and her hands moved towards the zip of my slacks. Although my whole body was brimming with anticipation for the moment her hands and mouth would make contact with my skin, her amateurish fumbling with my zipper and then my briefs as she tried to pull them down was thrilling. It was clear she was not as experienced as I had imagined, and for some bizarre reason the idea excited and thrilled me.

I watched as she took in my size, jutting out from the dark briefs. And then her eyes lifted upwards to steal a glance. To my shock her eyes were filled with desire. She *wanted* to suck me off!

I lifted my butt off the bed and she quickly hooked her fingers into my briefs on either side of my hips and pulled them down. For a second she did nothing, just stared at my erect cock as if hypnotized, then her hand slipped up my thigh. I watched in fascination as her pale fingers snaked through the dark hair smattering across my crotch towards my cock. When she made contact with my cock, it jerked and pre-cum flowed out.

"Lick it," I rasped.

Gently she curled her slender fingers around my cock, and moved her swollen mouth towards my cum. Her tongue flicked out and she let the tip run along the drip. It was all I could do to sit still while she played around with my dick like a little kitten. But sit still I did. No woman had done that to me before. Explored my taste with such curiosity.

Her plump, pink lips parted and I held my breath as she stretched it and covered the mushroom head of my cock. A groan rumbled in my chest as my head fell back, and for a moment I considered just giving in to the weakness that had overtaken my arms.

It would be a delight to just lie back and give in to the maddening sensation of her touch, but that would be not only leaving my guard down, but also missing the expressions fleeting across her face as she blew me.

I didn't want to miss that for anything.

My cock seemed monstrous compared to the size of her mouth, as she struggled to take a decent amount of me into it. She had never learned to deep-throat. The honest struggle was somewhat endearing, and I couldn't help reaching out to hold the back of her head in place.

Her hair was wet to the touch, and for a moment it distracted me, and an image flashed into my mind. She was sitting on the bed, and I was taking a dryer to the shiny gold tresses, working my fingers through it as I dried it.

A deep, guttural groan escaped my lips, but I couldn't tell if it was from the hard suction from her mouth, or from the image of the warmly romantic, but extremely unlikely situation that had floated into my mind.

I shook my head to clear it and focused my gaze on her lips, stretched across my width. I watched her careful and rhythmic sucking of the head, and the jolts of pleasure that zinged through my body made me quiver. I was meant to be minimally affected like I had always been, but the sweet agony was too much to bear.

"Fuck!" I hissed and clenched my eyes shut.

Tightening her grip, she slid her hand down my slick length and then began to milk me. Slowly at first, but as she became more confident, she increased her pace, and I was reduced to a breathless fool. Then she leaned forward again, adding her mouth to the tease and I was gone.

My back gave out and I collapsed onto the bed... and completely gave in to her magic. And it was magic. Witches magic. Very dangerous, but I was past caring.

CHAPTER 19

SKYE

Seeing him in this way was exhilarating.

I never wanted to be excited or turned on, but I was already soaked and dripping wet between my thighs. It felt as if an entire colony of hornets were buzzing in my belly. I wanted to squash them all dead, but I couldn't feel enough malice to attack them. What I truly wanted in that moment was revenge.

And not against them, but him.

Back in the dining room, he had reduced me to a spineless, mumbling mess and I wanted nothing more than to do the same to him. To crack through that impenetrable shell, and to prove to myself and him that he was just as susceptible as the rest of us.

I focused more on the thick, throbbing length of meat in my hand and mouth and once again marveled at the sight. I had felt how huge he was inside of me from being so thoroughly filled and stretched, but this was the first time that I was so close to it.

Salvatore's cock had been disgusting to look at, long, thin, and bent and hardly ever fully erect. Each time I even glimpsed it I'd gagged internally. One time, I couldn't hold back and nearly threw up when he had tried to shove that weak thing into my mouth. I then had to pretend I had a bad stomach.

With Luca, I couldn't look away, or get enough of how he looked, felt, and tasted.

His skin was silky smooth, and the slight whiff of musk mixed with the scent of tobacco and a spice... perhaps cinnamon swirled around my nostrils, and spurred my enjoyment of him. I sucked feverishly on the large head, drawing out as much of his cum as I could into my mouth. Adding both my hands into the task of blowing him, I quickly found a rhythm that made his back arch.

"Fuck," he cursed out again, his voice low and raspy.

And I loved it.

With my hand gripping the pulsing head, I ran my tongue down the thick length until I arrived at his balls, tight and heavy. I sucked on them, softly caressing the two sacks with my free hand before licking my way back up his length. I paused on the way to place sensual kisses along the bulging veins and his responding twitches spurred me on.

He was now slick with a mix of saliva and cum and it only made me greedier.

My knees hurt being pressed against the rug, but I could feel my own juices running down my thighs and I was desperate to have his cock inside me. I adjusted myself so I could take him even more deeply into my mouth, but about mid-way down his length, he hit the back of my throat, and I was forced to halt, but I didn't take things easy. Once again, I could sense that I was losing myself, but I didn't know how to hold back. I was just as aroused as he was and perhaps even more so, and the need to see him climax was even more gnawing than my own anguished need for a release.

My cheeks hollowed and I began to bob my head up and down his rock-hard length.

"Jesus," he muttered almost as if in disbelief.

My heart jumped and so did my pace.

He rocked his hips to my hard and rapid rhythm and soon he was fucking mindlessly into my mouth, the guttural groans that rumbled through his body sent electric tingles down my spine.

I was now desperate for his release so that I could get my own. Both my hands wrapped around his hardness and joined in the sensuous pumping towards his climax.

His groans drove me on, until suddenly he came, bursting into the back of my throat. Thick and hot and unbearably hot. I grabbed onto his clenched thighs as he pounded his fist onto the bed. His throat was strained, the veins popping, and his body was twisted with the intensity of his release.

As he took great gasping breaths I kept on sucking him, unwilling to let a single drop go to waste as his spurts kept coming. His eyes were wide open and glued to the ceiling as I slavishly licked every inch of his cock clean. When it was finally over I let go of him and stood looking down at him. He stared up at me and the seconds stretched. I could not tell what he was thinking or how long I stood there entranced by his translucent eyes. I only knew I could not tear my eyes away from him.

Without warning, he moved so quickly, it shocked me when I felt his grip capture my thighs and felt myself being dumped on the bed.

A startled cry escaped my lips but before I could gather my wits, he rolled on top of me and licked my mouth.

The act was so animalistic I froze in shock.

He hooked my tongue with his and sucked it into his mouth. I was so astonished I couldn't even respond. Then he began to suck on my tongue, greedily, hungrily, as if he couldn't get enough. My belly contracted and it felt as if my soul was being sucked out of my body. Suddenly, I became afraid of the sensations inside my body. I recognized the undeniable fact that I was losing control of myself.

I was not a fool, so from the first moment I had laid eyes on him, I was very aware that I was wildly and irrationally attracted to him and it would be quite easy to fall maddeningly and senselessly in love with him.

But I had convinced myself that sleeping with him would be an ordeal I must endure for my father, just like I had with Salvatore. I pretended to myself that my greatest danger was not that he would break my heart and leave me inconsolable, but that I would feel like a prostitute. Now I could see clearly that I would not come out of this ordeal unscarred.

As the kiss went deeper, his taste began to filter into me. He was delicious. I pushed away the sad thoughts and with my eyes clenched shut I swung my arms around him, determined to have my fill before I lost him forever.

I sucked wildly on his tongue and it took me to another plane of bliss and intimacy. The barrage of emotions and sensations were overwhelming and I felt as if I was close to passing out.

Stop... my mind vaguely registered my weak plea, but he didn't listen.

It was clear that we were both wrapped in a cocoon of dangerous attraction and molten lust and it was a state that neither of us wanted to come out from. But I was actually frighteningly dizzy and I broke the kiss and turned my face away from him. I felt hot all over and I could feel my blood pounding in my veins.

"Look at me," he snarled.

I heard his command, but I couldn't.

I felt his hands part my thighs roughly and I let him.

His cock arrived, silky and pushed at my entrance, and I held my breath in anticipation of his violent thrust, but he slid into me, slowly and purposefully. I expelled the breath I was holding. I turned my head to look at him and the look in his eyes shocked me. I gasped.

Possessive. God, so possessive.

He pumped into me slowly, deliberately until I was writhing across the bed, one hand in my hair and the other gripping his shoulder.

My head rolled from side to side. Then he reached down once again and captured my lips with his and I forgot the look in his eyes, the feel of his body on top of mine, the way his cock reached the depths of my core. I even forgot the exquisite sensation of blazing lust spreading through our bodies.

I climaxed. So hard my eyes rolled to the back of my head, my whole body froze, and I saw colors.

I was so lost I did not realize that he had stopped fucking me, and was ravenously drinking in my juices. He lapped it all up while I panted and gasped my way back to reality. I felt weak and exposed. His mouth kept on sucking at my sex until I lay my hands on his head.

"Enough," I whispered, my pussy felt as if it was swollen to twice its size.

He raised his head and body then. I could feel something change between us, as he held me tightly in his hands and tasted every inch of my body like he worshiped me.

As I watched, he returned his cock back into me. I swallowed. His cock felt unbearably big in my swollen flesh. As if he knew he was hurting me, he traced searing, deep kisses along my torso and breasts.

When he started to move I expected him to slam into me violently like he always did, but he didn't. His strokes were languid and gentle. I buried my face in his neck to muffle my whimpering at the emotions that spread through me as he rocked his hips into me.

I wanted to open my eyes and look into his beautiful light eyes, but I wanted this moment to be untampered with. What if I saw something there I didn't want to see? I wanted this moment to remain the perfection it was. One day I would be abandoned, left high and dry, and I knew it would be this moment that would be etched forever into my mind, into my old age, and finally to my dying moments, and I refused to allow any rocks of reality to spoil it.

I wanted to bask in the lie that this was the sweetest thing I'd ever experienced. It didn't matter if it was a lie.

Slowly, slowly, I lost my mind again. And it was beautiful. It never registered whether he came or not because I was too far gone. All that occurred to me was my own disintegrating, shattering into tiny, tiny pieces in his arms.

I cried out, my throat burning with his name.

For a long time, he remained glued to me, inside me. I felt an exhaustion deep in my bones that I hadn't felt in so long and it was shutting my entire system down.

CHAPTER 20

LUCA

*T*he lamp cast a warm glow on her skin and hair that was somewhat dried now and lay in tangled waves around her face like a golden halo. For the hundredth time, I asked myself what I was still doing here, staring down at her while she slept.

But I simply couldn't pull away.

There was a ceaseless stream of liquid fire coursing through my veins from wanting to be still inside her. I hadn't shared a bed with anyone since my wife Alessa. And I was planning on keeping it that way for the foreseeable future. The lure of her body throbbed and called as I forced myself to turn away. I warned myself that she was a siren, one of those dangerous creatures that made men crash their boats into rocks with sheer madness.

Suddenly she moaned, and like an addict being offered another shot, I turned helplessly, eagerly, but she was only stretching in her sleep. One breast poked out, the nipple pink and innocent, I was transfixed to the spot at the beautiful and vulnerable scene.

The tenderness of my thoughts clearly showed I was beginning to develop a kind of affection for her and it stopped me cold in my tracks. I didn't even wait to slip my feet back into my shoes, barefoot, I fled from her.

Back in my own room, sleep didn't come as easily. My mind was abuzz with the evening I'd just had. It was the first time I'd been rewarded so handsomely for coming to dinner here. I'd have to come more often. Perhaps every night. There was no need to change my plans. They were still good.

As planned, I would fuck the living daylights out of her until I lost interest. Yes, she was something special, I'd give her that much, but there was absolutely no way I wouldn't be bored in twenty-nine days. No woman had kept my attention beyond two weeks. In fact, by the first week I would already begin the process of tiring of them.

My flight to Sicily was at six am, and feeling confident the infatuation wouldn't last I shut my eyes. This time sleep came.

CHAPTER 21

SKYE

"*S*orry, apparently, the head gardener doesn't have approval to let you into the greenhouse today," Mary Jane announced regretfully, as she came back into the sunroom bearing a jar of cranberry juice.

I stopped munching through the slice of smoked salmon on sourdough toast. Placing my half eaten toast down on my plate, I took a deep breath and addressed the situation head-on. "The head gardener doesn't have approval? Whose approval does he need?"

"The boss, I guess," she replied. "But he left before dawn this morning so John won't be able to see him now until he returns and nobody knows when that will be. Mind you even if he does return, as I explained to you yesterday, it is almost impossible to see him, let alone meet with him."

My mind went to the man who had ravished me to the point of exhaustion, then pulled the duvet over my drained body last night. I shook my head to shake off the steamy flashbacks that immediately came flooding back.

"Can I meet John? I want to speak to him."

"Ooo… I don't know about that," she said, and began to needlessly rearrange some of the dishes on the buffet table.

"What's the problem?"

She made a face and spoke in a hushed voice. "Um… Madam Mitterand is not very… open to guests wandering across the grounds. It's a very security tight compound so it's usually preferred that everyone stayed within the confines of… um… their own areas."

I stared at her, unable to come up with a response beyond astonishment. Did that mean I couldn't even walk on the grounds? Was I meant to be a prisoner indoors for the duration of my stay here? No, that was not part of my contract. I was to make myself available to Luca for… sex, but otherwise I was free to do as I pleased.

I'll find him myself, I decided. And Madam Mitterand could stick it.

AFTER BREAKFAST, I returned to my room. I secured my hair in a ponytail at the back of my head and stood before my expansive new wardrobe.

I was going to bury my hands in the soil, but appeared I only had designer gear in my wardrobe. As much as it hurt to think I would be ruining thousands of dollars worth of luxury items, I had no other choices. I opted for a pair of black Armani skinny jeans, a neon green sweatshirt from Dolce and Gabbana and Gucci boots. I found myself taking care not to glance at the tags as I broke them off. I pulled on a thick jacket with faux fur on the collar, jammed a beautiful black and white baseball hat with a Chanel logo on my head and I was done.

Still vaguely disturbed by the idea of dressing in such expensive clothes to do some gardening, I quickly left the room.

I got out through the sunroom and began to make my way across the rolling landscape of lawns covered in pristine snow. I had always lived in the city and I had never had the privilege of walking on such pristine ground where there were only my own footsteps in the ground and such silence.

Although I was inside a winter wonderland, I did not feel the chill. The air was crisp and exhilarating and I wished I could bring Dad here. Away from that house that smelt of medicine and poverty. Maybe, before I left, I could get Luca to agree to such a visit. It would do my father good to be here in this beautiful part of the world, that much I knew for sure.

I crossed over a narrow bridge underneath of which was a stream. I was tempted to follow the running water, just to see where it would end, but I pushed away the distracting course and focused on following the instructions that Mary Jane had given to me.

Soon the steel frames and glass panels of the greenhouse came into view and my heart jumped with excitement. All my life I had loved plants and growing my own stuff. When I was young I did try to grow tomatoes and chilies in the back garden, but for some weird reason they would never do well. They would be doing really well, and then for no reason at all they would become brown, shrivel up and die. I could never understand it and after many tries I finally gave up and stopped trying to grow my own vegetable garden.

I saw the man I supposed must be John, since Mary Jane told me he was the only one working in the greenhouse that day, pushing a wheelbarrow full of soil into the glass encased space. She also told me he was jealous about his space, so I did not immediately enter the greenhouse, but stood outside and called out politely. From where I stood I could see big healthy looking cabbages and all kinds of plants that you would only get in summer growing abundantly.

I knew I could be happy here.

The man with very bushy gray eyebrows and leather skin appeared from behind a row of tomato plants. He was holding a trowel in his gloved hand and scowling at me as though I had intruded on his sacred space.

"What do you want?" he asked. His voice was as hostile as his face and stance. If he thought he could get rid of me by this show of unfriendliness, he could think again. I was used to my father being grumpy and knew there was no real harm behind it.

"I'm staying at the house for a month," I explained politely, "and I was hoping I could potter around here for a little bit. I want to pick up some skills about gardening and if possible plant some flowers."

I looked around as I spoke, and noted there weren't any flower plants. It was all vegetables and herbs and it filled the green house with a clean and earthy scent.

"No," was his immediate and seemingly incontestable response. Without waiting for a reply from me, he ducked back behind the tomato plants.

I smiled. Now I knew for sure he was no big bad wolf. He was actually hiding from me! I walked towards him and found him behind the plants. He was filling little pots with healthy black soil.

"Why not?" I asked.

He didn't look at me. "We don't plant flowers in the greenhouse. You'll spoil your fine clothes."

"Alright, I'll plant some vegetables instead, and I don't care if I spoil my fine clothes."

"You can't grow anything in a month," he muttered.

"I know, but I still want to start the process."

"It's hard work and you'll break your nails."

I held out my hands. "My nails are already all broken and I love hard work."

He turned then and looked at me from under his bushy eyebrows. "Why do you want to work here?"

"Because I love gardening. I used to try to grow things in my father's backyard when I was a child, but they always died and I just want to know what I did wrong."

Something flickered in his eyes. A professional's desire to help me understand my mistakes, but he blanked it. "You'll have to ask Don Messana's permission first."

"Okay, I will," I said and smiled at him.

He grunted and went back to his work.

I then wandered in the snow for a long time. It was beautiful to be so alone in such beauty. A robin landed on a branch close by. He was so near I could actually look into his eyes. He was so beautiful I wanted to reach out and stroke him. In the distance, I saw a small herd of deer, but I didn't try to approach them. My hands and feet were frozen, but I felt totally at peace with myself.

By the time I went back to the house it was already lunchtime and feeling ravenous I headed straight to the orangery. Mary Jane was waiting for me there. She smiled at me. "Shall I serve lunch now?"

I ate an exquisite meal. There was freshly baked bread with cold butter and a shank of lamb that Mary Jane said the Chef was famous for. It was so tender you didn't need a knife to eat it. All you had to do was pick it up from one end and shake it gently and the meat would fall off the bone. I tried it and she was right. The flesh simply slid off the bone. I tucked into it hungrily. It was delicious. Then I polished off a small bowl of crème brulee and tried to call the number Luca had given me the first night we met, but the phone appeared to be turned off. I couldn't imagine his phone was off, so I guessed he must have more than one phone.

"Is there a way I can reach the Don?" I asked Mary Jane, as I sipped my coffee.

"I have no idea." Her tone was laced with incredulity at the very suggestion. "I told you I don't even—"

"Know what he looks like," I finished for her.

And then I felt bad because it was not my intention to mock her. It was just the way everyone spoke of him made him seem like he was a god or a ghost. I smiled at her. "It's okay. I'll ask him when I eventually see him."

Once lunch was over I went back to my room, flung my coat on the bed and collapsed next to it.

Immediately, thoughts of our night together flowed into my head. I blushed to think of the way I had sucked him. As if he was the most delicious lollipop I'd ever tasted. The things we had done to each other in the dark seemed unutterably sensual in the daylight. My fingers moved to the crotch of my jeans, but I pulled my hand away. I had to stop it. I was on the way to becoming a sex addict.

With a sigh I pulled my phone out of my coat. First I called my father and made sure all was well with him and his tests, then I called Katie, but she was busy at work and promised to call me later. With nothing to do I began to research all I could about the kinds of flowers I would be able to grow given the season.

I was filled with excitement as I went through countless photos of seedlings and read up on all that I could about growing vegetables in greenhouses. Mary Jane knocked on my door to ask if I would like some tea and cakes. I said yes and went down to the orangery again. There were scones with thick cream and jam; egg and cress finger sandwiches; and some kind of French cake which looked like a tower or flaky pastry layered with custard and fresh fruit.

Mmmm... delicious.

Afterwards I wandered into the vast library. There must have been tens of thousands of books in there. I stood in the middle of the room and marveled at all the books lined up on the walls all the way up to the lofty ceiling. I guessed the contents of the library must have come with the house too, because I couldn't for the life of me imagine Luca choosing these books. It must have taken years to make this collection.

They were all old books and as I walked along I noted the categories. Ancient European architecture, philosophy, anthropology, medicine, alchemy, and a whole section on esoteric and occult knowledge. I pulled out several and looked inside them. The pages of the books were all yellow with age, and the language used was archaic and difficult to understand.

It was a strange thing, but I liked being in that library. It was like I had gone back in time. Any moment the door would open and a man or a woman wearing clothes from times gone by would walk in. To my surprise I actually found an old book with a lot of illustrations about growing exotic plants in cold climates. I would have loved to have stayed in the library and read the book there, but the fireplace was not lit and it was too cold.

I returned to the large living room that faced the front of the house. Its walls were painted a sunny yellow and a fire had been lit in the elaborate marble fireplace. I curled up on the sofa next to it and opened *The Intrepid Gardener* by Samuel J Snowden.

Luca was not expected for dinner so I ate a solitary meal in the great dining room. It felt strange and lonely without him. The noises I made with my knife and fork seemed to echo all around me. I wondered where he was, if he even thought of me. Of course not, a little voice taunted. I knew the voice was not wrong. I was just a plaything for an obscenely rich man. The fact that he didn't even bother to turn up on the second night told me everything I needed to know. He was not desperate for my flesh like I was for his.

Madam Mitterand looked at me with disapproval but didn't say anything as I carried the decanter of blackberry wine and my glass with me to the sunny yellow room I'd spent the evening in. I settled myself next to the fire and prepared myself to wait for Luca. I figured it would be easier for me to hear his arrival here than if I remained in my room. I didn't want him to return in the shadows and leave in the same way with me none the wiser.

But two glasses of berry wine later I felt drowsy and slightly tipsy. It also didn't help that I was sitting in what was probably the toastiest room known to man. I didn't want to fall asleep so I roused myself and walked to the foyer. Despite the estate having numerous security, there was no one about and it was eerily quiet and once again I noted how cold and lonely it seemed. My room had been decorated in warm colors and was enough to keep this feeling at bay but being here right now, with nothing but infinitely tall ceilings and sprawling limestone steps was too ominous.

I turned away and decided to get a drink of water for my parched throat. I found my way to the kitchen; the space I'd never bothered entering in order to avoid Madam Mitterand's glares. I found the light switch and as light flooded the space I saw that it was just as magnificent as the rest of the house with its granite countertops and shiny chrome appliances.

I opened the doors of the huge refrigerator and I found some bottles of water. I uncapped one and lifted it to my mouth. The water was cold and welcome and I shut my eyes to savor it. A sudden sound behind me made me jump back in shock.

"Oh my God," I gasped in fright, as I whirled around. Cold water spilled over my body.

It was someone that I hadn't seen before. It was a big man with a shiny bald head. He was dressed in a dark suit and was carrying something that looked like a walkie-talkie and I immediately pegged him as part of the security detail.

"You shouldn't be in here," he said in a neutral tone. It wasn't a rebuke, just a simple statement of fact.

"I was thirsty."

"That's alright," he said. "Get what you need and I'll escort you back to your wing."

At a loss for words, I shut the door and exited the kitchen. He walked silently behind me. As we reached the living room where I had spent the evening, I said, "I can find my own way back from here."

He nodded. "All right. Good night."

"Er… your boss," I said hurriedly. "Am I going to see him? Tonight?"

"He is currently away on business."

That word away held many possible connotations. "Away, like he'll be back tomorrow, or away, like he'll be back in about a week."

"I don't have a response to that," he said.

"Is that because you do not know or you just don't want to give me a response?"

His expression did not change. "It's because I am not privy to the knowledge."

I chewed my lower lip. I felt my patience running low. Everybody in this house was so cagey. "Is there a way I can reach him then?"

"Give me a moment," he said and pulled a phone out of his pocket.

My heart jumped into my throat. I had expected a refusal. Was I going to get to speak to Luca?

But no such luck. He quickly typed out a text into his phone then he put it away. My eyes lifted to meet his.

"I've sent your request," he said. "Goodnight, Miss Morrison." He turned around to leave.

"Wait a minute. Aren't you going to wait a little bit to see if he responds?"

He turned back, wry amusement in his eyes. "You have your phone with you, don't you?"

"Yeah."

"He'll contact you directly… if he wants to."

CHAPTER 22

LUCA

J was on a conference call with Angelo and my father in our family's mansion in Sicily when the text message came in. Seeing that it came from Luke, who was based at Torrington Hall, I immediately opened it and read what he had to say.

Miss Morrison wants to speak to you, boss.

All kinds of thoughts flashed through my mind as I stared at the message until it registered that Angelo was trying to get my attention from one of the two screens in front of me. I put the phone away.

"Everything alright?" he asked.

I gave a brief nod.

My father didn't comment on the interruption. My father had always been laser focused on the job at hand and despised any kind of emotion or weakness. The way he dealt with Alessa after she did what she did would forever be etched in my mind. "What's the status with that idiot Fisher?" he asked coldly.

I focused my mind on the conversation, but my awareness of the request waiting for my response distracted me more than I would have thought was possible. As soon as the conversation concluded and my father signed off I picked up the phone and was about to answer the message when I realized that Angelo was still watching me.

"Everything alright?" he asked again silkily.

I tossed the phone aside casually and frowned at him. "Don't you have a fiancée to get to?"

"She's not home right now. She went grocery shopping. Ever since we moved in together she's fallen in love with experimenting with meals when she's not at work."

"Is that a complaint?"

"It's not," Angelo denied instantly. "Actually, it's very interesting to see her excited about creating something new for me to try. I've had to double my workouts at the gym otherwise she's going to make me fat while she keeps her heavenly body."

My mind immediately went to the contours of Skye's body. Of all the dips and curves and flesh in all the right places. She was perfectly heavenly.

"Something's different about you. What's going on, Luca?"

I leaned forward. "Nothing's going on. I have things to do. Speak to you tomorrow." Before he could protest I ended the call and the screen became black.

I stared at my blurry reflection as my fingers thrummed against the table.

I shouldn't call her. It was not her place to make demands on my time. In fact, it had annoyed me greatly that I hadn't been able to get her off my mind all day, not completely. In the little moments when the chaos had settled, she would appear in my head as very vivid memories. I saw her moaning, panting, in the throes of passion... calling out my name as she climaxed.

I wanted to see that mouth say filthy things. I thought about how it had felt like to kiss her and it made me shake. I still couldn't understand why I had been driven by an almost desperate need to taste her. With that one kiss she had broken down walls I had spent years building. Walls I did not want to come down. My life was fine as it was. I had no dependents. No one who truly loved me. One day I would die as I had lived, violently, but I was okay with that too.

I didn't need her, or anyone else.

It was best like this. I picked up my phone and rose to my feet with it. I found her number from my list of contacts and headed over to the door overlooking the room's balcony. It overlooked the ocean. From this vantage point I could see the dark waves rolling in and crashing against the rocky banks. I opened the door and stepped into the freezing cold night air. The strong ocean wind rushed into me and swept back my hair. I was only wearing a thin dress shirt and the cold bit right down into my bones, but I did not really feel it.

I gazed unseeing at the dark ocean. It was unknowable, full of weird and wonderful secrets, and all the souls it had stolen through the centuries.

Hear what she has to say, a voice whispered to me.

I pressed the call button and placed the phone to my ear. I let it ring for five rings and when she didn't pick up, I ended the call.

That's it, I thought. I had given her a chance and she had missed it. I'd had a long day and tomorrow would be even longer and I should get to bed. However, I couldn't bring myself to go back inside. Angelo was right. I was not myself. Something was happening inside me. The more I tried to stop it, the worse it became. I gripped the balcony railing, closed my eyes, and leaned out towards the ocean. I thought of her calling me as she came. Like a Siren.

And then I did the strangest thing.

I willed her to call me back.

When my phone started to ring, I opened my eyes and stared down at it with astonishment. The hairs at the back of my neck were standing. I told myself not to be so silly. It was not me who had called to her psychically, it was just her returning my call. I accepted the call and lifted my phone to my ear.

I didn't speak and for the first few seconds neither did she.

"What is it?" I asked.

She cleared her throat. "Um, sorry for disturbing you, but I wanted to ask you about the greenhouse."

The greenhouse? I had considered at least fifty other reasons why she would have been asking to speak to me, and the greenhouse would not have come on the list if I had listed a thousand. "What about it?" I asked curiously.

"Well... um, because I don't have much to do here when you're not around and I want to... I want to grow some flowers."

Her voice filled my head. I almost imagined all those hesitant words dropping from that delicious mouth. "And what's the problem?"

"The head gardener, er... he says, he can't give me access to the greenhouse without your approval."

I pondered on the request. "The greenhouse has been under his jurisdiction from before I bought the house. He doesn't need my approval at all."

She went silent.

She was so far away and I wanted so desperately to hear her voice fill my ear. With any kind of conversation. Even if it was just to say, she had found a dress or a piece of jewelry she wanted me to buy for her, which was bizarre because it bored me stiff when women started talking about stuff like that. Because I craved it so very much I said, "If that is all..."

"Wait, wait, I mean don't go yet!"

I waited.

"I..." she began. "Is there a way you can at least speak to him on my behalf? I can help him around the place. Just sitting around and idling away the time is really not the best for my mental health."

I resisted the urge to smile. The idea she might want to spend her time gardening was novel. I would have thought she would want to go shopping at the best boutiques. "I've given you my response, Skye," I said. "John does not need my approval. If he said he did, it means he doesn't want you in his space."

"Oh!" she mumbled and it was impossible to miss the disappointment in her tone.

"I do have a suggestion for you."

Hope lifted to her voice. "Really? What is it?"

"He's just a man. Hang around the place. Smile lots. Bring him little treats and break down his resistance with charm."

"You really think that would work?"

"It would work on me," I said dryly.

"Okay," she almost sang with happiness. "I'll start the charm offensive tomorrow."

I was aware now it was time to go, but I didn't want to. The pleasure I felt at speaking to her made every nerve in my body come alive and tingle. "Good night," I said and without hearing her reply, ended the call.

CHAPTER 23

SKYE

J stared down at my phone in surprise. Just when I thought we were getting along he goes and ends the conversation so abruptly. Why on earth did he have to do that? I tossed the phone aside and it bounced across the bed, but to my relief, settled just shy of the edge of the big bed.

The last thing I needed right now was a broken phone. There were not too many helpful people in this house. I thought of the gardener once again and how my charm project should be.

I had to admit Mr. Snob was totally right.

Building a sort of relationship with the gardener was much better than barging into the greenhouse and claiming a share of his real estate. There were also several things he could teach me so it was indeed a good idea to win him over.

With that thought I luxuriated in a long soak in the bath, then slipped into the silkiest nightie I had ever worn in my life and climbed into bed. Katie called as I was about to switch off the bedside lamp.

"How's it going," she asked.

"It's okay. I'm going to try and win over the heart of a crusty old gardener tomorrow."

"What?"

"There's this gardener here. He has bushy eyebrows and eyes that are rheumy with age. I think he must be at least eighty. I'm gonna try and get him to let me work with him in his greenhouse."

"Are you drunk, Skye?"

"I've had a few glasses, but I'm not drunk. Honest, I'm not. Did you not know I've always wanted to garden? I love the feeling of soil running through my fingers, and watching the seeds start to sprout. The sad thing is I don't think I have very green fingers because all my plants always die and I'm going to ask John, that's the old gardener, why that keeps happening to my plants."

"How strange. I've known you for years and I never knew this about you."

"Ah, well. I've been busy earning a living," I said.

"Anyway, how's it going with the Don?"

I frowned. "I don't know."

"What do you mean?"

"I mean… there's something there. Something I cannot explain. It's like an invisible rope that connects us. And the sex… the sex is just out of this world."

"Jesus, Skye. You're not falling for this guy, are you?" Her voice was incredulous.

"No, of course not."

"You better not be. You have a one-month contract with this guy. And then it's over. You're out of there. And you go back to living your life the way you want to. Not as some sexual slave to a rich man."

I chewed my bottom lip. Of course, she was right, but I had to make her understand how I felt. "I know I've not had much experience with guys, but this feels good and right, Katie."

"Two guys and that idiot Salvatore is not 'much experience', Skye. It's almost no experience," Katie stated firmly. "Maybe he's good in bed, but you seriously need to stop fooling your-self that this is going to lead anywhere."

"I know it's not going to lead anywhere," I muttered.

Someone called to her then, and she said, "Look, I got to go, but I'll call you tomorrow."

"Speak tomorrow," I said.

"Bye."

"Bye," I echoed softly and the line went dead.

I switched off the light, and lay staring at the wall. The joy I had felt about gardening again was gone. Katie was right. I had to guard my heart. This would come to an end, this grand house, this luxurious bed, the greenhouse, and my amazing surroundings would be gone, and I would have to go out there into the world again and be Skye, the waitress.

From now on I had to remember that.

I was not a princess in a fairytale.

I was just Skye, the waitress.

CHAPTER 24

SKYE

*I*t was still dark the next morning when I got out of bed and went to the kitchen. There was no one else around, but Madam Mitterand was already up and sitting at the table drinking something from a cup and looking into an open notebook. She looked up at me and frowned.

"Is something wrong?"

I shook my head. "Nothing is wrong. I was wondering if I could have some cake or cookies."

Her eyes widened. "Cakes or cookies?"

"Yes, I wanted to take it to John."

She looked at me as if I was mad. "You want to take cakes and cookies to John?"

"Yes, I spoke to Luca last night and he said I could."

For a second she seemed lost for words, then she pushed her chair back and disappeared through a door. It must have been the pantry or something because she came back with two silver tins. Silently, she boxed some chocolate chip cookies and a few slices of butter cake into a white cardboard box. Then she tied the box with a red ribbon and handed it to me.

"His favorites," she said.

"Thank you so much," I said with a grateful smile.

She didn't smile back, but she didn't look hostile either. She just nodded formally.

The light outside was blue and I ran through the snow like a child. I felt full of hope. I knew now I was Skye the waitress, but it was okay to be Skye the waitress. Life was still good. My father was getting the best treatment money could buy, and I was here in the most beautiful place on earth. And I was going to learn to garden again.

The greenhouse came into view. There were no lights in it so maybe John was not there yet.

However, when I peeped through the glass walls I saw him already bent before a row of vegetables on the ground.

Right. Smile lots. I straightened my back and was about to go to the door when he turned and saw me watching him.

He sighed elaborately.

Smile lots.

I grinned at him like a fool and lifted my box of goodies to show him that I had something for him.

With another sigh he rose to his feet. When he started to walk towards the entrance I quickly ran over to meet him at the door. He stopped a few feet away from me.

"I brought you cookies and cake," I said and smiled again.

"What kind?" he asked.

"Chocolate chip cookies and butter cake."

A smile cracked on to his face. "Madam packed it?"

I nodded and quickly closed the distance between us, handed him the box.

"What exactly do you want to do in here?" he asked, his old fingers stroking the red ribbon on the box.

"Help you out," I said softly. "Learn how to plant some flowers."

His tone was gruff. "I don't need you to help me out. What flowers do you want to plant?"

"Sweet peas, Alliums, Bugleweed. Anything. Even vegetables if I can't grow flowers."

"Do you have the seedlings?"

My heart rate picked up. "I... I'll order them tomorrow."

He gave me an exasperated look, then turned around to walk deeper into the greenhouse. My heart swelled with excitement as I followed him into the huge glass encased paradise that smelled of earth and good things.

"There," he pointed to an uncultivated patch of soil.

But to me it seemed especially beautiful because it was demarcated by a small pond which I crossed over on a planked platform that acted as a bridge. On the pond's surface were huge floating lily pads and the occasional flick of a fish's silvery fin as it swam around in bliss. I squealed inside and pressed my hands together in gratitude.

"Do you know how to prepare the soil?" John asked from behind me.

I nodded. "I think I do."

"There are tools in those trays over there."

"Great," I said moving towards them.

"Have you done this before?"

"When I was a child."

He arched a brow but I refused to give in to the doubt.

"Alright. Get what you need and get to work. And no yammering in my ear."

"Got it. And thank you," I said and got started.

Soon, the available trays were laid out on the platforms of the areas I was given so I began to prepare them. I cleaned the platforms which seemed to have been quite neglected for a while, as well as the potting trays that I would need. The next few hours were happy ones while I logged and cleaned all the pots, even the ones that I would not be using. I couldn't remember having a better day in months. Then I began to sweep the whole area.

Midway through the job, I heard Mary Jane calling out to me. I almost wanted to hide from her so that I could keep going, but the thought of her brought to mind all the delicious food that I had indeed missed out on by choosing to slave away here instead of going for breakfast.

"You missed breakfast," she said kindly. "You can't miss lunch too."

I stretched my stiff back and smiled at the glass of golden, iced tea she brought for me. The air outside was frigid, but the warmth in the greenhouse had made it feel anything but, so the refreshment from the cold iced tea was extremely welcomed.

I downed the whole glass before releasing a deep breath. "I won't miss lunch. I could eat a horse," I told her. "What are we having today?"

"Madam said since you have been working hard you will need something substantial so you are having rib-eye steak and crushed new potatoes."

"Sounds delicious," I murmured.

"It will be," she said as she gazed around at the space. "Wow you've really cleaned it up."

"You've been in here before?' I asked, as I continued with my sweeping.

"Of course. I used to come here sometimes to collect vegetables for the Chef. There used to be a lot more variety growing in here, but since John..." she looked around to make sure he wasn't in sight and whispered. "Lost his daughter earlier this year, he's been quite grumpy and detached from all of us. He also lost a lot of interest in his plants. Nowadays the Chef buys most of the stuff he needs, and I don't come around much."

At the information, I looked towards the direction of the man and my heart softened as I thought of his loss. Losing a loved one was the most devastating thing in the world. I knew that first hand. The many, many nights I cried myself to sleep. Something I thought that I still hadn't got over the loss of my mother. For the last couple of years I'd lived with the terror I would go to sleep one day and get a phone call the next morning telling me my father was no more.

"Let's go," Mary Jane said.

I put the broom away and followed her out.

"I can't believe you're working in the greenhouse," Mary Jane said. "I would have thought that you'd take this visit as a vacation and just lounge by the indoor pool."

"Indoor pool?" I asked.

"Yeah. It's gorgeous. I'll take you there after lunch."

The idea sounded very promising because after my work at the greenhouse, stretching out my limbs and relaxing would surely be an incredibly rewarding event.

"That would be great, thank you," I said.

Madam was waiting for us in the Orangery. "You're going out to dinner with Don Messana tonight. Please be ready by 6.p.m."

CHAPTER 25

I took her to Boston's harbor hotel with its sixty-foot stone archway and its panoramic views of the city's skyline. It was also a personal favorite for other reasons. Security was easily monitored by my men, and my requests for privacy were always immediately fulfilled. As I mostly moved in the shadows and appreciated places that helped me maintain things that way.

Across the terrace, private and heated transparent igloo-like boxes had been erected to both tackle the frigid winter air, and to provide privacy. One of the things I liked the most about these encasements were how the glass made it possible for you to see out, but for no one to see within.

I sat at my usual enclosure with my customary glass of Dirty Martini and tried to imagine Skye working in the green-house… and couldn't. I'd never even been inside it. I had to admit I'd never given the idea of gardening much thought, but I had formed the general impression gardeners were gardeners because they couldn't find better jobs. The idea that Skye, who could have filled her time in a million other ways, chose to work hard in the greenhouse surprised and intrigued me.

I glanced at my watch. A minute to seven. I knew she would be right on time. My men wouldn't have allowed anything short of that. When I looked up Mateo was escorting her over to my table.

She was wearing scarlet lipstick and wrapped up in a long jet-black coat that made her hair shine like gold. I stood and offered to help her out of her coat. For a moment she hesitated, her hands clenching the soft wool. Then she let go of the material and turned around so I could help her out of it and hand it to Mateo. He would keep it with him in the next enclosure. She turned around to face me.

And my breathing quickened.

To all intents and purposes she was covered up with long sleeves and a high neckline that delicately encircled her neck, but that was as far as the illusion of decency went. The entire thing was made of lace and thus bits of her skin and sometimes whole sections of her were very clearly visible through the fabric.

I was quite certain she was naked underneath because I could see the full swell of her breasts, and the only part hidden with thicker lace designs was the areas surrounding nipples and her crotch. My eyes skimmed over the skin of her hips that was exposed through the little holes in the patterns of the lace.

And I was instantly hard.

"Good evening," she greeted as she took her seat without quite meeting my eyes. Her hair was pulled away from her face with a thin, glistening diamond headband. On her ears were simple stone studs.

I lost my appetite for food and was ravenous for something else.

Ideas about stopping the service and taking care of my hunger began to swirl in my head. All I needed was twenty minutes. And then I stopped myself. What was this attraction that made me behave like a hormone ridden teen? I had come across women whom had been more naked than she was, but I had never felt like fucking them on the restaurant table.

I had been this way since the first time I laid eyes on her. I had attributed it to curiosity then, but I'd fucked her long and hard and yet my hunger showed no signs of waning. If anything the need was becoming worse. To distract myself, I picked up my glass of Dirty Martini and emptied it.

The sommelier arrived together with a waiter. With a great sense of theater, they opened a bottle of Dom and poured it into the two flutes. Then withdrew and closed the glass doors.

When I lifted my gaze to Skye's I found her watching me. The candle light cast a beautiful golden glow on her skin. She was absolutely breathtaking.

I raised my glass. "To your flowers."

She smiled and raised her glass. "It might not be flowers. It might be vegetables."

My gaze went to her lips.

I took a sip and watched the muscles in her white throat move as she swallowed. She caught my eyes and sank her teeth into her bottom lip. God, how I wanted to fuck her. I picked up my menu without a word, and she did the same.

I didn't actually need to study the menu at all. I was well acquainted with it, but I needed those few seconds to get myself in order. The lust for her was incredible. After a little while, I set it down and she followed soon after. I pressed the call button and pretty soon there was a light tap on the glass.

"Come in," I responded and the waiter slid the glass door open.

He smiled. "You are ready to order?"

I nodded and made a gesture for him to take Skye's order first. He turned to her attentively.

"I'll have the—" she began, her eyes still on the menu.

But the waiter suddenly exclaimed, "Skye? Skye Morrison?"

Her head jerked up. "Oh, my God, James," she cried as she rose to her feet. She threw her arms around him, and he hugged her back just as tightly. She pulled away slightly, but still within the confines of his arms. "It's so great to see you. It's been years."

"About four now, right?"

"Yeah," she replied and the soft expression on her face as she stared up at him stunned me. It was full of deep affection. I'd never seen such an expression on her face. Seeing her stare at him in this way had a strange effect on me. My chest burned with irritation.

"How are you doing?" she asked.

"I'm alright. But you, Jesus. You look—"

"We need to catch up," she said quickly, and as if only then remembering me, threw a glance at me. She saw the look in my eyes and took a step back from him, but of course, the moron was totally oblivious.

"God, you look amazing. What are you doin, I mean?" He sent a smile in my direction, which I didn't acknowledge. And he too finally felt the chill coming from me and slightly cleared his throat.

"I'm sorry," she apologized, as she returned to her seat.

He threw another apologetic glance at me. "I'm sorry. We're old friends." He turned back to her. "Do you still have my number?" he asked quickly.

I knew there was nothing sexual in their relationship, but I wanted to rip him to shreds.

"No, I lost my old phone a while ago and couldn't retrieve my contacts."

"No worries. I'll be serving you for the rest of the dinner so I'll definitely hand it over before you leave."

"That would be great."

"I saw your sister about three weeks ago when I was with my friends at Sinkhole. She's still as crazy as ever."

"Yeah," she replied, and I noted the flash of sadness that passed through her eyes.

"Oh, look at me just yapping away. What do you want to eat, Gorgeous?"

I knew there was nothing to the endearment. That it was harmless. A friendly thing, but I had to forcibly keep myself from leaping out of my chair and socking the fool.

She was all smiles as she gave him her order and so was he as he finally took his leave.

I was boiling with anger, but didn't ask her about him. After a few tense moments of silence, she explained herself. "We used to work together, at a diner a few years back. I haven't seen him since. I apologize for the interruption."

I decided that she needed to be punished for being so brazen and so defiant before me.

"Get over here," I commanded, and her eyes widened slightly in shock.

CHAPTER 26

SKYE

A shiver crackled through my spine at his words.

Because I knew that look in his eyes, the almost ferocious gaze and I knew what usually followed after that. The last time he had had that look in his eyes and told me to get over to where he was, I had been fucked against a door and left in a puddle at his feet.

"Um," I swallowed. "I need to go to the Ladies first?"

"You're going to be sorry if I have to repeat myself."

"Please. Someone could come in." All I could think about was James and the fact that he worked here. This was not how I wanted someone from my past to see me.

"No one will come in until I allow them to."

Through the glass, I could see the other igloos around us, and people passing in between. I was pretty certain that they couldn't see into our own encasement, but they would definitely be able to hear us especially since there was no way that I would be able to stay quiet after he touched me.

"But people can hear us," I whispered.

His gaze darkened even further, and I had to accept the painful truth that I didn't have a choice. This was what I had been paid for. I rose to my feet and circled the table until I was standing in front of him. He watched me intently with those wolf eyes. He placed his hand on my ass, and then pulled me close to him till his face was before my crotch, and then he inhaled. I had gone without any underwear in order to do the dress the justice it deserved, so I knew he could smell me.

His grip on my ass tightened, as he slipped his hand into my dress and up my thigh. Then he palmed me, and I quivered. In that moment all I could think about was hoisting my dress even further up to my waist and then riding his face. I had done it in the past and it had blown my mind but this was a public place.

"You're so wet," he murmured.

The very thought of him and perhaps the reaction he would have to me in this dress had already turned me on hours earlier so he was right I was already soaking wet for him. Things had however taken a wrong turn when I must have annoyed him by being overly familiar with James. But I couldn't help it. James had been a friend to me for a long time, though at the moment it felt like another lifetime ago.

He pushed his glass and cutlery away from him. "Sit on the table."

I wanted to act stubbornly, to make things difficult for him, but I knew there was no point because it was either I got rid of the tension that had so built up inside or I was going to literally explode in a ball of frustration. Silently, I obeyed.

"Open your legs and show me your pussy," he commanded.

Slowly I spread my thighs and he saw for himself how wet I was.

Reaching between my legs he began to stroke me, his fingers sinking between my folds and tormenting the swollen bud of my arousal. I pursed my lips to keep all of my whimpering at bay, but then his middle finger slipped into my sex and I held unto the edge of the table, the glasses on it softly rattling at the sudden movement.

He began to finger me, and soon another finger joined the intrusion. I almost cried out. What would never get old was just how delicious it felt to have his fingers inside me. A couple passed by us and they felt so close that I could have reached out to touch them except that they couldn't see us.

"Oh God," I muttered, my head thrown back and my eyes clenched shut, as his thrusts became faster.

I tightened my hand on the table to stabilize myself when he didn't slow down his pace. In no time my body was wound as tightly as an instrument, and then I was coming. My toes curled and my frame writhed as the orgasm tore through my body.

I would have completely fallen over if he hadn't caught me. He held me with one hand around my midriff, while the other continued to play with my pussy. I could see I had stained the table cloth. It was embarrassing, but he seemed not to care at all. He pulled my thighs further apart and ran his tongue on my wet slit. I let him lick me clean. It felt good to see his head between my legs.

"Sit astride me," he ordered suddenly.

I shook my head in horror. At this point, I was sure that we had been heard enough. I knew I could never have sex with him without screaming the whole place down.

"I want to… I have to go to the Ladies," I said as I began to get off the table. Before I knew it, he bodily lifted me and put me on his lap. Although I struggled with him I was mindful of not making too much noise. The last thing I needed was to cause such a ruckus that every eye on the roof top would be on the commotion coming from our space. I watched his hand quickly and expertly release his cock. Before I knew it, I was astride him and being lowered onto his thick angry cock.

I couldn't believe that we were doing this here, but as soon as I felt the hardness of his length as it curved into me, I couldn't help riding on it. With my ass thrust up, I smeared my slickness all over the smooth mushroom head.

"Stop," I whispered, but my words no longer meant a thing.

He shoved the hardness into me and a deep gasp escaped my lips as I felt how tightly sheathed he was inside me. My hand slapped over my mouth to muffle any other sudden exclamations. Slowly, I began to bounce on his cock, and the plush head of his cock prodded at that elusive spot inside of me. I whimpered with shock, my head falling onto his shoulders until I was on the verge of another orgasm.

"Fuck," I cried out, unable to control myself.

I hated that he could reduce me to this state, but there was not a thing I could do to stop myself. This was beyond me. I was helpless to stop my body from betraying me. I was just going to let my body ride him just as hard and take what it needed from him. My fingers found their way into his hair and I pulled as hard as I could. My punishment was a painful smack to my ass.

"Let go!" he commanded harshly.

I did, but to my surprise, the burn of his smack had been a most welcome ache. I felt myself leak out even more down my thighs. With my feet solidly positioned on the floor, and my hand gripping his shoulders, I began to ride him. He pumped his hips up to thrust brutally into me and I met every vicious drive. Then he ground his hips into my groin. With hands around my waist he pulled me up until only the broad mushroom head of his cock was inside me. Staring into my eyes he pushed me down his shaft, until I was balls deep. I gasped with shock.

That was just the beginning.

He fucked me harder than I thought possible. The sounds of our moans, harsh breathings and of flesh smacking against flesh filled the space around us and surely escaped the enclosure. I gazed out to the skyline as he took me to the heights of ecstasy, and it was breathtakingly dreamlike. The sparkling lights, the dark cloudless sky, and the half-moon hanging up above. I would never forget it as long as I lived.

He gripped my waist, as his thrusts came faster and pretty soon I could no longer keep up. He was furious and I could hear it in his grunts. He cursed into my ear and my eyes fluttered closed to savor the sounds. It had been two days since I had last seen him and the truth was that I had missed him, and it was pure bliss to have him inside me.

My hand moved to stroke my clit. I circled the swollen bud at a maddened pace until I burst. Surprisingly, he was the one whose hand came over my mouth to muffle my scream. I bit his hand hard.

I heard the gruff announcement of his own release as he buried his face into my neck, while his seed shot thick, and hot into me, flooding my sex.

I stood and stumbled away from him as quickly as I could. As he zipped himself back into his trousers, I returned to my seat. I felt confused and embarrassed. I could see the wet patch on his tablecloth I had left. Still far away from normal, I picked up my glass of champagne, drained it, and placed it back down.

"I want to leave," I told him.

"Not till after dinner," he said, as he retrieved his napkin. He took his time unfolding the cloth and then laying it on his lap before returning his gaze to mine.

I couldn't hold back my tongue.

"I can't eat here."

He cocked his head. "Why not?"

"Everyone heard us!"

He refilled my glass. "Eat your food and walk out as you normally would. No one knows you and no one cares."

"Someone knows me here." I lashed out before I could stop myself.

His eyes narrowed. "Is that why you're embarrassed?"

I realized then what had provoked him. I shook my head in disbelief. "Is that why you did it? Because I met a friend here? I didn't realize that you were insecure."

His expression didn't change, however his hand slowly unwrapped from the stem of the glass and rested on the table. His gaze darkened as the fingers began to tap one after the other and I knew then I had crossed a line, but I would never apologize… not even if he hurt me.

My hand trembled as I reached for my drink so I immediately pulled it back and hid it under the table. The fact that he wasn't an ordinary person and didn't manage a garbage disposal company like Salvatore began to dawn on me.

What if he put out a hit on James? Men like him were capable of anything without blinking an eye. Jesus, what on earth was I playing with here?

The words spilled out from my lips in a rush. "I'm sorry," I said. "Please… please don't hurt James. I'm sorry for what I said."

He looked at me curiously. As if I was a creature he did not understand. There was a soft tap on our door and I jumped.

"Come in," he called, and the door was slid open.

Two waiters, one pushing a trolley stood outside. He had a tight smile for us and began to lay our order across the table. I didn't pay attention because my gaze was solely on him and on the fact that he wasn't James.

"Enjoy," he said when he was done, but before he could move away, I asked, "Where's James?"

He seemed startled at the question. Then his eyes shifted nervously between Luca and I. "He had to attend to a personal matter," he said apologetically, before shutting the door and leaving.

I knew that someone who guarded Luca's best interests had seen James and me hugging and thought it was inappropriate or disrespectful to Luca. Before I could speak Luca intercepted me.

"I want to enjoy this meal," he said, picking up his cutlery. "So eat. Don't piss me off more than I already am."

I could feel his cum leaking out of me as I picked up my fork.

CHAPTER 27

LUCA

*W*e were riding back to Torrington Hall. Our bodies at least two feet apart. I stared out at trees, all cast in darkness, as we left the city.

Who was I angry at? Was it at myself? For reacting like a jealous fool. Or was it at her for pointing it out? I couldn't decide, but either way it didn't feel good.

I knew she was scared for her friend's safety, but I had no intentions of doing anything to him. At that moment when I saw him touch her so casually I wanted to throttle him, but now that my blood was no longer boiling, I could clearly see he was only a little gnat. Even the tiny effort required to squash him would not be worth my time.

" I… uh… I wanted to speak to you tonight about the greenhouse," she said hesitantly. Her tone was soft and docile.

I turned my head to look at her. In the soft light coming from the console, her skin looked like alabaster.

"Thank you for allowing me to work there," she continued. "I need to buy some seeds. I will purchase them on my own of course, but I want to confirm that they will be able to deliver it to the house."

Before I could respond a call came in. It was not an urgent call, but I picked it up anyway and deliberately began the conversation in Italian as a way to shut her out. I ended the call five minutes later, but by then she had completely given up on a response. I left it that way.

She ran into the house the moment we arrived, and I stood and watched her. It was hard for me to understand what was going on inside me. Why I felt so possessive over her. I had never felt that way about any woman before. Not even for Alessa, and I married her.

I stayed back for a few minutes to give some last minute instructions to the men. Afterwards, I walked in, shut the door behind me and walked into the foyer. She was waiting for me at the bottom of the stairs.

"What will it take?" she asked passionately. "To stop you from hurting James?"

I gazed at her curiously. Her loyalty first to her father and now to her friend was quite remarkable. It was clear she was worried senseless. It made me feel like a schoolyard bully. I was never that.

"Go to bed. Your friend is safe. I'm not going to touch him," I said coldly, as I went on my way.

A few moments later I heard her footsteps behind me. I stopped and turned around to see that she was indeed following me.

"What is it?" I asked.

"I… um… I want to spend the night with you," she blurted out. Her hands were hidden behind her back and the look in her eyes had changed from fear to gratitude.

I didn't need her fucking gratitude and I would have rejected her, but then I considered the chill of the night. There was also the fantasy I'd had of fucking her on the plush white rug in front of the roaring fire.

"Alright," I heard myself say. "Come with me."

She nodded and immediately came forward.

My hand reached out, but before it connected with the small of her back, I pulled back. There was something too tender about the intention that I most definitely did not want. A little later we reached the elevator that would take us underneath the building. The doors swished open outside my den.

I walked ahead of her, opened the wide door, and headed straight for the liquor cabinet. Just as I grabbed the decanter filled with old whiskey, it dawned on me just how often I'd been reaching for it these days. It wasn't because of her I reasoned as I poured out a generous measure. I lifted it to my lips and took a whiff of its smoky scent of burnt heather and wood.

The burn of the liquid as it slid down my throat was most welcome. It seemed to restore a sense of ease and control back to me. *It wasn't because of her, I* affirmed, as I turned around to give my attention to the stranger I'd brought into my most private space. Until now, other than the staff who clean and refill stuff, no one had been allowed into this place.

She was standing awkwardly in the middle of the room, her arms wrapped protectively around her waist, as her eyes roved around my den.

Bringing her here wasn't the smartest move, but here we were, so I was damn well going to do my fantasy justice and fuck her through the night on that furry rug. The logs were already crackling in the hearth, handled ahead of time by one of the men so the expansive space was already filled with its warmth. There was a raging fire in my belly. I knew it was seeing that fool touch her, but I refused to admit it even to myself.

I downed the whiskey. "Take your clothes off."

I turned away and put my empty glass down, then shrugged off my jacket and flung it away. I turned back towards her and saw her stepping out of her shoes. My expression twisted. Sometimes it was hard for me to believe she was that sexually inexperienced. Never had a woman I'd ordered to undress in this kind of situation taken her shoes off first. Every one of them was smart enough to walk towards me naked but for their high heels.

"Leave the shoes on."

Her face flushed a pretty pink as she put them back on.

Not taking my eyes off her, I pulled the tails of my shirt out of my slacks and began to unbutton. Her arms were behind her back as she struggled with a stuck zip.

"Come here," I invited softly.

At first she hesitated, then she walked towards me, her hands still behind her back still trying hard to get it down. As soon as she was a foot away, she turned around, her hands falling to her sides. I gazed at her creamy skin already exposed. The middle of her shoulder was dotted with a tiny brown mole. I couldn't take my eyes away from the detail that I'd never noticed before. My hands went to the zip, but my fingers encountered her warm skin and I felt a jolt of static electricity zap me. She felt it too because she jumped. I fiddled with it carefully. I didn't want to ruin another dress. It gave and I started to pull the tab down. The material fell on either side. She didn't have a bra on underneath and the dress opened up to reveal flawless skin.

My hands slipped into her dress, curved around her smooth shoulders, and pulled her dress down her arms. Then I watched as she wriggled out of the material. Only the mood lights were on, so the room was lit mostly with the bright yellow flames in the massive fireplace. The mood was intimate and fiery and every movement seemed simultaneously too slow and too fast. I peeled the dress down her flaring hips and it puddled around her feet. She was left completely naked before me and I couldn't help but stare at all that beauty. My eyes traced the beautiful and delicate curves of her body, the dip of her waist and the curve of her ass.

Tenderly, I brushed her hair over one shoulder, and lowered until my lips connected with her creamy flesh. She was warm, incredibly so, and she smelled like heaven. A sweet mix of roses and some other notes I couldn't quite identify. My arms slunk around her waist.

I heard her light gasp at the pressing of skin against skin, her head tilting to the side as I continued my trail of kisses across her shoulders. They were unhurried and heated, and with each soft suction I savored the taste of her skin. She grew restless, her body squirming and with my lips I began to suck at that tiny mole on her back. She turned in my arms and I let her. She gazed into my eyes, hers heavy-lidded with a need that sent a painful jolt of arousal to my already aching cock.

"Fuck me," she said, her eyes sliding away. "There's no need to pretend this is anything more than... just sex."

My heart thundered loudly in my chest, and for a muscle that had been trained over the years to maintain its calmness regardless of what external dilemmas I was facing, my reaction to her was disappointing to say the least. I grabbed her chin and turned her face till her gaze returned to mine.

Don't tell me what to do, I wanted to say to her, but the words wouldn't come to my lips in that moment, because I was entranced by her eyes. Suddenly in the blue pools I saw unimaginable depths of selflessness and resolution.

I stared into her eyes and without realizing it my grip had become too hard. Her hands wrapped around my wrist in protest and only when I saw her pained expression did I realize that I was slightly out of control. I released my grip of her and she staggered backwards, her golden hair bouncing.

She straightened and stared back at me, her chest heaving.

I couldn't look away at the picture she made. She was an angel and I was a sinner. I didn't deserve to even touch such pure flesh. Well, what did it matter? Luca Messana was going to hell and there would be no angels there for me to fuck. All the angels I got would be here, on God's beautiful earth. This was all I was getting and it was damn well good enough.

"Go lie down on the rug and open your legs," I commanded harshly.

171

CHAPTER 28

SKYE

https://www.youtube.com/watch?v=JF8BRvqGCNs
-Stay-

I could barely catch my breath.

My jaw still tingled from his grip, but it was not that which caused me concern. It was the almost violent tug of the desperate need to have him thrust so hard into me that my fingers claw down his expansive back. He had turned his back to me and I watched his sculpted muscles hungrily, every movement of his arms caused a shift in his muscles that was simply mesmerizing.

I knew I shouldn't have been so rude to him, but the kisses down my back had scared me. It was the kisses of a lover, someone who cared. I was already in a place where I kept forgetting he had bought me and planned to discard me in less than a month, but if he was going to take his time and start devoting his attention to every part of my body, then I was finished.

Detachment was what I needed. I desperately needed him to be the distant, cruel man who saw me as nothing more than a body at his disposal for the coming weeks. That was how I needed my perception of him to remain.

I headed over to the plush rug. It was white and furry, and deliciously sensuous. I almost moaned when the exquisite fabric came in contact with my skin. I didn't want to be caught staring at him so I deliberately moved my gaze to the crackling hearth before me. I watched the logs burn and had a surreal impression that I was not on earth anymore. I was in some fantasy world or inside a fairytale. Maybe a castle in the middle of a dark forest filled with tall, narrow trees.

My thoughts were interrupted by the sound of the metal buckle of his belt.

It seemed to pierce the atmosphere of the room. I looked up at his undeniably beautiful face, even the scar only added to his mystery and beauty. His face was focused and on guard as he worked the fly of his pants. I was stiff and on alert as I watched his trousers slip down his muscled thighs. He stepped out of them and continued towards me in his dark briefs bulging with his aroused cock.

My heart caught in my throat and I quickly moved my gaze away from it to the muscles in his thighs, then to the flat of his stomach. There was a light smattering of hair coursing through the region, and disappearing into his briefs it completely struck me with wonder at just how sculpted the man was, with barely a trace of fat anywhere on his body.

"Lie down," he ordered as he lowered himself to the rug.

I obeyed, and he kneeled astride me and moved up until his groin was poised over my face. I licked my lips in uncontrollable anticipation of what was to come. His hand slid into his briefs. His cock was pulled out and I couldn't help staring at his angry cock as it throbbed and pulsed in his hand. Before he could even lean towards me, I had already lifted my weight onto my elbows and parted my lips to capture the wide head.

Whatever he had been about to say died in his throat as a raspy groan at the contact made his chest heave. My hands curled around his hips and I pulled him forward so my back could return to softly rest against the fur as I sucked him… hard. I tried to keep my eyes open however, the deep rhythmic hollowing of my cheeks as I milked the first small spurt of cum out of him had me intoxicated. With one hand closed around the base of his thick width I let my head bob continuously.

Up and down. Up and down.

I knew I was driving him crazy. I could tell by the bob of his Adam's apple, the beautifully twisted expression on his face, and his clenched fists. I couldn't help myself from touching him. My hand moved upwards and I laid my hand on the flat of his abdomen.

Pushing at that slab of muscle I tried to slide out from underneath him, but the breathless moan died in his lips.

"Stay" he rasped.

But like a little eel I wriggled and completely came out from under him. To my surprise, he didn't protest and just watched me with his wolf's eyes. I decided then that I was going to do whatever I wanted to him. I knelt just as he did and threw my arms around his neck. He watched me as my head tilted to nibble lightly on his jaw line. I didn't miss his sharp intake of breath.

"Listening is not one of your strong suits, is it?" he asked drily.

I mumbled my answer against his overheated flesh as I trailed kisses down the thick muscles of his arms. "It is. Obedience is not."

He made a muffled sound. It might have been laughter, but it could have been annoyance too.

I straightened once again, my breasts pressed against his chest and his cock poking hard against my belly.

"I'm going to kiss you," I told him and he frowned, however he didn't try to stop me.

My audacity came from a driving need inside me to possess him in the same way he had done to me. We were in his private space and just as he had come into mine and shattered me to pieces I was desperate to do just the same to him.

I caught his bottom lip between my teeth and nibbled softly on the delicate flesh. His eyes were still open and watching me, and it sent chills down my back. But it also stoked a fire in my gut that consumed me from the inside. I sucked softly on that tasty bottom lip, then moved on to the upper. Soon his lips parted to catch his breath and I slipped my tongue in. My arms tightened around him as I stroked his tongue with mine, and then delved even deeper to draw out as much of his taste as I could. His eyes fluttered closed at the long and deep kiss that followed, and I felt my body weaken. It was not supposed to be that shattered, but here I was again. Falling apart.

With a hand around my waist, he lowered me gently onto the rug.

I wanted to take back control and began to kiss every inch of skin that I could reach. When I felt his finger slide into my sex the jolt to my heart was excruciating and I almost wanted to give in to the exquisite pleasure I knew he could give.

"No," I muttered, and pulled his finger out. "You first."

He frowned, but before he could get the chance to refuse I moved out from underneath him once again and sat astride him. I could feel his cock on my wet pussy and the temptation to just let him fuck me was almost too much to resist, but I pushed at his chest. He allowed himself to fall back against the fur. With the pad of my thumb, I flicked the disc of his hardened nipple and then leaned forward to cover the bud with my mouth. I sucked deeply on it, then moved to the other.

By the time I came up for a breath his arm was over his eyes.

With a smile, I followed the light trail of dark hair down his torso till I returned once more to his cock.

I closed my hands around the slightly curved length, gently and almost apologetically for the neglect and then once again took him in my mouth, my lips hollowing to pull him deep, all the way to the back of my throat. I had never had a man this deep before and I was afraid I was going to spoil it all by gagging, but to my surprise I didn't gag. I loved him so deep in my mouth. His heady scent filled my nostrils and I couldn't stop.

"Fuck," I heard him swear.

My tongue flicked out and licked hungrily along the damp flesh. With my hand at the root, I began to fist him as my lips sucked feverishly on the head.

His hips bucked, his hands finding their way to my hair and I relished the tight tug as more than anything it relayed the effect that my teasing was having on him.

"Faster," he growled.

I obliged him.

As he pumped his cock into my mouth I met every thrust with a tighter, deeper hollowing of my cheeks.

It was so stimulating I could feel my sex begin to clench with pure lust. I focused on milking him, spurred by my passion and his and in time he was releasing into my mouth. I kept my lips firmly locked around him as his burst shot down my throat, the liquid deliciously hot and thick.

I swallowed it all, and his growl of pleasure reverberated through the room.

His arm was still over his eyes, hiding his face from mine, but I sat back on him and pulled his arm away. He looked into my eyes then. What I saw shocked me. He wasn't a monster. He was beautiful. Unbearably beautiful. Like a fallen angel. I didn't want to see him like that and it was clear he didn't want me to see him as he really was either.

I didn't know what to do. I tore my gaze away from his and turned to the only thing I knew could move me from that place I was in. Sex. I was here for sex. What we had was just sex. Yes, I was so wet and aroused I could no longer remain still so I began to rub my sex against his semi-hard cock.

His hands came to my hips and suddenly strong arms gripped my waist and I was lifted clean off his body.

I gasped in shock. Before I could even recover my pussy was hovering over his face. Then his mouth covered the soaked, pulsing flesh, and I cried out, my yearning finally attended to. The wave of molten pleasure spreading through my body was incredible.

My back arched and my breasts jutted out as his tongue drove into me, then curved. While I moaned helplessly he lapped at the juices leaking from me, before he moved over to my swollen clit and sucked hard in a maddening rhythm.

My fingers dug into my own scalp as I writhed wildly against his face and soon I was coming. I completely gave in to the climax that tore through me. It sent violent tremors through my body and my cries resounded inside the underground chamber.

His lips burned a trail along my inner thighs and then back to my sex for one last kiss. I gasped in surprise as he slid me down over his chest and stomach until my cleft was stroking the length of his cock. Pulling me forward he rolled me until the soft fur was on my back.

The head of his cock slid into my slickness, and the crackling of the fire was like fireworks going off in my ears. I gripped his ass, the thought occurring to me that at some point he had taken his briefs off, but I was so out of it I hadn't even noticed. He pushed the rest of his length into me, and a long moan tore out of my throat.

He sunk deep. God he sunk deep.

My heart was full, my bones felt like warm wax, and my core wound deliciously tight around his hardness.

He cradled my head in his arms as he began to thrust into me, starting with slow, heart melting strokes which later translated to a more rapid pace. From here onwards, all I could do was feel; his searing warmth all around me, the harsh sounds from the depths of his throat entwining with the soft whimpers and cries from mine. And the squirming, the shameless squirming. I was like a fish out of water. Not gasping for air, but him. I wanted more, more of him, more sensation, more friction.

As I edged closer to my release I swore and thrashed in his arms, but instead of letting me come he slowed his pace. Again and again, he did that. His hips worked me and my pussy with a level of expertise and familiarity that left me shaken and battered. My vision blurred despite being wide open as I stared up at the ceiling.

"Luca, please, let me come," I breathed, gasping as the head of his cock stroked that elusive spot inside of me.

"Fuck!" he growled as if he had been holding himself back until that moment. His hips bucked and so did mine as I shattered into a million tiny pieces.

He kept fucking me, his motions although jerky, were relentless. Now I understood why the French called it the little death. Because there was no more of me. No body, no mind, no separation from the rest of the world. I was just a wave of pure bliss connected to everything in the universe.

His hips rocked into mine, milking out every ounce of ecstasy between us until he collapsed onto me with a groan.

"I can't believe you're paying me for this," I whispered. In that moment I realized that if I had known that sex with him could feel this way, I would have gone on my knees to beg for it.

For a second he froze, then he raised his head and chuckled.

I stared at him in shock. My God, he was so beautiful when he laughed. So utterly beautiful. A small answering laugh bubbled out of me. With my arms around him, I crushed his frame to mine, my legs tightening around his waist. These were things that I shouldn't have dared to do, but I no longer cared.

He didn't protest so I shut my eyes and basked in the magic of our joining. I don't know how it happened, but before I knew it I was asleep. When I woke I guessed it must already be morning. The fire was still burning, and around me was the thick biceps of the man I had drowned myself in last night.

The realization immediately squeezed my heart and my chest tightened with emotion.

I had fallen asleep in his arms.

I had fallen asleep in his arms.

I was almost too afraid to breathe. The wonder I felt of being pressed so intimately to him, every inch of my skin plastered to his, and his soft breathing in my neck. Last night I had given myself completely to him.

And now, I didn't know how to feel.

We still had three weeks left of our arrangement, but I was acutely aware that if things kept going this way, I wasn't going to be able to depart unscathed. I released a careful sigh again, but then a gentle sound began to thrum across the room. With my heart slamming against my chest, I shut my eyes and went as still as I possibly could.

CHAPTER 29

LUCA

The ringing of my phone roused me from sleep.

At first I was disoriented, almost perplexed as to where I was which was unnerving. I shot up, immediately on guard. I realized then that I was in my own den. I ran my fingers through my hair sheepishly.

Damn, that was a bad way to start the day.

I realized why things had felt so off balance. For the first time in a very long while, I'd woken up to the warmth of a woman burning against my skin and it had sent a jolt of shock through me. I vaulted to my feet and padded over to my phone and placed it against my ear.

"Pronto," I said in Italian, and lifted my gaze to watch her.

She was still asleep on the rug, her body lightly covered with one of the thick blankets I had pulled from one of the armchairs and draped over us last night. Inside that intimate warm cocoon I had sunk into the deepest and most invigorating sleep I'd had in years. Her. It was strange and if I was honest, rather wonderful to see her gold head on my rug. I felt a yearning then. To have her here with me at all times, and the very thought made me uncomfortable.

I kept my eyes on her as she stirred in her sleep. Dawn had hardly broken so I thought she would sleep for a few more hours, but she stretched, and a corner of the blanket fell off her, revealing the delicate curves of her naked body.

She got up then, and I couldn't pull my gaze away.

Only half-listening to Mateo, I watched her shyly and hurriedly, wrap the blanket around herself. It was such a sharp contrast from the wanton woman of last night that it made my lips curl with amusement. Without looking in my direction she began to gather her discarded clothes. She jumped when there was a knock on the door.

"Come in," I called.

The door pushed open and Luigi came in with an envelope in his hand. If he was surprised to see me naked with a woman down here, he didn't show it, and he was smart enough to keep his eyes well away from Skye too.

"I'm off to the greenhouse. See you later," Skye called out as she sailed past him towards the door.

Her shoulders were exposed, her hair tousled, and she was clutching a big blanket around her naked body, but she could have been a queen for the regality with which she exited the room.

Luigi put the envelope on the desk and withdrew silently. Once the door was shut behind him an eerie silence settled over the room. Or perhaps it had always been there, but I just had never truly noticed or been bothered by it. Until now.

I pushed away the thought impatiently. I'd always loved it here on my own. My solitude was not a burden, on the contrary it was something I cherished and nurtured.

I opened the envelope. The receipt of messages about the things that could not be sent electronically was a necessity in my business, but I felt no interest in the contents. It fluttered from my hands.

Skye

I COULD NOT BELIEVE I was running around that massive house naked under a blanket. Whatever had possessed me to run out of his room like that?

Idiot.

I kicked myself mentally, as the lift opened. The wide corridor was empty, thank God. I hurried down it, the blanket trailing. Maybe, it would be okay. I would get to my room without anyone seeing me. After all, it was still dark outside, and surely no one would be up at this time.

I was wrong.

As I was halfway down the corridor, Madam Mitterand appeared at the end of it. It was clear she saw me, but she pretended as if she hadn't and quickly disappeared into the first door she came to. I breathed a sigh of relief. It would have been embarrassing for both of us if she had carried on down the corridor and had to pass me.

I reached my room without meeting anyone else. I wanted to keep Luca's scent on my body so I didn't shower. I quickly changed into a thick hoodie and a pair of skinny jeans. Then I pulled on my coat and shoes and ran down the stairs. I went into the kitchen and Madam Mitterand was now sitting in the same chair I found her in yesterday morning. She was drinking from the same cup and looking down on her notebook.

On the edge of the table closest to me were two small boxes tied up with a red ribbon.

"Oh, are those for John?" I asked, surprised.

She looked up, her face calm and expressionless. "Mini oatmeal muffins and an almond croissant," she informed.

"Thank you, Madam. Thank you so much," I whispered gratefully.

She nodded, and returned her attention to her notebook.

Clutching my boxes I ran to the foyer and opened the great big door. Outside it was now light, snowing softly and incredibly quiet and peaceful. With a song in my heart I began to walk to the greenhouse.

Today I was going to plant something. Something beautiful.

CHAPTER 30

LUCA

I went into the adjoining bathroom and showered. Then I walked through into the dressing room, pulled on a pair of jeans and turtleneck sweater, and went to sit at my desk. I tried to work, but I kept glancing at the empty rug.

After a while I leaned back in my chair and stared at the fire. It was beginning to die. The embers glowed red among the ashes.

The greenhouse.

It had never even crossed my mind to go see it since I bought this house and yet it held such a fascination for her. As I stared at the dying fire, a seed of curiosity sprouted within me. I realized I'd never ever walked across the grounds of the house. When I had first bought it the estate agent had flown me over it to show me the exact boundaries, but since then I had never bothered about it. It was extremely rare for me to take things at a slower pace even while I was on vacation, but maybe this morning I could explore the grounds of my own house.

I rose to my feet, and after pulling on a warm jacket and walking shoes, I strolled out of my den.

Outside it was snowing steadily. The dark silhouettes of the trees beyond were covered in the soft white tufts. I breathed in the cold air. Strange, how different everything felt. Mateo and two of my other bodyguards suddenly appeared behind me shocked to see what I was doing. They knew I only ever went from the house to the car so guarding me was easy. This time because of the size of the estate they had no plan for me just strolling away from the house.

I told them to relax and remain at the house and started to walk in the direction of the greenhouse. It was as if I was a blind man seeing for the first time. I saw things I normally would not have noticed. There was beauty everywhere I looked.

It was actually breathtaking.

I told myself I should do this more often. Soon the greenhouse came into view. The moment I arrived in the glass encased space, I heard the sound of shuffling and ceramic clanking exertion. It smelt of moist earth in here. And it was warm. I strolled through the rows of plants and soon she came into view.

The sight she made was quite interesting.

She had just emerged from the storage room holding a tray of pots. The moment she spotted me however she dropped the tray and all the pots crashed onto the ground. While some survived the fall, a few didn't make it. There were broken shards, whole pots, and dark soil all around her.

Ignoring the mess, she stared in shock at me. "What are you doing here?"

I shrugged. "Just came to see what you were doing."

"Oh."

Small teeth sank into her bottom lip. It was not a sexual gesture, but one of uncertainty, but as my cock hardened, I turned away quickly and focused my attention on my surroundings.

She crouched down and started to put the unbroken pots back on the tray. Standing, she put the tray on a wooden platform nearby and ran the palms of her hands down the sides of her jeans. My eyes were immediately drawn to the curve of her hips.

I took a step towards her. "What are you planting?" I asked. My voice sounded strange, foreign almost.

"Flowers."

I took another step towards her. "Why?"

"Because I love flowers," she said, taking a step towards me.

"Why not just buy them?" I asked as I stepped closer.

"Because I like the idea of putting a seed into the soil and watching it grow."

We were only a couple of feet apart now. Daylight had filtered in through the glass now and she looked incomparably beautiful.

She was wearing a bulky, dark blue hoodie that stopped at her waist. The rest of her lower body was then encased in skin-tight dark jeans that molded to her flesh, revealing to the eye every dip and curve of her body. My libido was already thrumming at the sight especially when she had turned around to pick up a shard earlier. At the jut of her ass, I felt a painful ache in my balls. I needed to slip my cock between those cheeks and plunge into her depths.

However, I knew better than to give in to the crazed urge. I was not an animal. I could control myself. As I watched her however, I wondered if that ship hadn't already sailed, and of what consequence that would be to me to sail along with it.

I had long cultivated the habit of deliberately denying myself of something I wanted in order to strengthen my will. It served to expose any vulnerability inside me and for me to take steps to kill whatever it was. However, she was exposing a vulnerability inside me that was startling and there was not a thing I could do about it.

I was like an addict. I knew it would destroy me, but I couldn't help myself. With my fists clenched I said, "Well, have a nice day."

I turned around to leave but she stopped me.

"John's not here, and I need some help with a bag of soil in there. Could you help me, please?"

For a second I didn't do anything. No one had ever asked me to do something so menial. Ever. In my whole life. Those things were done by servants. Slowly, I turned around.

"Could you help me, please?" she asked. Her eyes were enormous.

I should tell her to wait for John. Dirt and soil were not my thing, but to my surprise I found myself saying. "Where is it?"

CHAPTER 31

SKYE

https://www.youtube.com/watch?v=b_zHQ6kFuQ0

*W*hat the hell was I doing?

There was no freaking bag of soil in there! I had already taken most of it out the previous day and spread them across the available pots and trays that I had in preparation for the seeds. However, from the moment he had walked into that greenhouse, I had lost the ability to think with my brain. My sex was pulsing, wet with arousal, as though it recognized the person that had lavished it with attention the previous night.

And then there was the attire that he had on. Thus far, I had only seen him in the corporate looking suits and jackets, but today he was dressed luxuriously but casually in a leather jacket and a black cashmere sweater. But it was the hip hugging black jeans that made me want to peel everything off him and lick every inch of his body.

I was nervous about the lie I'd blurted out and thought of what to do to cancel it. With my heart in my throat I finally blurted it out. "Luca, actually, there's no need. I... I just remembered that I've already used it up yesterday. I'm sorry for the trouble."

He frowned.

"I'm sorry," I apologized again.

He cocked his head "Are you playing with me?"

"No, no," I quickly protested. "I just..." I couldn't finish the sentence.

But he stood there waiting and didn't let it go.

I turned around to escape but he caught me by the arm and pulled me roughly towards his body. I slammed into the hardness of his chest tearing a gasp from me.

"Luca," I breathed as one hand came around my waist but there was nothing delicate about this.

"What are you doing, Skye?" He whispered in my ear.

I shook my head, my body trembling. "No I just... I wanted to be in a somewhat smaller space with you."

He stilled. "Why?"

I felt heat rise up my throat. "I... I wanted you to... to... kiss me."

"Kiss?" he asked, something dark flaring in his eyes.

I pressed my trembling lips together and nodded.

"Where's John?" he murmured.

"He had to leave to pick something up from the hardware store that he had ordered. He left about ten minutes ago." My voice was breathless.

His answer was to undo the button of my jeans, unzip it, slip his hand in and grab my mound. I fell against him like a limp noodle.

I was soaking wet so his fingers immediately sunk into my slickness. Tremors of ecstasy began to broil in the pit of my stomach.

All I needed and could think about now was the delicious release that only he could give to me, but I couldn't help but panic that he was going to tease me and then let me go without taking things to the end. After all this was morning and it was only a few hours ago since we'd been in each other's arms.

"Is this what you wanted?" he asked as he roughly stroked the engorged bud between my thighs.

I nodded, my eyes fluttering shut, but I also wanted to kiss him, to have my legs wrapped around him and him pounding into me. I had started to feel empty without his thick cock stretching me, filling me, and soothing the almost maddening ache that his absence created. It was becoming so that being filled with him was normal and not having him inside me was unfamiliar and strange.

He slid two fingers into me, but there were too many barriers in his way. I peeled the skin-tight material down my thighs, exposing my ass to the cold. I couldn't believe how shameless I was being, but my desire for him had completely taken over my mind and I fully gave myself to it.

His arm tightened around me, his back curving with mine as he began to drive his fingers deeper and faster into me. I cried out at the rapid onslaught as I was finger fucked into a delicious release. I nearly crumbled to the floor as a mind-blowing orgasm shot through me, but he caught me and instead led me towards one of the wooden platforms.

The moment my ass connected with it, he pulled off my left shoe and yanked the jean leg from my foot. Then he got onto his heels and jerked my thighs even further apart. He moved his head forward and with his lips covered my sex and drew my sensitive, engorged clit into his mouth.

The delicious suction tore a long moan from me and with my fingers clawed into his shoulder it became too much quickly and I fought to be loosened from his hold, but he didn't let go till he had tortured me to his satisfaction and I was whimpering and begging for release.

It was only then that he rose to his feet and for a few seconds he did nothing, just looked at me sitting there with my legs wide open and my body trembling. Then he slanted his head and captured my lips with his. The kiss was decadent and filthy and I savored it with a desperation that had my head spinning. His tongue sunk into my mouth to take my fill of my own taste. Then he nibbled and sucked at my lips and my tongue.

By the time he pulled away, my lips were bruised and swollen.

"Have you got what you wanted yet?" he rasped.

Only one request came to mind and it repeated itself over and over in my head. "No, I want you to fuck me," I gasped as I jumped off the bench. I fumbled at the button of his jeans. I yanked the zip down hurriedly and reached into his briefs and pulled out his cock. It was as hard as a piece of rock. In moments the whole head was sheathed with my lips. I lapped him up from the base to the root and then took as much of him into my mouth as I could. I felt so greedy. So greedy for his taste.

For a while he let me suck him. And suck him I did. I sucked him as I had never sucked anyone before. Hungrily, as if I was devouring him. As if I couldn't get enough. As if my life depended on it.

I was thoroughly enjoying myself when he wrenched away from my mouth and pulled me to my feet. "I want to come inside of you," he growled. In seconds I was flipped around, my hands flattened against the platform and my legs spread apart.

He was going to take me from behind and my chest nearly collapsed with excitement.

Somewhere in the back of my head it registered that the room had a chill breeze blowing from somewhere, but in that moment I was surrounded by the waves of heat and urgency radiating from both our bodies. Desire was boiling through my bloodstream and my ears thrumming with the maddened pace of my heartbeat. He didn't waste any time.

The head of his cock stroked through my cleft as he positioned it where it was always meant to be. From the first moment my eyes met his, my body already knew that. He slid in and my jaw clenched at the excruciatingly tight intrusion. Then grabbing my hips with both hands and bending his knees he plunged into me so hard that my whole body jerked forward.

I cried out.

He began to thrust. There was nothing slow or controlled about his pace as he drove his cock in and out of me, and my moans rang across the space. All I could do was clench my fist and slam it into the wooden table.

"Luca," I cried out his name, sweating and quivering.

But he didn't let up. He drove harder, his grunts urging me on to the force of his fucking. I worked my hips to meet the slam of his and the sound of his flesh smacking against my flesh was a song I knew would forever be etched into my mind.

At this pace, neither of us had any hope of lasting long and soon enough our hips were bucking. He gripped me, his hands wrapping around my waist to hold me in place as he sent a rapid burst of hard plunges into me. My entire pelvis went numb and the orgasm burst through me in a wet, heavy rush. My eyes rolled to the back of my head as my brain shut down. I felt as if I was floating above my body. All that registered in the surreal moment of pleasure was his hot release flooding my pussy.

I reveled in every moment of it.

He buried his face in my neck to muffle his own groan and I would never know how long we remained in that position, tightly glued to each other and joined together as one, but he was the first one to move and with it came an overwhelming disappointment that he was once again about to be separated from me. He pulled out and a flow of cum dripped onto the floor. I stared down at the drops as I tried to catch my breath, unable to face him.

I stood there naked from the waist down, with one jean leg and my panties still attached to my foot while the other foot was shoeless. I couldn't move so I just stood there like a dummy as he readjusted his clothes. I hoped with all my heart that he wouldn't leave without saying anything further to me. He didn't.

He went and picked up my shoe. Then he knelt down in front of me. As if I was a child he lifted my foot so he could pull my panties and jeans over it, before he put my shoe on. Then he stood and pulled my jeans up, zipped it, and even buttoned it up for me.

For some bizarre, totally inexplicable reason, I felt like crying.

"You okay?" he asked.

I shook my head.

I don't know what I expected him to do, but I definitely didn't expect him to freeze the way he did. Startled, I lifted my head and looked him in the eye. I knew my eyes were wet. He stared at me as if in shock. Then he took a step backwards, as if I was dangerous to him, or I had some communicable disease. I could only stare at him in confusion. What was going on? What had I done?

Suddenly, he turned around, and without a word, exited the greenhouse.

I turned my head and I watched him walk through the snow. A black figure in a white landscape. He looked alone and somehow hurt, almost wounded. It was strange because of course, he wasn't alone or wounded. I wanted to reach out and bring him back to me, but he soon disappeared from sight.

Slowly, I sunk down to the floor, my head buried between my knees. I was in deep shit. I sat in that position for a long time. I felt dazed and stupid. It was only the sound of John returning that made me stir my stiff limbs.

He looked at me on the floor and came rushing up to me. "Did you fall?"

"No, no," I whispered hoarsely.

"Are you all right?" he asked, his voice concerned.

"Yes, I am. I think I just felt a bit faint, but I'm okay now."

"Shall I bring you some hot tea?"

"No, no, I'll be fine. I'll just go back to the house now, I think."

"Let me take you back in the truck."

I smiled at him gratefully, guiltily. "Thank you, John. Honestly, it was nothing. A walk in the fresh air will do me good."

He nodded and I quickly started walking towards the entrance. I knew he was watching me so I kept my pace brisk and sure so he would know that there was absolutely nothing wrong with me.

CHAPTER 32

SKYE

I returned immediately to my room and got dressed. I needed the day out, away from Luca and this cocoon of crazed lust and the mental gymnastics I needed to undertake to pretend to myself that everything was still all right. That my heart wasn't about to break into a thousand jagged pieces. I called Katie and we agreed to meet up at the mall where we usually met, and do lunch together afterwards.

Once I was ready I called my father. He was taking a nap, but he roused himself and insisted on talking to me. He was in good spirits and it cheered me to know that in a couple of days he would be going in to start his treatments. I told him I would come by in the next couple of days as I didn't want him to see me as I was today. Confused and disorientated about my future. We said goodbye and I put the phone into my purse and looked at my reflection before I left the room carrying my present for Katie.

Obviously, I didn't want to contact Luca again with the request to let me leave for the day so I headed towards the surveillance camera that was hidden in one corner. I looked up at it and waved, hoping that the home was indeed as tightly guarded as Mary Jane had implied it was, because thus far I'd only met one of the guards when he had found me ransacking the fridge in the middle of the night.

Turning around, I leaned against the wall of my room and waited. For more than a minute that followed there was no response, then my phone began to ring. The number was of course, unidentifiable.

"Miss Morrison," a male voice came through the receiver. "Is there a problem?"

I was impressed. The house really was even more tightly guarded than Mary Jane knew.

"I need to meet up with a friend in the city," I said with as much confidence as I could muster.

He went silent.

"Hello?" I said into the silence.

"One moment please, Miss Morrison."

The line went quiet, and I guessed he was checking my request with his boss. I took a deep breath. There was nothing in the contract to say I couldn't go meet my friends and I knew Luca wouldn't say no, but even so I felt slightly nervous.

There was a clicking sound before the male voice came back. "Certainly, Miss Morrison. If you want to come out now, a car will be waiting for you out front."

I headed down the stairs and out. Indeed, a tinted, black SUV with its engine idling was already waiting for me. The driver came out and opened the passenger door for me.

I got in and settled down as he closed the car and slipped into the driver's seat.

"Where to?" he asked, as he shifted the gears into motion.

"Starfield Mall."

"Okay," he replied, and did not say another word until we arrived at our destination.

As I waited for Katie outside the Japanese tea store we had agreed on, I spotted her come up the escalator in her sales manager attire of a striped dark pant suit, my mood immediately lifted. It had been three weeks since I last saw her so I couldn't even remain still. I started waving and walking towards her.

"Oh my God, Skye," she screamed, her hazel eyes becoming as round as saucers. "Look at you. You look amazing. Where did you get that coat? It's divine."

I grinned at her. "You look pretty hot yourself."

"You, crazy person, you. Of course, I don't. I'm in my ugly old uniform," she scolded as she slapped me across my arm.

I pulled her into a tight hug. Her lavender bob smelt familiar and returned to me a sense of security and peace. I really had missed her and it felt so good to see and hold her again. The restaurant was only a couple of shops away so we strolled towards it while we chatted.

"So are you going to tell me where you got the coat from?"

"It was brought to me by a stylist Luca Messana hired to dress me."

She stopped mid-stride. "You're serious, aren't you?"

I stopped too and nodded. "Yeah. They live in a completely different world from us, Katie."

"I bet they do. Come on. Let's go sit down and you can tell me everything."

We were taken to our table by a friendly waitress. She gave us menus and hurried off. Instantly, Katie honed in on me. "Come on then. What's going on. You look fabulous, but you sounded so strange and tense on the phone. Tell me what the hell is going on?" she asked.

"I will once we order." I passed her a sealed bottle of water and she accepted it.

She lifted the bottle to her lips, and took a long drink. "I ran all the way over here, so this better be some sort of real emergency."

"It is," I said with a smile.

Her gaze narrowed as she searched in mine for any trace of mischief. Just then a waiter arrived at our table. I ordered a glass of white wine and she settled for a Coke since she had to get back to work. The waiter went away and I turned to Katie. She was staring at me. I pushed the menu at her.

"Get whatever you want," I told her. "It's Luca Messana's treat."

She raised her eyebrows. "What do you mean?"

"Well, I found some extra dollars in my bank account yesterday."

Her eyes widened dramatically. "How much?"

I lowered my voice. "Twenty freaking thousand."

"Whoa!"

"Yup, and this is also for you." I pushed her present towards her.

She grabbed the bag eagerly. "What is it?"

I didn't need to say anything. I just watched as she tore the wrapping paper with the eagerness of a child and gasped in wonder at her gift.

"Oh, my God! I can't believe it. It's a classic Burberry jacket." She pulled it out and gazed at it in disbelief. "It's gorgeous, Skye. It's exactly what I've been lusting after for years."

"Don't I know it," I agreed with a laugh.

She looked up. "Oh, Skye. I can't accept this. It must have cost thousands."

"Well, it didn't cost me anything. As I mentioned Luca got a stylist to get me a whole designer wardrobe. One, I might add, I will hardly be able to use once I go back to my old life of being a waitress."

She looked down at the jacket again. "But wouldn't you like to keep this for yourself though?"

"No, not at all. As soon as I saw it hanging on the rack I decided it was yours. I'm not such a big fan of Burberry anyway."

"Yeah, you're a fan of Target," she said dryly.

"What's wrong with Target?"

"If you have to ask that, there is no point." Then she reached out and curled her hand around mine. "Thank you, Skye. It's an amazing present."

"I'm glad you like it. Now what are you going to eat? I'm having the spaghetti with lobster."

Katie's eyes widened. The price of the meal at forty-eight dollars was absolutely extravagant by our standards. Then she grinned. "Twenty thousand, did you say?"

I giggled. "I did."

"Alright, I'll have the same. I've always wanted to try that dish."

"Forget me drinking by myself we should have a bottle of wine to go with it, shouldn't we?"

Her eyes twinkled mischievously. "Yes, lets. It's not the end of the world if I go back a little sloshed. I don't have anything too important to do today."

The waiter came and took our order.

"Before I forget," she said, as he went away. "I met Diana the other day and she said she was trying to reach you."

I was surprised at the mention of my stepsister. "She was trying to reach me?"

"Yup. She was actually quite friendly. Tried to find out if I had seen you recently."

"What did you tell her?"

"Relax. I didn't tell her anything, but you should call her."

I sighed. I could feel my appetite leaving at the thought of calling her, so I pushed it out of mind, and refocused on Katie. I saw precious little of Katie and I wasn't going to let Diana spoil my lunch with my bestie.

The wine came and we toasted each other and took a sip. I had ordered their most expensive and it was delicious and cool on my tongue.

"So… why did you sound so tense and unhappy this morning?" Katie asked over the rim of her glass.

"I think I'm falling for Luca, Katie."

"What?" she blurted out, spraying wine all over the tablecloth.

I couldn't help it. I had to laugh. She was so funny.

Red faced, she mopped at the table. "Are you serious?"

"Yeah, I'm serious."

She looked at me incredulously. "How can you possibly fall in love with someone after less than a week?"

"I don't know how, but from the first moment our eyes met at the party it was as if I am connected to him at a deeper level. And every time we have sex I feel myself slip just a little more."

She was speechless. "He's that good?"

I shook my head in despair. "Sometimes I even cry real tears."

"Woah," she said and leaned back into the chair. "That's not good."

"See why I'm panicking now."

"You can't have feelings for him," she said. "You're meant to be out of there in what? Two weeks?"

"Two and a half," I answered. "It sounds like nothing, but that's a long time for me. I can't explain it, but when I am at his house, it's like being in a different world. I just..." I sighed in frustration. "I guess I just want to know how to switch me off. How to not react so intensely to him every single time. How would you do it?"

Her gaze on me softened. "I have absolutely no idea. I've never been in a relationship like that."

My mouth slightly parted in disappointment, even though it was what I should have expected.

"Isn't there any way you can get out of this early?"

I shook my head. "I can't. I've signed a contract and Dad needs this."

"You know something, Skye. It's not the end of the world. I mean, if I were you I'd go for it, and if my heart gets broken so fucking what? Most people live the kind of lives that they might as well be dead. At least you are really living now. To be perfectly honest I'd love to be in your shoes right now."

I shook my head. "I thought you disapproved of my relation-ship with him."

"That was before I saw your coat," she said with a laugh.

206

At the moment the waiter arrived with our food and we both turned our attention to the food, but her words kept ringing in my head.

If I were you, I'd go for it.

I wondered what would happen if I did go for it…

CHAPTER 33

LUCA

The door to my study burst open suddenly, but I was already with my gun drawn and cocked. I'd heard the unfamiliar footsteps. Unrecognizable as any of my house guards. One much heavier than the other. What had alerted me was the way they were creeping forward. I felt calm. No emotion. My gun was cocked and pointed to the door. I was ready to shoot the motherfuckers dead the second they opened my fucking door.

It happened so fast. If my reflexes had not been so quick I would have shot Angelo. For it was my brother who stood at the threshold of my study

"Are you fucking insane?" I growled, fury coursing through my veins. "I could have blown your head off."

"That's what I told him," a soft female voice said from behind him, and I realized then that there was someone behind him. She stepped forward with a bright smile on her face and both my brother and his fiancée stood before me. My gaze moved between the both of them, as I swallowed my anger at my brother. I could have killed him.

Angelo laughed. "Be thankful, big brother. I was testing your reflexes."

"It looked more like you were trying to win the Darwin award," I muttered. Then I turned to his fiancée. "Sienna," I greeted.

"Hey," she said with an easy smile, as she moved her hand to entwine her fingers with my brother's.

She was everything Skye was not. Tanned, confident, sure of her place in the world. She never had to sell herself to pay for her father's medical bills. A great sense of protectiveness filled my chest. At that moment I made myself a promise. When our thirty days were over I would make sure she was financially secure for the rest of her life. Never again would she have to sell herself to low lives for anything she wanted to do or buy.

"Can I get you both a drink?" I asked.

"Sit down and relax. I'll get it," my brother said, as he moved towards the bar.

I led the way towards the leather sofas by the fireplace. I lowered myself into the armchair and left the sofa for them. I wasn't in a very chatty mood, but fortunately Sienna launched into a comment about alcohol and a story about the state of my brother's fridge when she first met him.

The following half hour was spent catching up with the both of them. It was almost dinner time when Melania came in to ask me if guests were staying for dinner.

I threw the question back to Angelo and Sienna. "Do you guys want to have dinner in the house or head out?"

Angelo looked to Sienna who rested in his arms. "I'm easy. What do you want to do?"

"Let's go out to the city," she said. "I've hardly seen anything of Boston."

I looked at Melania. "No food for us." Then I pulled out my phone and rose to my feet. "I'll get Matteo to call ahead."

We left the study immediately and were approaching the front door when it suddenly opened.

My breath caught in my throat when I saw Skye.

For a moment we all froze, as neither of us had expected to see the other. The last time I had seen her was in the greenhouse. When I had asked her if she was all right. She had shaken her golden head and my heart, that I thought was dead forever, began to hurt again.

I was well aware of my brother and his fiancée's eyes on me. They were both expecting an introduction, but I didn't want to introduce her to them. She was my glorious secret. As if she knew I didn't want to introduce her, she stepped aside to allow us to pass, as if she was one of the staff or someone unworthy of being introduced. Her action sent a jolt of unease through me. She was not my staff and she was not unworthy of being introduced to anyone. I had selfishly not wanted to introduce her because I wanted to keep her to myself, not because I was ashamed of her.

"Well, well," I heard Angelo murmur under his breath.

I cursed underneath my breath. He understood me well, and he knew he was on to something. He walked ahead of us with his hand outstretched.

"I'm Angelo, Luca's brother," he said with a charming smile.

"Oh," she exclaimed and glanced uncertainly at me.

"Don't mind him. He's a grumpy old bear," my brother said encouragingly.

Her eyes widened. "Oh. Well, I'm Skye."

"And this is Sienna, my fiancée."

"It's nice to meet both of you," Skye replied shyly.

"We were just going out to dinner. Why don't you join us?" Angelo asked, his voice sly and cajoling.

Her eyes slightly widened at the invitation. "Uh… I don't think…" Her gaze found mine. She was looking to me for guidance.

Again, that strange feeling of protectiveness filled my chest.

Before I could answer though, she touched her hair self-consciously, and said, "I was out walking so I'm not exactly dressed for a night out."

"Don't worry, we're not going anywhere fancy. If they'll allow my brother in, they'll allow you," Angelo said.

"Yes, do come with us," Sienna added, and went over to lightly touch her arm.

"Yes, come with us," I heard myself say.

Skye came forward then and with my hand on the small of her back I walked out of the house and towards the waiting

Rolls. Cullinan's old body moved fluidly and gracefully to open the door closest to Skye. Ahead, I could see my men jumping into their SUVs. One of the vehicles began to move while the other waited to follow us from behind.

Skye hesitated at the doorway, her gaze on the polished leather seat as though she was being sent into a snake's hole.

"Well, are you coming or not?" I whispered in her ear.

"Yes," she said, and climbed into the vehicle. The rest of us joined her inside, Cullinan put the car into motion and we were off.

There was no time for the atmosphere in the car to get awkward.

"What do you do, Skye?" Angelo asked Skye.

"I'm a waitress."

"Really?" Sienna said. "I used to be a waitress when I lived in London. It was okay, but I wanted to kick some of my customers."

I was surprised at her revelation. Being the only daughter of one of the biggest Mafia families in the states, she most certainly would never have needed to have a job while she studied abroad.

Skye smiled. "Well, it pays the bills."

Sienna laughed softly and the talk turned to how they had met.

Knowing Angelo to be an extremely quiet and reserved person, I'd expected the person he chose would be as quiet as he naturally was, but I was discovering that that was not the case.

As soon as we arrived at the exclusive country club, we were whisked off to a secluded table in one of their restaurants. We settled, and a waiter arrived to ask for our drinks orders.

"I can't drink right now," Sienna said gaily, "so it's going to be cranberry juice for me all the way."

Angelo smiled and stroked her arm, and I knew immediately she was pregnant. I felt a sharp pain. He would have been seven years old now. I dropped my head and pretended to study the menu until the moment passed. It always did.

After we had put in our orders and received our drinks, Sienna rose to her feet. "Please excuse me, I have to use the restroom," she turned to Skye. "Skye, do you want to come along?"

She placed her glass of wine down. "Sure," she said and both women left.

"Want to tell me who she is?" Angelo asked as soon as the girls were out of earshot.

I gazed at the unreal green of grass of the golf course that stretched as far as the eye could see. "Why don't you tell me? You seem to have already added her to the family.'

He chuckled. "If you had not wanted her to come with us she wouldn't be here."

This was the truth and he knew it. So did I. "Maybe I just didn't want to offend her."

He laughed outright. "When have you ever given a fuck about offending anyone? You're the guy that pointed a gun at dad four years ago and told him to step down or else you'd break his knee and make him."

The memory caused me no pain. "He was spiraling out of control. That was a needed call."

"Exactly," he said with satisfaction. "Now, are you going to tell me who she is?"

"No." I wasn't ready to talk about Skye to anyone, not even Angelo. Not yet. Maybe not ever. Maybe she would become a ghost like my little boy.

CHAPTER 34

SKYE

*I*t was a bit awkward visiting the bathroom with Sienna.

For one, we seemed to be the only two in the expansive space and our activities within the stalls seemed to bounce against the walls. Even my weeing seemed too loud. I was washing my hands when she exited, a smile on her lips for me through her reflection in the mirror.

She was a petite, gorgeous woman with long, raven hair that almost reached her waist. She was not showing at all, but I knew from her comment about not drinking that she must be pregnant.

"How far along are you?" I asked turning off the tap and reaching for a thick white hand towel.

"About twelve weeks." She pressed her hand to the tucked in white sweater she had on, her voice going soft and dreamy. "I can't wait for the time when I will get really big. I know it sounds strange, but I've always loved the way pregnant women look. Even that waddling walk is attractive to me."

With a soft laugh she began to wash her hands.

"In that case I hope you get really big," I replied with a smile. She seemed incredibly friendly and it made me like her, although I didn't know if we could ever truly connect. In spite of her stint working as a waitress in London we were clearly from different worlds, and I was especially aware that beyond the simplicity of her appearance in a sweater and stone washed blue jeans, and almost no jewelry other than the rock on her engagement finger, she was most probably an heiress of some kind. In fact, I would lay money on that guess. She just had that look of someone born into money. Lots of money.

"How long have you known Luca?" she asked as we got out of the Ladies and walked passed a seemingly endless fish tank in the hallway.

"Not long at all"

"Ah," she said softly and lightly touched my arm. "I invited you because Luca never brings guests into that house after an… an incident in the past. I think Angelo was quite shocked to see you there."

My mind went to the face of her fiancé when he had first seen me. I hadn't caught any expression on him that supported this claim, but perhaps they could read each other better than anyone else could.

"You will come to my wedding, won't you?" she asked. "We don't want to rush things so we're thinking of having it after the baby is born."

I didn't quite know what to say as I couldn't tell her that I wouldn't be around by that time. In fact, I would be gone in about two weeks. Thankfully, we had reached the table by then and her fiancé distracted her by rising to gallantly pull her chair out. For the first time in my life I felt the sharp pinch of envy. How lucky she was. She had found a man who obviously and truly adored her.

Luca didn't even look at me. I felt a painful chill pass through me and instantly turned to my still unfinished glass of wine.

"Skye, you did not answer me," Sienna continued.

"If the stars align," I said cryptically and took a sip of wine.

"That's good enough for me," she said with a beaming smile.

Our starters arrived then.

I most certainly didn't know about the stars aligning later on but right now, they seemed to be aligned well enough to keep my father in the best treatment money could buy so I tried my best to relax.

My starter of Spanish baked prawns was delicious. And afterwards the filet mignon was buttery with just a hint of rosemary. Sienna chatted enough for all of us and I suspected that it wasn't particularly because she was a chatterbox, but because her fiancé seemed to be generally the strong silent type, Luca hardly spoke two words and I couldn't help feeling like a fish out of water.

Her fiancé had his arm around her waist throughout most of the dinner and his eyes gleaming like stars in the night sky as he watched her adoringly. Many a time it took my breath away just watching them and the striking difference between the warmth and adoration that shone through his eyes and the cold, detached gaze of Luca's.

Then she started talking about the shoe business she had started, and with my still sprouting dream of working with flowers I asked genuinely curious questions when appropriate.

It was however extremely hard through all of this to ignore the presence of the man sitting so still beside me. His scent, combined with the warmth of the restaurant and the soft ambience blues, made my insides burn and burn.

With every one of his slight movements, my chest would contract, and at the delivery of his clear and curt responses a strong awareness would prickle underneath my skin. At one point a glimpse of his fingers as they handled the cutlery would bring flashbacks of those very same hands opening my legs, and pushing his fingers into my sex.

A gasp escaped my lips. Our two companions were too far away to hear it, but he turned. I didn't dare look at him, but he watched me for what seemed like forever, before returning his gaze back to his brother, and my hands nearly ripped the napkin in my lap to shreds.

"It was good to see you both again," he said as he signaled a waiter over.

I released a deep sigh of relief.

After he had signed for the bill, he rose to his feet. To my surprise, Angelo and Sienna did not come with us. They had another car waiting for them. Sienna pulled me into a warm hug.

"I hope to see you again soon," she said.

I just nodded, even though I knew I would most probably never see her again unless it was by accident on the street or if I was waitressing at a party she had been invited to.

In the car Luca lapsed into somber silence. I got the impression that it had nothing to do with me. He was preoccupied with something else.

The moment we got in, Madam was waiting in the foyer. She offered to get us drinks and refreshments, but Luca waved her away and walked in the direction of his den.

I made my way back to my room. I felt strangely lonely and abandoned. I hoped Luca would come to my bed later that night so I ran a scented bath and soaked in it. I also washed my hair so it would be sweet smelling.

By the time I climbed into bed an hour had passed.

I lay on the bed and stared at the ceiling. Perhaps he would not come. Perhaps he was already bored of me. I curled my body into a ball and remembered Sienna mention the 'accident' and how he never invited guests to his home.

As I raised my hand to switch off the bedside lamp, the door opened and there he was. For a moment we stared at each other.

"Leave the light on," he said, and came forward.

My hand fell back down on the bed.

He put his nose in the curve of my neck and inhaled deeply. I thought I heard him say something, but it was muffled. Then he raised his head.

"You are a witch, Skye," he growled, as he pulled my nightgown up.

I was not wearing any underwear so he got on the bed and buried his head between my thighs. I sighed with pleasure. After he made me climax, he fucked me. There is no other way to describe how brutally he thrust into me. When it was over, he pulled his pants back on and left without a word.

I felt a sob rise in my throat, as the door closed. I switched off the light.

And the tears came.

CHAPTER 35

LUCA

https://www.youtube.com/watch?v=u9Dg-g7t2l4
-The Sound Of Silence-

*L*aughter surrounded me.

It was unrestrained and endless. A beautiful sound. We were in the pool, with floats strapped around his chubby toddler arms and his cheeks flushed from the heat of the sun. I held onto his waist while he kicked his legs underneath.

"Don't let me go," he cried out in his chirpy voice.

I felt my chest swell. Never. Rocca. Never.

I counted to three in my mind and once again loosened my hold from his. He let out a small scream as he began to sink into the water. "Keep kicking," I told him. "Remain calm."

He tried, but still continued to smack his face into the water because of how nervous he was.

"Papa, save me. Save me. I'm dying!" he screamed with fear.

The sound pierced my heart. I caught him, pulling him towards my chest... but as if he was smoke he disappeared. All that was left was his scream of terror. *Papa, papa, save me, save me. I'm dying.*

My eyes flew open.

I was lying on my bed, and my body was slick with sweat. It had been many years since I remembered him with such detail. All around me was darkness and I stared at the ceiling blankly. For the longest time I didn't even blink. I dare not. I could still hear his happy laughter, and I wanted to keep that for as long as I could. But it went. The same way he had disappeared in my dream. Like a wisp of smoke.

All I could hear was my heart slamming into my chest. And then the terrible, terrible sorrow of his loss came. It filled my body. Every cell was infected with the loss. I squeezed my burning eyes shut. No, not that again.

I had long ago closed my heart towards the memories, even pushing them out of my mind because the pain was too unbearable. The only thing I truly loved in the world had been ripped away from me, and although I felt the lingering emptiness every single day that passed since then, it meant life was bearable.

Now, it had returned with a vengeance.

I knew it was because of Angelo's child. I didn't begrudge him his child, I just wanted my boy back. After all these years, I still missed him as if he had been taken away from me yesterday. I felt my hands clench. I wanted to smash everything up and howl with the pain. I thought of the bottle of alcohol downstairs. For months after Rocca died I'd been so drunk I didn't even know my name. I was in such a rage even the bodyguards, uncertain of what I might do at the slightest mistake on their part, kept their distance. I was a drunken madman in charge of a violent empire.

Inhaling deeply, I counted to three, and pushed my body upwards. Then I swung my legs out of the bed and sat with my head buried in my hands. Slowly, methodically, I regulated my breathing. When my state was somewhat back under control, I walked away from the room without thought. I didn't even know what time it was, but that didn't matter either.

All I could think about was getting completely lost in a different kind of emotion. A heady, tumultuous rush that would take me out of my state of despair and bitterness and back into the realm of the living again.

I pushed her door open and was surprised to see that her lamp was on and she wasn't in her bed. The bathroom door was open, but it was in darkness so I knew she was not in there. I could feel a cold wind and I realized with shock she must be out on the balcony. I walked over to the open door and saw her standing there in her thin nightgown. My bare feet had made no sound, but she turned suddenly.

She gasped and staggered backwards. Her face was pale, her mouth opening in a silent scream. I reached out and caught her before she could fall and hurt herself.

"What are you doing here?" she whispered.

The horror was so real, I slammed her into my body and hugged her hard. Her skin was cold. It reminded me of his skin that day. Oh, God! I nearly gagged with horror. Without thinking I buried my face in her neck, so the warmth from my skin would seep into hers, but she was frozen. I could feel her body trembling. I pulled her into the room and shut the door.

"Luca," she whispered, but I was already moving towards the bathroom. I needed to make her warm again. I needed to make her skin stop being so cold. I switched on the shower and turned it up so it was hot. Then I pulled her under the cascade.

She didn't struggle or argue. She let me. The stream was powerful and warm, and slowly it began to warm her. Looking into my eyes she reached out a hand and touched my scar. I shuddered slightly, but I didn't catch her hand or pull away. Part of me couldn't believe I was letting her.

"Is it true a tiger gored you?"

I shook my head. The truth was more prosaic and less romantic. "A knife fight when I was fifteen. I got careless."

"You are the most beautiful man I've ever known," she whispered.

I frowned. "I'm not. My soul is ugly beyond redemption."

"I know you were beautiful once. What happened to you, Luca?"

Suddenly, it was too much. I turned away from her.

But she wrapped her arms around me and laid her cheek on my back. Then she began to kiss me, her lips tracing down my back. Then her hands in front began to move, across the muscles of my torso and then downwards into my track pants.

She gripped my cock and began to pump it, gently at first but then increasingly faster until she settled into sweet, rhythmic strokes. I clenched my eyes shut and reveled in the enthralling feel of pleasure coursing through my veins. He was not gone from the cavity in my chest but the pain in my chest was gone. She coaxed out all of the tension from my limbs. She knew exactly what I needed in that moment without even having to say a word.

Her strength and her pace would never be enough alone to get me off, and I needed to see her beautiful face, so I caught her hand and turned around to gaze at the woman before me.

She was a goddess, with water pouring down her hair, her alabaster skin looked even more pale and perfect. Her eyes sparkled and as I stared down at her, I felt something shift in my chest.

Before I could pay too much attention to analyze what it was, I tilted my head and took her lips in a deep kiss. My heart slammed painfully into my chest at the contact and it fueled my craving for more. Holding her face in position, I sucked hard on her lower lip. She whimpered like a little animal. I slipped my tongue into her mouth to dance with hers.

I pushed her against the tiles. There, I ran my hands possessively down her body and then her behind to grab her ass.

"Take me," she breathed.

I hoisted her off the floor, and her legs wrapped perfectly around my waist. My cock thick and hard, curved against her wet pussy. She rocked the slick flesh against me eagerly. With a hand supporting her body I slipped my hand into the small space between us and positioned my cock at her entrance.

Now I truly wanted to disappear... into her depths, into the bliss that she was. Where there was no pain, no thoughts, just heaven on earth.

She tore her mouth away from mine with a cry when I slid into her and stretched her walls taut and grated deliciously on the sensitive tissues.

She moaned as I sucked and nipped on the exposed skin of her neck. I was gentle with her. I could tell by her swollen eyes that I'd made her cry. I didn't want to make her cry. Her life was sad enough without that. When I was a boy I once rescued a small squirrel that had its head stuck in a can. It struggled and scratched my hands until I cut it free. When it was free it did not thank me. It darted away as fast as it could up a tree and disappeared, but when I looked at my bleeding hands I felt good.

It felt good to have saved Skye. In the end my hands will be bleeding, but it would have been worth it.

I drove my cock into her until the fire of our joining burned so bright and beautiful she opened her mouth in a scream and lost her mind. Her head thrashed from side to side under a cascade of water and her body twisted and writhed. Her scream became mewling cries that resounded in the enclosed space as the orgasm rocked her to her very core.

That was when I let myself go over the edge.

I shut my eyes and savored every last bit of the fire in our joining. I burned it into the archives of my memories as vividly as a brand, needing it to be there and available for the time when she would no longer be mine. Out of my mouth came a growl, wild and impossible to contain and it combined beautifully with her unrestrained cries.

We collapsed against the other, limp and spent and neither of us wanted to move. She clung to me like a second skin, shaking her head when she felt I was about to peel her off me. It was the first time she'd held on so tightly and it flooded me with a dangerous warmth.

I stopped trying to get away from her. This was only temporary. One day it would be no more. Why shouldn't I enjoy it. There was so little happiness in my life. Until she had come it had been completely barren. All I had was money and power, but my soul was broken and crying out. I would never trust a woman again, but for now, she was here and so was I.

The warm water crashed down on us until she reluctantly unhooked her limbs and tried to stand on her own. We both avoided the other's gaze, but neither of us were willing to let go. She turned slightly and reached for the shower gel.

Then she caught my hand and turned it over and squirted some of the blue liquid onto my palm. The message was clear. She didn't want me going anywhere just yet. She was not done. Neither was I.

Rubbing both of my hands together till soft soap suds grew between them, I pulled her slightly away from the cascade once again and covered her beautiful breasts.

She gasped softly.

CHAPTER 36

SKYE

https://www.youtube.com/watch?v=LBMXephwd6w
-When You Came Into My Life-

First he ate me out in the shower, then he carried me back to bed, dried my hair, and afterwards he worshipped my body. He kissed, sucked, and licked every inch of me. He even sucked my toes. One by one, as if they were the most delicious things in the world. Then he turned me over and even parted my ass cheeks and licked me there while he played with my clit. I was shocked, but at the same time my whole body began to feel as if it was vibrating with some kind of electricity.

When I climaxed, it was so intense, it actually felt as if I'd died and gone to heaven.

Afterwards, when I came back to earth, he turned me around and made love to me. His cock moved deeply into me. I knew small cracks were gradually forming in my heart. Not out of hurt, but out of… longing. I wanted him now, more than ever, and much more than I could have believed would ever be possible.

With a shuddering breath, I clenched my eyelids tightly shut as he sank further into me. When he came inside me I pulled him even closer and I held my grief at bay at what couldn't be. I fell asleep with him still inside me.

The next time I came awake he was gone. I sat up and looked around the empty room. Last night seemed like some dream I'd made up. But when I turned around to look at the rumpled pillow next to me I knew it was not. I threw my face into the pillow and breathed him in.

Oh, Luca, Luca, Luca. What will I do when you throw me away?

After a while, I got out of bed and began to dress. The dark soil and the little seeds that held the promise of blooms would heal me. I went to the kitchen. I thought it would be too early for Madam to be there, but she was at her usual chair drinking from her cup. The two boxes of treats were also already prepared.

"Thank you, Madam. You are very kind," I said walking towards the boxes.

"Not at all. It is nothing."

"No, it's something. John really appreciates it. I see how much he enjoys the cakes and cookies when he stops for his breaks. You always know exactly what he likes. He eats one box for his coffee break and saves the other for his tea break."

"Really?"

"Yeah. You've really made his day."

"No, it is not I who did that. It is you. It was your idea. I only wrapped the sweets." Then she allowed a smile to touch her thin lips. It was only small, but it was the first smile I'd seen on her face, and it made her quite pretty.

I beamed back at her. "Have a nice day, Madam."

She nodded. "You too." Then she went back to studying her notebook.

It was still dark when I left the house and began to walk towards the greenhouse. When I got closer I could see the lights were already on. John must already be there. As I walked through the entrance he came out from behind some plants and stood peering at me anxiously.

"Good morning," I greeted brightly.

"How are you feeling today?" he asked.

"Great. I'm ready to do a full day's work."

"Hmmm," he said doubtfully.

"Really, I am," I said with a grin.

"Well, I went into town yesterday afternoon and got you some flower seeds." His voice was gruff.

My eyes went wide. "You did?"

"I see that you've prepared the soil in the pots, and the moon is waxing, so it would be a good day to plant today."

"Why does the moon waxing matter?" I asked curiously, as I walked towards him.

We walked together towards my section of the greenhouse.

"Don't ask me why but the moon affects the way plants grow. Always plant when the moon is growing and prune back when the moon is waning."

"I see. I never knew that. Maybe that was why all the plants I ever tried to grow died on me. Every single one," I admitted gloomily.

"That's strange. The moon can make your plants healthier or make the harvest more bountiful, but it doesn't kill the plants. Maybe your soil was wrong."

"I don't think so. They would be growing fine, then one day they would simply shrivel up and die. All of them at the same time. And it happened every time no matter what I tried to grow."

He stopped and scratched his chin. "Hmmm... that's strange. The only explanation I can think of is sabotage. It happened once to me while I was growing the biggest turnip ever recorded. One of my competitors came to visit, and after that my turnip plant started to die off. I was suspicious so I sent off samples of the turnip and soil to a lab and the results came back that the samples were poisoned."

The first thought in my head was so unworthy and so unkind I immediately kicked it away and refused to even consider it any more.

THE REST of the morning was spent helping John. I actually loved working for him. He knew so much and it felt wonderful to work with someone so knowledgeable. Plus, I got the feeling he enjoyed having me around since I was quite happy to clean up after him.

It was nearly lunchtime when I flopped onto the tiled floor and laid flat on it. I felt exhausted, but in a good way. Then my gaze settled over to that place Luca and I had had sex and a sharp pang of arousal struck my core at the very vivid reminder. I shut my eyes and pulled my thoughts away from him. It was time to go back to the house, take a shower, and go visit my dad. I heard footsteps on the tiles and quickly opened my eyes.

"Refreshment for you," Mary Jane said with a smile.

"Thank you," I replied gratefully and rose to my feet.

I drained the tall glass of ice tea she had brought me and when I was done, relished the chill as it seeped into my bones. She'd already gone off to look at my rows of hard work, her words filled with compliments.

"You did all this," she asked admiringly.

"Well, it's all still soil" I laughed. "Nothing has germinated yet."

"But the seeds are already planted right."

"Yeah they are."

She nodded, but her eyebrows furrowed at an unspoken thought.

"Can I ask you a question?" she asked, chewing her bottom lip.

"Sure."

"I'm not trying to be smart or anything, but why are you planting these when you're only staying for a month? I mean, are you taking them with you, or are you staying for longer?"

Just a few days earlier, hearing that last part of her question would have made me shrug and tell her I was planting because I loved the feeling of soil between my fingers, but now I felt a great sadness at the reminder of my impermanence in Torrington Hall.

I loved that greenhouse, I loved working with John, I loved walking the cold landscape, and more than that I was falling for the owner of the estate. Even while I was working on the plants I missed him. He remained in my mind, his voice in my ears and his scent so poignant around me that I wondered if it had clung to me or if it was just the very deep recollection of it in my memory.

Either way, it brought a restlessness to my soul that made me feel sad and lost. And I hated it.

I looked at Mary Jane. "I know I will not be here to see them bloom, but I have loved planting flowers all my life and the joy for me is to grow something here on this fabulous estate that will go on flowering for long after I am gone, and hopefully John will find the same joy in them."

CHAPTER 37

SKYE

I went with Mary Jane to the house and ate my lunch. I was hungry and as ever it was absolutely delicious and I cleaned the plates of every last bit of food.

Afterwards I went up to my room to get ready to go visit my father, but while I was coming out of the shower Laura phoned to tell me not to come that day because her sister was coming to take them for a day out at the park. She asked me to postpone my visit until the next day. Then she passed the phone to my dad. He was in a grumpy mood. He hated Laura's sister. I laughed and told him not to be so horrible. He grumbled some more then I blew him a kiss and laughingly told him I would see him the next day.

But once the call was over I stood in my towel in the middle of that beautiful room and felt sad all over again. I pulled on a warm jacket and went for a long walk. I ended my walk at the greenhouse. John was in his little office/storage room. He had a two-bar heater on and his feet were up on his desk. When he saw me through the glass he waved me over. He made tea and we had it together with one of Madam's cakes in his warm cozy office. We talked about plants, and then he told me about his home country. He was born in Scotland and had come to the States when he was five. He was a good man. An honest and simple man. It felt good to talk to him. I would miss him. A lot.

Afterwards, I helped wash out the mugs we had used and while I was there I cleaned his dusty desk.

"You're a kind lass," he said to me unexpectedly.

I smiled at him.

"You remind me of my daughter. She looked nothing like you, of course, but she had a heart of gold. Like you."

I went up to him and lightly kissed his weathered cheek.

"Are you really leaving in a month?"

"There is less than a month left, John." I could hear the sadness in my own voice.

"Oh," he said, and scratched his head in confusion.

"I should be going. See you tomorrow."

It was already starting to get dark as I trudged back in the snow. My heart felt heavy and when I went back to the house I couldn't concentrate on my gardening book. I kept listening out for Luca to arrive. He did not. I had a solitary dinner in the big dining room. I carried my sweet dessert wine into the living room with the big log fire and waited for him.

But he did not come back. Knowing now there were guards prowling and always watching, I was forced to return to my room to sleep, but I couldn't sleep. I waited for him throughout the night and only fell asleep sometime after two in the morning.

I woke with a jerk at dawn and hurried to the kitchen to pick up John's cakes. As usual Madam was ready with the boxes and I took them and walked in the snow to the greenhouse. John was waiting for me and we worked together. I never let myself think of Luca. Where he was or where he had spent the night. I couldn't let myself think of him wrapped around another woman's body. The thought burned me like acid.

After lunch I went to see my father. He was asleep when I went through the door, but Laura seemed excited and flustered as she showed me the first-class plane tickets, and told me my father and her were going to be flown to a special hospital in Switzerland so that my father could have mineral and vitamins given to him intravenously to build back his immunity, and have a course of blood transfusions from young people. Apparently, it was a new way of regenerating a sick or old body that was all the rage with the rich and famous.

With tears in her eyes she hugged me tightly.

"One day," she sniffed. "One day, you will be rewarded for being such a good daughter to your father. I love my daughter and I would die for her, but I can see that you are the daughter every parent dreams of."

Then she wiped her eyes and took me to see Dad. I thought he looked slightly better than the last time I had seen him but I couldn't tell for sure.

He gripped my hand tightly. "You've done so much for me."

I shook my head. "I've done what any daughter would."

"Don't Skye," he whispered fiercely. "You've sacrificed for me. I know you have. You're one in a billion, Skye. One in a billion. And I love you, Skye. I love you."

Tears filled my eyes. At that moment, I knew it had all been worth it. All the times I had let Salvatore into my body. All the times I had taken him in my mouth. It was all worth it. Even knowing everything I knew now I would do it all again... without a second thought.

"I love you too, Daddy."

Laura said she had something to do and went out of the room then, but I think she just wanted to give us some privacy. When they first got together she used to be jealous of the relationship Dad and I had, but after a while she put it aside and learned to love us both. She knew I was no threat to her.

I put my hand into my coat and pulled out the chocolate truffle the Chef had made and served me with last night. It was so delicious I had wrapped it in tissue paper and saved it for Dad. I unwrapped it and placed it into his mouth.

"I know sugar is no good for you, but just a little bit won't hurt."

He rolled it around his tongue, and his eyes widened. Poor thing. His food was deliberately bland and without spices or sugar. It was a long time since he had eaten anything truly delicious. I watched him slowly suck at the chocolate, his eyes misting over with love. I laid my cheek in his lap and cried then. For him. For me. For the way life was always so unjust. Everything I wanted was always taken away from me.

He stroked my hair gently. "Don't cry, my little angel. Everything will be alright."

"When you come back, I'm taking you and Laura out to a nice restaurant."

He chuckled. "Do we have to take the old witch?"

"Dad," I admonished, lifting my head.

He pretended to sigh. "Fine, we'll take her along."

Laura came back into the room and started making tea. We sat around talking, drinking tea and eating biscuits from a tin. Afterwards, I went back to the car and got in. Silently, the driver put the car into motion.

CHAPTER 38

SKYE

$\mathcal{A}$s soon as we arrived back at Torrington Hall I ran up to my room. Sitting on my bed, I pulled out my phone and dialed his number. My heart was beating so fast, my chest felt fluttery and strange. What if he was with a woman? What if she picked up the phone? What if he told me fuck off? I was gripping my phone so hard my hand hurt.

"Skye," Luca's deep, smooth voice said into my ear.

I launched into my prepared message. "I'm just calling to say thank you so much for what you are doing for my father. I am truly grateful."

In the silence that followed I wasn't sure if the line had dropped. Then he spoke. "No need to thank me. I'm just keeping my side of the bargain."

"Sending my father on a first-class flight to Switzerland to regenerate himself is not part of the bargain."

"I have a ball, a charity event for the Charington General Hospital that I have to attend today. You'll come with me."

"What time?" I whispered.

"You will be picked up at 7pm."

"Okay."

"Right. See you later."

The line went dead and I rose to my feet and went into my new closet. I went through the row of dresses. They ranged from vibrant reds, greens, pinks to the more neutral shades of grey and beige. Some were sexy and some were cute, but a dress wasn't really what I was in the mood for. I knew the party would be filled with socialite women like Sienna, and I wanted to look sophisticated and confident. I wanted to show them that I didn't need anybody's approval. I wanted to wear something nobody else would be wearing.

I turned towards the sets of pantsuits that hung from the rack.

My eyes were immediately drawn to a tailored white number with a soft blazer. It came with an incredibly beautiful, lacy high-necked blouse. I ran my finger along the delicate material. Never in my life had I imagined I'd own or worn something so beautiful. I did not try it that day when Anna had brought it. It was so similar to another black one I had tried that Anna said, it should fit in exactly the same way. I took it down and changed into it.

It was a perfect fit, of course, but it turned out to be nothing like the black one.

The black one was flawlessly grown-up and professional looking. This one. This one clung to every curve and dip of my body. I could only be awed by the clever tailoring and the way the gorgeous lace made scallop like shapes around my neck.

I took the outfit off and went to have a quick shower and wash my hair. Once my hair was dried I put it into a ponytail high on my head. Then I dressed in the pantsuit and stood in front of the mirror. Something was missing.

I opened the accessories drawer and decided on a plain string of pearls with a gold clasp. The beads were lustrous and luxurious and it was the perfect accompaniment to the outfit. I sat in front of the vanity mirror and painted my lips a stark blood red, and finished off the attire with bright red Louboutin stilettos.

When I stood in front of the mirror, I could hardly recognize myself. I looked like a stranger. A glamorous, confident stranger. Would Luca be proud to have me on his arm?

Maybe. I hoped so.

I checked the time, happy that I was about twenty minutes early. I felt nervous so I thought I would go down to the Blue Room and get myself a drink. I slung my coat loosely over my shoulder and went out. As I was halfway down the stairs my phone rang. I didn't recognize the caller. When I answered it, I found it was one of the guards at the front gate at the other end.

"There's a woman here who says she's your sister. Would you like me to let her in?"

I was stunned speechless. What on earth was my step sister doing here? How did she even find this place?

"Miss Morrison?" the guard reminded politely.

I gripped the banister hard and my voice was strange, as I said, "Yes, let her in."

I hesitated in the vast foyer undecided if I should go to the front door and let my sister in or would that not be the done thing, but the staff at Torrington Hall ran a well-oiled ship. The guard must have called ahead to let Madam know for she was already coming in from the direction of the kitchen. Her eyes widened at my appearance, then she nodded politely at me. "I will show her into the music room."

I walked on the stone tiles, my shoes echoing, and went into the music room where there was a grand piano and went straight to the bar. I needed a drink more than ever. I poured myself a glass of neat whiskey and downed it. The effect was instantaneous. It ran into my empty stomach like fire and spread through my body, giving me warmth. There was a soft knock on the door and Madam came in.

"Miss Diana Morrison," she said formally.

I was shocked. I never thought Madam would ever treat me as if I was the lady of the house receiving a visitor. This was the woman who deliberately took me up the servants' stairs when I first arrived here.

"Thank you, Madam," I replied with a grateful smile.

Then my sister came into view. "Hey," she said, her bright smile losing its luster when she laid eyes on me. Her eyes became round. I knew it was because of the way I looked. As I watched she struggled to get her equilibrium back.

"Hello, Diana," I greeted softly.

"Should I bring some tea or refreshments, Ma'am?" Madam asked me.

"No thank you, Madam. I have a car coming for me in a few minutes."

She withdrew and shut the door behind her. I turned to my sister.

"Wow, so you're living here now. Must be nice."

"How did you know I was here?" I asked.

"Katie mentioned it so I thought I'd pay you a visit. See how the other half lives and all that," she said nonchalantly and ended with a false laugh.

"What can I do for you, Diana?"

She didn't answer me. Instead she walked over to a large painting and stood gazing up at it. "Beautiful, isn't it. I bet it must have cost the earth."

I said nothing.

She turned towards me, a fake smile stretched across her face. "So... are you his mistress?"

I shrugged. "I guess you could call it that."

"You must be very proud of yourself. Landing such a big fish."

I wasn't going to give her the satisfaction. I lifted my chin. "Yeah, I got lucky."

I saw the flash of jealousy in her eyes, but it was gone in a fraction of a second. "I like your outfit. The blouse is from Dior, isn't it?"

"I think so."

She nodded. "It is. I saw it in their fall collection. Kim

Kardashian has it too." She came closer. "Mom told me you've arranged for Dad and her to go to Switzerland for some sort of experimental treatment at an expensive clinic for the rich and famous."

"I didn't arrange that for them," I corrected. "Luca probably got his assistants on the job."

"Right. Must be nice to have minions to do everything for you."

I glanced at my watch. "I have to be somewhere else soon. Did you come here for some other reason than to see how the other half lives?"

"Yes, as a matter of fact, I did." She flashed another fake smile. "I was wondering if you would be able to lend me some money, Skye. I promise I'll pay it back as soon as I can. I have some unexpected bills to settle."

"Yes, I can do that. But first I need to know something."

Her eyes narrowed. "What is it?"

"Did you... kill my plants?"

She had not expected that and her jaw dropped with shock. "What?"

"When I was trying to make a little garden for myself did you kill my plants?" I repeated slowly.

Then she snapped her mouth shut and denied the accusation strongly. "Of course not. Why would I do something like that? I don't even like plants."

But I had seen the truth flash in her eyes. It *was* her. She was the jealous poisoner. How she must have hated me even all those years ago. So much that she could not bear to see me succeed at even the smallest thing. Not even something she had absolutely no interest in.

"How much money do you need?" I asked softly.

She hesitated. "$5,000."

I looked into her greedy, sly eyes. "Why so little? Look around you. There is so much here. Why didn't you ask me for ten or twenty or even a hundred thousand?"

She stared at me aghast. Worried that she had asked too little. "Well, I didn't' want to ask too much, but it would really help if you gave me, I mean, lent me $10,000."

I started to laugh.

"What is so funny?" she demanded.

"Ah, Diana. I cannot believe how desperately I wanted to be your little sister, wanted you to love me. For years, and years, I tried to please you, but all that time you just treated me as if I was a piece of dirty gum on your high and mighty shoe. And now you come here wanting *me* to lend *you* money that I've earned from whoring myself. Is the irony lost on you?"

"Look, I know we haven't really got on, but I'm willing to try… for our parents' sakes. Let's try to be a family again, okay?"

"No," I said. "You are poison, Diana, and I truly wish I will never again run into you. But no doubt at some time I will see you at Dad's house, and when that happens I want you to completely ignore me, don't even look in my direction, and I will do the same to you."

Her face turned white with anger, and she showed her true colors. "How dare you take that tone with me. You're all dressed up like a Queen, but you're just a prostitute. No better than a hooker on a street corner turning tricks for cash. Don't you forget that."

"And what do you call a woman who tries to borrow money from said prostitute?"

Hate made her ugly. With a snarl, she lunged forward, her clawed hand stretched in front of her. I knew exactly what her intention was. She wanted to destroy. She wanted to tear my lovely lace blouse. Just like she had killed my plants and convinced me that my hair, which everyone always complimented me on, was ugly and I should dye it brown or black.

I was too fast for her. I stepped sideways, but the momentum of her lunge carried her forward relentlessly, and she crashed onto the floor with a scream. She screamed with a mixture of frustration, fury and pain.

I looked at her sprawled figure and felt sad. She had let her jealousy eat her up. I never wanted to hurt Laura so I never told on Diana even when she hurt me, but enough was enough. I never wanted to see Diana again.

I turned away and walked towards the door. She shouted at me, called me a whore and a cheap bitch, but her insults were water off a duck's back. I didn't care what she said or thought anymore. I did not turn back. We were finished.

Madam was standing just outside the door. She smiled grimly at me. "You go on ahead, Ma'am. Sergio is waiting outside for you. I'll take care of her."

"Thank you," I said quietly, and walked outside into the clean crisp air. I had done the right thing and I felt lighter. No more pretending to be her friend. Not even to make Laura happy.

CHAPTER 39

SKYE

*A*t eight on the dot, we arrived at the ball. There was a huge banner outside and there were people in fine clothes milling around.

I was nervous, well aware that I did not belong amongst this crowd of elites and socialites and didn't know where to go, but a woman in a black dress stepped out of the crowd.

"Miss Morrison, I'm Tina. I'm here to escort you to your table," she said with a smile.

She took my coat from me and handed it over at the counter to the girl minding coats. Then we walked into the grand hall. It had a stage at the far end and the middle of it was a dance floor.

The bright golden light of the room, the small orchestra by the corner of the stage, the vibrant smiles, the seemingly inexhaustible stream of champagne being passed around, proved that this was an important event indeed.

I spotted the Mayor of Boston, the founder of Reebok, and a couple of Hollywood celebrities as Tina and I walked through the room. Everyone was immaculately dressed in evening dresses and tuxedos, but many heads turned to stare at me. I guess I was the only one who wore a pantsuit to a ball. Tina led me to the main table right in front of the stage. She swiped away the place setting with my name on it, and pulled out the chair for me.

The round table which had about ten seats was already half filled with people. They looked at me curiously as I took my seat. Inside, I was close to panicking, but I smiled at them distantly and as regally as I could, as if I was a Princess from an obscure European country. It worked because they nodded and smiled back at me politely. Before they could engage me in conversation and find out I was a waitress, I turned my head and began to look around me.

I was looking for Luca.

In fact, I was so intent on my search I almost jumped when the chair beside me suddenly moved. I looked up into Luca's mesmerizingly luminous eyes. He smiled slowly at me and my heart started to crash against my ribcage. His hair was slicked back and he looked utterly dashing in a crisp white shirt, an exquisite tuxedo and bow tie.

He took his seat and I could tell that all the others at the table had stopped their conversations and turned their heads to watch us avidly, but he didn't even bother acknowledging anyone. His eyes were on me. My stomach did little flips and I could feel the heat rising into my cheeks at the look in his eyes.

"Luca!" a soft, breathless voice called.

I felt her voice in the pit of my stomach. I felt it the way a woman feels when she realizes a hooded man is walking behind her in a deserted car park. I knew she was trouble. With the hairs at the back of my neck standing, I turned to look at the owner of the seductive voice.

She was beautiful. Her dazzling red dress clung to her sexy figure.

"Irene," Luca said, and rose to his feet for her.

I had to lower my head because I couldn't trust what my expression would reveal.

"You didn't tell me last night you would be here," I heard her say.

"You didn't ask," he replied.

Was he flirting with her right in front of me? I saw red. It was pathetic but I wanted to scratch her eyes out. I got to my feet.

"Excuse me," I said needing to be out of there but not before I caught the finger that she had pressed teasingly on his chest.

"Who is she?" I heard her ask as I hastened away.

The moment I was out of the massive hall, I leaned against a wall. There were signs ahead giving directions to the washrooms, but I needed a moment to just calm down. I felt a wreck. I was so jealous it was like acid pouring into my stomach. So this is what Diana felt for all those years. I could almost understand her now. Why she had killed my plants. I wanted to cut her finger off. I hated even the thought of her touching Luca. I closed my eyes. I needed to get a hold of myself.

"It doesn't matter," I whispered to myself. "Nothing matters. It'll all be over soon."

"You look amazing?" a voice I hoped I would never hear again drawled close to me.

My boiling blood froze over. Disbelief ripped through me and for a moment I was too afraid to open my eyes. It couldn't be. But I opened my eyes and there he was. My worst nightmare. I could do nothing but stare at him, my entire body tingling with disgust.

A sick smile spread across his face. "Wow," he said with a strained laugh. "Anyone would think you hated me."

He took a step towards me and I jumped away.

He feigned hurt. "What? You don't want me anymore?"

Bile rose to my throat. I swallowed hard. "We're finished, Salvatore."

"You don't understand, Skye. His month is nearly up and then you're coming back to me. I've made good, Skye. I'm earning big bucks now. I can take care of you... and your dad. I'll be good to you. I'll take you shopping and buy you more stuff like this outfit you're wearing now."

CHAPTER 40

LUCA

I got rid of Irene and glanced impatiently at the empty seat next to me. I felt ridiculous. Was I truly this eager to see her after one night away that I couldn't bear for her to be out of my sight for a simple bathroom break?

Every decent cell in my body told me to sit there and wait for her to return, but I couldn't sit still. I felt agitated and even angsty. I rose up from my seat and strode out of the hall. I could see my men hanging around the edges of the room. They stared at me with guarded expressions.

As I got out of the room I saw her. Then I saw him. The fury that burned inside me was like a ball of lava.

"You don't have a choice?" I heard him say, his voice malicious and bitter. "The moment he's done with you I'm taking you back."

"I'd rather die," I heard her spit out.

"Oh no you won't," he shot back. "Your father will. If you don't come back to me, I'll hurt him."

"Move away from her," I growled. Hell would freeze over before I let him have her.

He turned around to face me. Our gazes collided, his wide and shocked as he began to back away from me.

"Don Luca! I wasn't. I was just..."

I swung my fist and socked him on the jaw. He flew backwards and landed on his back. I glared at him, but he didn't move at all. He was out cold. There were shocked gasps around us. From the corner of my eyes I could see my men. Keeping their distance, but ready to do battle. My knuckles stung and I inhaled deeply before I turned my eyes to her.

Her hands were covering her mouth. I felt a surreal pain when I saw the tension in her face.

I went to touch her, but she instantly flinched away.

"Are you okay?"

She nodded. "Don't mind me. It's been a long day."

I hooked my arms behind her knees and back and swept her off her feet. She gasped, but immediately curled her arms around my neck.

"What are you doing?" she cried.

I didn't respond, just began to walk towards the entrance.

"Let me go!" she insisted. "I can walk on my own."

I didn't respond but instead held her tightly in my arms. When she realized that she couldn't get herself away from me she pounded her fists into my chest, but when she realized they had no effect on me, her attack became softer and softer. Eventually she buried her face in my neck, her body still shaking. My men had already radioed Cullinan and he was already waiting outside the steps.

Even Cullinan could not stop the astonishment from showing on his usually stoic face when he saw me carrying her down the steps. I put her into the back of the car and went around the other side. As soon as I shut the door I pulled her back into my arms. She clung to me.

"Did you sleep with her last night?" she mumbled against my neck.

"What?"

"That woman, Irene? Did you sleep with her last night?" Her voice sounded pitiful.

I pulled her away from me so I could look into her eyes. "Irene is the wife of a business associate of mine."

"But you saw her last night," she insisted.

I couldn't believe I was explaining my movements to a woman, but I could see how hurt she was. "Yes, I met her briefly last night when she came to pick her husband up from the business meeting we were having."

"But she touched your chest."

I shrugged. "Irene is naturally flirtatious. She does that to everyone."

She licked her lips and I felt my cock twitch. "Um... so why didn't you come back to me last night?"

"I worked very late and I had an early meeting in the city."

"I waited for you," she whispered.

I wanted to tell her I couldn't sleep thinking of her, but the words were stuck in my throat. I just pulled her close to me and just listened to her even breathing. It felt like the walls I had so painstakingly erected around myself over so many years were crumbling to dust. One brick at a time. But I told myself the plan had not changed. Soon it would be time to let her go. She would go back to her life and I would go back to mine. And that would be that.

"I'm sorry," she mumbled.

"What for?"

"Your event," she said. "I ruined it for you."

"You didn't ruin anything," I murmured. For a while there was silence. Then I broke it. "Did I tell you how beautiful you look tonight?"

She lifted her head. "No. Do you really think I'm beautiful?"

I smiled at her innocence. "You were the most beautiful woman in the place." I paused. "I think you might even be the most beautiful woman I've ever known."

Even in the dim light inside the limo I could see her blushing at the compliment before she buried her face in my chest. Neither of us spoke after that. My thoughts were too jumbled and difficult to decipher. It was a long, long time since a woman hid in my chest. And if I was truly honest, it felt wonderful.

We arrived at the house and we strolled in together. None of the men came with us as though it was some sort of unspoken command that the both of us simply needed to be left alone. I shut the door and turned to watch as she walked ahead of me. From the start it had been her walk that first arrested my attention. Something slinky and sensuous about the way her hips moved.

She stopped and half-turned to look at me.

"Are you coming up?" she asked and the slight tremble in her lower lip made me want to fuck her right there and then.

"Are you hungry?" I asked.

"Starving," she confessed.

"So am I."

Her eyes twinkled. "Shall we raid the refrigerator?"

I smiled slowly. "That might be the best suggestion I've heard all day."

The refrigerator was fully stocked, but all she wanted was a ham and cheese toastie.

I went into the cellar and found an old bottle I was saving for a special occasion. It was almost a sin to drink it with a ham and cheese sandwich, but there was no one else in the world I wanted to share the bottle with. By the time I got back our sandwiches were ready.

We went down to my den and sat on the rug in front of the fire, eating and drinking. The wine was really good and she was fascinating. I could not stop staring at her. The way the firelight licked her rosy cheeks, the way her mouth moved, the way she laughed.

When she asked me about myself I clammed up. I wasn't ready to talk about him and nothing else about me was important. So she talked about her family. Her father, whom she obviously loved dearly, her mother who had passed away when she was very young, her stepmother who she had great affection for, and almost nothing about her step sister who she didn't get on with.

But I already knew that. Mateo had already informed me about the incident that afternoon and how Madam had to throw her out while she tried to ruin Skye's reputation by hurling vile insults and accusations about Skye.

I felt relaxed and mellow, just lying in front of the fire listening to her voice.

A part of me began to wish this was real. That there was no expiry date on us. To stop the sensation from spreading I reached blindly for her and covered her plump mouth with mine.

There was only this. No more than this. And the sooner I understood that the better it would be for both of us.

Skye

I woke up to the red glow from the dying embers in the fireplace.

I knew it was time to go to the greenhouse, but for the first time since being given permission to work in the greenhouse I found it hard to jump up eagerly at the prospect. I just wanted to stay under the big blanket with Luca's warm strong body glued to mine. Then I thought about old John waiting for me, his packages in the kitchen, and I very, very slowly, millimeter by millimeter moved away from Luca. Not slow enough apparently, because he stirred and turning his head, opened his eyes.

Immediately, the wolf-like eyes became alert.

My cheery greeting died on my tongue.

He looked… rested and handsome. While I must have looked a horrible mess with yesterday's make-up all stale and smeared around my eyes.

"Where do you think you're going?" he murmured, as he turned on his side to face me. A thick healthy slab of hair fell across his forehead making his eyes appear even more piercing even though his mouth was relaxed and sensuous. I wanted to reach out and comb his hair back with my fingers and cradle his gorgeous face in my palms. I could hardly believe this was the stone-cold, heartless, mythical Luca before me. Yet, once he left this warm hearth and put on his clothes he would once again become an unapproachable stranger.

"To the greenhouse," I mumbled.

He looked at me curiously. "You're really committed to growing your plants, aren't you?"

I smiled. "Very much."

"Okay, I'll be quick. Ten minutes tops," he promised, and suddenly dived under the covers. I felt his mouth clamp down on my clit and gasped. Well, he was much less than ten minutes. I think the earth beneath me shattered in five.

To my credit I was even faster. Took a lot less than five minute to shatter his world. With a laugh, I evaded his grabbing hands while he was still too disorientated to move as fast as me, I whipped the blanket off him and scrambled away. With the big blanket clutched around my body, I ran out of the room.

Again, I saw Madam as I was running down the corridor. This time she didn't disappear into the first room she came to. She passed by and respectfully greeted me, "Good morning, Ma'am."

"Good morning to you too, Madam," I called out, as I whizzed past.

CHAPTER 41

SKYE

One week later

The days were passing quickly. My father was doing well in Switzerland, and Laura called everyday during their morning break. He was swimming and eating well, getting his transfusions regularly and generally seemed to be stronger and in a much better mood. My plants had become tiny little seedlings with pale green leaves. Every day when I woke up I ticked off another day in the calendar in my head and grieved for its loss.

Luca left last night for Brighton Beach, but he said he would be back in time for dinner.

I spent all morning in the greenhouse with John. There was not much to do with my plants any more other than watch them lovingly so I had taken to helping him with his chores. I could see that he was old now and his back would start to hurt by mid-day. Before I left this house I promised myself that I would talk to Luca about getting a little assistant for him. He was too proud to admit it, but he desperately needed one.

This morning, John had to run some personal errands and he left about 10.00am. I walked back to the house feeling exhausted. Not from physical labor, which I welcomed, but from the constant thoughts of leaving this place. The torment just wouldn't stop, even though I had prepared myself so hard for this. It was impossible for me to think he would no longer be in my life in just over a week. Or that I would never step into the greenhouse again, or lie on the white rug in front of the fire with Luca. I would even miss Madam.

The last week had been a kind of dream. Sometimes he would hold me as if he was never going to let go, then other times he withdrew as soon as our bodies were spent. I wanted to hold onto him, but I knew better. He was not mine.

I sat on my bed and pulled up his number, but before I could send anything I stopped myself and instead sent the message to Katie.

Let's have lunch.

A few seconds later, she replied.

"Oooo where?

I smiled slightly.

You choose.

Her reply was instantaneous.

Mr. Chow.

I typed back.

Done. 1pm okay with you?

I didn't have to wait long for her reply.

See you there. Btw when is your contract over again?

I stared at the message, a dull ache in my heart that almost left me feeling numb. I couldn't bear to write the words down. I typed the four letters with a frown on my forehead.

Soon.

Her reply was quick as a flash.

Are you ok?

Mine was just as fast.

Yes. See you at 1pm

I thought that would be the end of it but another text came through.

I want to get my nails done before lunch.

I texted back.

I'll come with you.

She took a little while longer to respond, no doubt she had to deal with a customer or something.

At the mall? Onora's?

I replied.

Sounds good. Will you book or shall I?

Her reply came back with five angry face emojis.

I will but gotta go. Bitch client. Ugh. See you there.

WITH A SMILE I tossed the phone on the bed and collapsed next to it.

CHAPTER 42

SKYE

*A*n hour and a half later I arrived at the chic nail salon at our favorite mall. Katie was already there and having an animated conversation with the staff. They were all from Thailand and good friends of hers and always applied great discounts whenever we went together. It felt strange to think I didn't need those discounts as much as I used to.

"Skye" she called and got to her feet to rush over to me

I smiled at her, but her expression twisted with concern. "Hey, are you okay?"

"Yeah," I croaked. "Why?"

"Your eyes are sunken, and you're deathly pale. Have you eaten today?"

"I have, I'm fine," I said and reached up to slap some color into my cheeks.

"Well, you don't look it," she muttered. She stared at me, an amused frown digging into her forehead. "What's happening? You're not pregnant, are you?"

My eyes widened. "Don't be silly." Even the idea was ludicrous. "I'm on the pill."

"And you're sure you haven't missed a day?"

"Not a single day," I said firmly.

"In that case, come on." She pulled me with her into the salon. "We're having a nibble. Sushi. It's amazing."

I opted for a simple pedicure and settled into the low seat. The girls began to work on us and the intimate space echoed with their friendly chatter and laughter. Thankfully nothing whatsoever about me came up so I just listened to the other girls as they spoke about their lives; their work, their kids, and the reprehensible men in their lives.

As I listened to them it seemed to me every one of them had a solid grasp of their reality and where they were going. Whilst I on the other hand felt as if I was in a dream. The fever that was Luca Messana was burning wildly in my heart, but even a fool knew every fire must come to an end.

When our nail session came to an end we began to stroll through the mall towards Mr. Chow

"So…" Katie began. "You'll soon be done with your contract. How do you feel?"

I couldn't hold back anymore. My throat constricted as I tried to stem the tears but she had already seen them. With burning eyes, I stared down at my feet. We were both still wearing the throwaway sliders from the nail bar and my beautifully pedicured nails looked blurred.

"Skye."

Katie positioned herself in front of me and waited for me to get myself back together. She didn't rush me. She just placed a hand on my shoulder and waited.

When I could eventually get the words out, they were delivered in a whisper. "I already miss him so much it hurts."

I was afraid to see her expression. Afraid she would laugh at me being so idiotic. Who fell in love with a man like Luca? It was like an ant that dreams of driving a car. It was just so dumb. Dumb. Dumb. Dumb.

I could feel my tears run down my face and splash on my slides.

"Oh, Skye," she muttered, and pulled me into a hug.

I held on tightly and cried my eyes out. Right there in the middle of the mall with all the people moving around us.

"It'll be okay. You'll see, it'll be okay."

"I feel so ridiculous. How could I have let myself fall in love with him? I am a nobody." I sobbed.

"Look at me, Skye," Katie said firmly, pulling away.

I looked into her kind eyes. "How could you not have fallen for him? It was the classic Beauty and the Beast scenario. You sacrificed yourself for your father and went to live in this big lonely castle, where you fell in love with the beast. I think I would have done the same, especially since he's such a sex-on-a-stick type of beast, and he's been showering you with all the lovely things you never had in your life. If I were you, I would go back to your castle and enjoy the time you have left. I'd live intensely, and make every precious moment count. And when it was time to leave I would then start to grieve. I wouldn't spoil my time now with sorrow for what might not happen."

"What do you mean by might not happen?"

She shrugged. "Nothing is set in stone. You could walk out of here, get run over by a car and die on the spot, Luca could fall in love with you and ask you to stay."

I shook my head sadly. "It's not that kind of relationship, Katie. He doesn't want to get close. Anytime we get a little closer, he immediately pulls away emotionally, but you're right. I'm ruining the little time I have left. I should enjoy it. It will never come back."

"That's my girl."

Afterwards, Katie said, "I've kind of lost my appetite. Let's just have a massive pretzel instead of Chinese food."

"Are you sure?"

"Yes, I'm sure. We'll go to Mr. Chow next week or something."

We bought large pretzels at a kiosk and sat on one of the benches to eat them. I didn't feel any better, but I knew Katie was right. I had to stop moping around and live as intensely as possible. Enjoy every second because all of this was going to disappear in less than two weeks.

"I forgot to tell you that Diana called me," Katie said, as she dipped her pretzel into a container of sour cream.

"I'm finished with her. I never want to see her or talk about her again."

Her eyes widened. "Wow! That's drastic. What happened?"

"She came to Torrington Hall and it was not pretty."

"Oops... I shouldn't have told her you were living there, should I?"

"It's okay, you weren't to know."

"Sorry, Skye, but she kind of tricked me into telling her. I had no idea she would go there and cause trouble for you."

"Don't worry. I'm glad it happened. Now it's all out in the open. No more pretending. For years I put up with her condemnation and sarcasm. I don't need that in my life anymore. She's welcome to think I'm a whore. Her opinion doesn't bother me one bit."

With our pretzels eaten, we changed out of our slides into our shoes. Katie turned and hugged me. "It's going to be okay," she whispered.

I smiled gratefully at her. She had managed to make me see my situation in a different light. I had already decided not to waste a second of the time I had left. "Of course, it is."

Then I followed her to the escalator and watched her go down it and turn off towards the car park.

I didn't want to go back yet. I wanted some time alone to myself. I strolled through the mall towards the ice-cream shop, bought myself a cone with two scoops, and went back to sit at one of the benches inside the main lobby. I watched the myriads of people coming and going. They seemed excited or perhaps it was the season's decoration in sparkling gold, green, and red that made everyone and everything seem so lively.

"Do you know where the Ladies is?" someone asked next to me.

I looked up and saw a middle-aged woman. She was plump and dressed in jeans and a thick sweater. She was wearing glasses and her auburn hair was a mess of curls and frizzy bangs.

"Over there," I replied politely, pointing in the direction of the restrooms.

"Thanks honey. Is it okay if I sit next to you for a moment? My feet are killing me," she said.

"Of course," I said and moved to make a space for her.

She sat and turned toward me. "Is it okay if I show you something?"

I was not really in the mood to be drawn into someone else's life. I just wanted a bit of time on my own so I politely smiled and said, "I'm sorry, but I actually have to go now."

"Just one moment, hun," she said and pulled out her wallet which I noticed was very much like those I had seen in many movies. My eyes widened. Then she opened the wallet. On one half, I saw her Federal Bureau of Investigation identity card, and on the other was a shiny FBI badge.

CHAPTER 43

SKYE

*S*he snapped it shut. "Please remain calm," she said to me with the loveliest of smiles. "Don't panic otherwise you're going to make things very difficult for us. And if you make things difficult for us we, in turn, will make things very difficult for you."

A shudder passed through me. "W-what is this about?"

She smiled sweetly. "Please smile back at me. There are always eyes on you to ensure your safety. Luca Messana is little else if not vigilant."

I looked around me in confusion. Were Luca's men actually following me around? Then it occurred to me that she didn't understand the relationship I had with Luca. I was not his girlfriend. He didn't care about me enough to have men following me around and guarding me. "You don't under-stand—," I began.

"No, you don't understand. If you do not follow my instruc-tions, you and your family will bear the consequences. I believe your father is away in Switzerland enjoying the perks of being associated with the Messana clan as we speak."

Something cold slithered through me.

"Smile at me then start to head straight down to the restrooms you pointed me to. Don't turn to look back, keep your gaze ahead, and look casual."

She smiled gently. To any onlooker it would have seemed genuine, only I knew it was far from the case.

"You'll get up before me and go over to the bathrooms, and there my colleagues will be waiting to speak to you."

I nodded blankly. I was not truly afraid, just stunned.

She patted my knee kindly. "If you cooperate with us you have nothing to be worried about. We're on your side."

Taking a deep breath, I rose to my feet. I dropped my unfinished ice-cream into a bin and walked slowly towards the restrooms. My mind was whirling. What did they want with me? I had done nothing wrong. When I arrived at the Ladies, I almost knocked, but stopped myself and pushed the door open.

As it shut behind me I looked up and saw a man and a woman awaiting. They were dressed casually, but the moment they saw me they came over.

"I'm Sarah Yale," the woman said. She had thick dark brown hair, and carefully blank eyes.

"I'm Gregory Wang," the man introduced. He had an accent and was thin, gaunt almost, and black eyes.

I looked nervously between both of them. "What is this about?"

"Miss Morrison, we've become aware of your... relationship with Mr. Messana."

If he expected a reaction he got none. I had done nothing wrong and I was not going to let them intimidate me.

"We have been monitoring the criminal Messana family for a couple of years now for various criminal offenses like corruption, money laundering, suspect dealings with the Russian mafia, and even murder. However, we've not been able to get anything or anyone to rat on those slippery bastards. This is especially true of the Capo Luca Messana who moves about almost leaving no trace, even digitally. His operation seemed to be iron clad and impenetrable... until you came into the picture. We need your help."

My response was automatic: fuck you! I tried not to let it show and especially not to speak it out loud. "What do you want me to do?"

"We have solid reasons to believe a massive drug trafficking operation in collaboration with their associates in Italy is active. The biggest players in both countries will be involved in the deal so it is our big chance to catch them all red-handed. Having someone like you on the inside, who is on our side, would be invaluable."

"I'm not on the inside," I said calmly. "He barely speaks to me, let alone about his business."

Gregory Wang glanced at his colleague, then back to me. "We understand this, but at this point, any leverage we can get would be akin to a miracle. This potential bust is the largest case we have ever worked on, and it has also already caused the death of one of our officers and tears of too many of our members. Lives are at stake here. We hope that you'll be willing and able to assist us."

"You're not listening to me," I said. "He doesn't speak to me about business. Ever."

They shared another look with each other. Sarah Yale took over. If they were playing good cop bad cop I wondered who the bad cop was.

"We have a script that you would have to follow. It's very effective. Just follow it and for the most part it works. All criminals love to boast and they just need a bit of encouragement. It is especially effective after sex."

I took a deep breath. "So this is a honey trap?"

"Not exactly."

"How are you going to record the conversation? Do you plan to bug the house?"

"We will fit you with a wire now, and if you agree to help us we will send our operatives around disguised as your friends and fit up the place."

"You want me to wear a wire?" I asked in disbelief. This was just so out there. Never in a million years did I ever think I would be having this conversation with FBI officers.

"Yes, do not worry. Your safety will not be endangered in any way. We'll make sure that it is completely undetectable."

I could feel a deep frown working its way into my forehead. Anger churned in my stomach. "Do you understand what you're asking me to do?"

They nodded quietly.

"You tell me he's the head of one of the biggest criminal enterprises in the States. You tell me you have been hunting him for years with no results and then you ask me, a little waitress to wear a wire and to put my life and the life of my entire family in danger. Guess what? Based on that information he's smarter than you guys are and therefore smarter than me."

"Miss Morrison, we will be at your beck and call, immediately ready to respond should there be any issues," Gregory Wang said.

Sarah Yale's voice was soft and persuasive. "This could really help many people, Miss Morrison. You'd be making a great contribution to the bureau and society by helping put these monsters where they belong."

My laughter was dry. "Do you know exactly what my relationship with him is?"

"We are aware," Gregory responded. "Salvatore Picollo informed us of the details."

"Salvatore?"

"Yes. One of his men turned informant. We have him in custody."

I shuddered. Did Luca make one of his men turn on him? "If you know what my relationship with him is all about then you should also understand that I cannot wear a wire without it being discovered. Also my time with him is almost over."

"We know the details and this is why we need to give this a shot now. We—"

"I did this to save my father's life." I glared at them enunciating every single world. "I sold myself to two people because I couldn't afford to pay my father's medical bills. But now you're telling me to possibly sacrifice his life all over again just so I could... make a contribution to society? If I had asked society to help with my father's bills would they have given a damn?"

"Miss Mo—"

"What about after all of this? What if you're successful and his criminal enterprise is brought down? Doesn't that put a target on me and my family for the rest of our lives?"

"You'll be in the witness protection program. We will ensure—"

"I don't care what you will ensure. I know what witness protection means. You guys don't give a damn about the people you step on to get your big wins. You get to live your life while I have to look over my shoulder for the rest of mine? And what about my father? Do I leave him behind? Do I get to take him to a place that is completely foreign to him? Does he get to bring my stepmother? Does she get to bring her daughter? No? I thought so."

Fuming, I straightened my back and gave my final and definite response. "No! I will not do it. Please find someone else."

With as much confidence I could muster I turned around to exit the bathroom.

"We will prosecute you," Sarah Yale said coldly.

I stopped in my tracks. There it was: she was playing the part of bad cop.

"For income tax irregularities," she continued. "You received payments from both Salvatore Picollo and Luca Messana in cash, and you failed both times to put aside what is due to the IRS. Not declaring monies received in relation to services rendered is an offence that could get you incarcerated and will most definitely come with a hefty fine. And as we are government officials we are bound to report and act on such irregularities."

I turned around slowly. "You're threatening me?"

"No, Miss Morrison," Gregory spoke. "We're not threatening you. We're giving you a choice. You can either pay the amount owed, which at your tax rate we reckon would be close to a hundred thousand by the time all your dad's bills are taken into consideration, or… you could simply agree to collaborate with us."

Tears burned my eyes as I glared at both of them.

The bastards.

I swallowed hard, then spoke, every word even more painful as the last. "What exactly do you need me to do?"

"The first thing is to try to find a way to extend your time with him. This way we can work with you to obtain the specific type of information we need. Anything too sudden or direct will force him to become suspicious and clam up."

"And what if he doesn't want to extend the relationship?" I asked. "And anyway why do you assume our relationship is cordial?"

"Isn't it?' Sarah asked. "Based on Salvatore's report about the incident at the Hospital gala, it would seem to be."

"Salvatore insulted me and Luca helped Salvatore understand the error of his ways. Isn't that basic human decency?"

Sarah Yale hid a smile.

"Not for a man like Messana. Miss Morrison, as previously mentioned we have been chasing him for years and know more about him than his own mother probably does. This is not a man that is driven by affection or care for his fellowmen. He has sent his own men to their deaths."

"And yet this is the person that you're asking me to betray?"

Both had nothing to say to that. "The situation is the same. Do not help us and you are looking at prison time. If you don't want to do this for yourself, do it for your father. It would break his heart if you were incarcerated."

At the mention of my father I sighed. "All right. I'll help you."

The second I said that Sarah Yale pulled up a briefcase from the floor, opened it and took out her wires. Gregory went out of the room while she fitted me up. She worked quickly and expertly. Then she phoned someone. "Is it working?"

"Loud and clear," came the response.

"Good." She turned to me. "All you have to do is start talking to him. Start by complimenting his business prowess and show admiration for his skill, then show just a tiny bit of curiosity about his business. Don't rush it. Get him to talk."

I nodded. Then a sudden thought jolted my mind.

"What happens if he comes close enough to discover I'm wearing a wire and he's as dangerous as you suggest then I'm dead!"

"Don't let him get too close to you at the moment. Once you agree to let him let you stay longer we'll be able to bug the house properly, and then you can get as close as necessary," Gregory finished smoothly.

I was unconvinced, but I said, "Okay."

"Good. We'll contact you again tomorrow," said Sarah Yale.

"How?"

"Perhaps you can go to visit your friend again."

"All right."

She smiled encouragingly at me. "You're doing the right thing."

I did not smile back.

CHAPTER 44

SKYE

*O*nce I left the restrooms I wandered around the mall for a bit. I needed to think. I went into a shop and pretended to look through a rack of clothing. I felt eerily calm. I called Sergio and told him to meet me outside the mall.

The air outside was frigid, but I didn't feel it. Inside the car, I wrote out a long text. Then I closed my phone and looked out of the car. When we reached Torrington Hall, I came out of my daze and began to look around the snow-covered grounds. My hand touched the cold glass of the window.

"I will miss you," I whispered, as the car drove up the long, tree-lined driveway toward the house.

I knew Luca would not be back until dinnertime so I got into the house and was about to head straight up to my room when my name was called.

"Skye."

My heart nearly stopped. I turned around and was able to breathe easier when I saw it was just one of his other men. The echo in the foyer had made his voice sound almost identical to Luca's.

"Boss wants you in his study."

My eyes widened. "He's back?"

He nodded. "Come with me."

I straightened my spine. So the deed could not be postponed until later, but done now. They were listening in through the wires they had attached to my body. This meant I couldn't let Luca touch me intimately or he would find the device and everything would be ruined. I didn't think however that that was going to be a problem.

Nervously, I followed the man until he arrived at Luca's study and gave a hard knock on the door.

"Come in," I heard the response.

The security guard pushed the door open, and stood back to allow me to enter.

A fire was burning in the fireplace and the study felt beautifully warm. Luca was dressed in a black shirt with the sleeves rolled up and he was working on his laptop, but he slid it away from him and his searing eyes found mine. No matter how many times I saw him I always felt that strange attraction build inside my belly.

Taking a deep breath, I set in motion the events that would change my life forever.

Luca
https://www.youtube.com/watch?v=XVsWD1_GqwE
-Words-

I HADN'T SEEN her in thirty-six hours and I was desperate to crush her body against mine, but that look in her eyes made me stop and pay attention.

"What is it?" I asked softly.

She came forward. "Hello, darling."

My eyebrows rose. I stared at her as she walked to my desk, then placed her phone on it. She pointed at the screen, then very gently pushed it towards me while she carried on talking. "I missed you so much and I was wondering if it would be possible to extend my stay with you?"

"Why?" I asked, pulling her phone towards me. I could see that it was a text message that she had composed to me, but had not yet sent it. As I read, she talked.

"I want to spend more time with you. I realized that you are the best lover I've ever had and since you don't have anyone and I don't have anyone it would be a good thing for us both to stay together a bit longer. It makes sense, doesn't it? Well, I think it does. If you find someone, of course, I'll leave immediately. What do you think?"

I finished reading her note. Her note said.

The FBI contacted me at the mall. They want to use me to get intel on you. I didn't want to do it, but they threatened to put me in

prison because I have neither paid nor put aside the sums due to the IRS for the money I got from Salvatore and you.
I am wearing a wire right now.
So when I ask you to let me stay a bit longer, please say no. Maybe we can argue about something and you can pretend to throw me out of the house today. That way it won't be my fault and I will have no more use to them.

I lifted my gaze to hers.

"Also, I may need some more funds for my father. So if you don't mind me staying a bit more then… I'd really appreciate that."

I watched her quietly and she made a gesture of desperation with her hand.

"Marry me," I said.

She froze. For the longest time she didn't speak as she just stared at me, beyond stunned. Finally, her mouth opened and her voice came out in a croak. "What?"

"Marry me. I'd already decided that I wanted you to stay indefinitely so this is the perfect solution." I deleted her message and typed my own message into her phone as I spoke.

Then I went around the table, and gave her her phone with my message on it. Her eyes scanned my message quickly.

Say yes. They cannot ask a wife to testify against her own husband.

"So, what do you say?" I asked softly.

Her lips parted to speak, but they were trembling so much she shut her mouth and pressed them together.

"Say yes," I said persuasively.

"Yes," she murmured, but it was far from audible.

"Out loud," I mouthed to her and she repeated it this time a bit louder.

"Yes," she said her tone breathless. "I'll marry you."

"Today," I said.

Her eyeballs nearly popped out of her sockets. "What?"

"Right now," I told her. "Our family is very familiar with a reverend down at the King's Chapel. He'll be more than happy to wed us. Then it'll be official. We can have the big wedding later."

"Yes," she replied, in a daze. It was clear I had completely thrown her.

I linked my fingers with hers. "Now why don't you go up and change into something more... slinky. I like that white dress you have that shows off your shoulders."

CHAPTER 45

SKYE

I knew why he asked me to wear a strapless white dress when I didn't even have such a dress. The agents listening would understand that I couldn't wear the wire with such a dress. I ran upstairs to my room, closed the door, and leaned against it.

I closed my eyes and waited. Sure enough, my phone began to ring.

"Hello," I said calmly.

"Refuse him!" The order came fierce and harsh. "He cannot force you to marry him. Put a stop to this marriage now or you will be as guilty as him."

It felt as though I was on a high-speed train to an unknown and very possibly dangerous destination, but it didn't feel quite as terrifying as the second option, which was to jump off and roll into the sharp stones along the railway tracks, and that was what agreeing to betray Luca felt like. Because with that option I would be cutting my heart out of my body and feeding it to the ravens.

My lips trembled as I tried to speak, not out of fear, but out of a strange fury. How dare they? How dare government officials behave like thugs? I'd seen it in movies, the way the CIA and FBI went around threatening people to cooperate with them or have their lives destroyed and even then, I thought it was wrong, but I never dreamed I would be at the receiving end.

The end did not justify the means.

They shouldn't have the right to crush my life so they could have the kudos of catching someone who was obviously way smarter than them, judging by the way they had not managed to nab him even with all the high-tech digital surveillance and manpower power available to them. My life and my father's lives had value beyond the promotions and back slaps they would get for catching Luca.

"I can't put a stop to it," I replied calmly.

"Miss Morrison, this will bring the entire might of the bureau cracking down on the both of you."

With my phone close to my ear, I walked towards the window and stared out at the beauty around me. My gaze settled on a point far away. My heart fluttered in my chest. I wouldn't have to leave this place, the greenhouse, John, my plants. I could stay a bit longer with Luca.

"He is doing this because he thinks if you marry him you won't be able to testify against him."

"He's right, isn't he?" I asked softly.

There was an explosive moment of silence. "Skye, did you expose us?"

I felt as calm as a still lake. I found a pair of small eyebrow scissors and cut the wires of their listening device. There was not a thing these people could do to me. Not now. Not ever. "You heard every word. I did as you asked, but looks like he outsmarted you again."

"Miss Morrison, you don't—" he began.

But I had lost interest. "You failed. Better luck next time. Now I have to go. I have a wedding I must attend."

"Miss Morr—"

I ended the call and walked towards my wardrobe. I didn't know what the future held, I knew I was marrying a man who did not love me. I knew Luca was doing this because it was the best way for both of us to get out of the predicament the FBI had put us into for now, and after a time the agreement would be dissolved, but I didn't care. I felt as if my greatest dream had come true. For now, I was going to live in this beautiful house with the man I was in love with.

I wore a pale lemon and white Dior suit. As I buttoned the box jacket I saw myself in the mirror. Who was that girl in the mirror? My eyes were glittering with excitement. So much had happened in three little weeks. My lips moved and out came words. "Hello, I'm Skye Messana." The words didn't sound foreign. They sounded right.

I turned away from my reflection. I didn't dare feel happy, but as I reached for a pair of cream shoes I couldn't stop my hands trembling from sheer excitement and nerves. Taking a deep breath, I went out of my room and down the stairs.

Luca was waiting for me at the bottom of the stairs. I nearly lost my footing when our eyes met. His were dark and possessive. He was dressed in a black shirt and dove gray suit. He looked like heaven. God, I was so in love with him I felt almost dizzy. I reached the bottom step and stopped.

I felt the warmth of his flesh curl around on my wrist. I looked down and saw his hand, strong and tanned, against my own pale skin, and my heart thundered in my chest. What did this mean? What did any of this mean? My gaze lifted to his and he spoke.

"You look beautiful," he said softly.

I wanted to say thank you, but I couldn't speak. I couldn't make a single sound.

He led me to the car. Outside a cold wind lifted my hair and blew it into my face. I felt alive, every nerve was tingling. I was getting married to Luca Messana. The driver opened the door and I climbed in. I sat back on the leather seat. It had already been warmed in preparation for our entry. Luca slid his long body next to mine. I turned to look at him. A small smile lit his face. "Are you okay?"

I nodded.

After that neither of us spoke. It was as if the moment was too important to spoil with words. I felt as if I was on a cloud. When we arrived at the church, the door was opened and I stepped outside to look at it. It was an ancient stone church. There were gray angels and gargoyles guarding it. This was where I was going to marry Luca Messana. People passing by turned to look at me. Maybe I was glowing with happiness.

Then I felt Luca's arm around my waist. We went up the steps. His men were around us. The great wooden doors were opened for us and we went inside. It was cool and dim. Pale winter light filtered in through the stained-glass windows. Our footsteps echoed as we walked towards the altar. I felt as if I was in a dream. A portly man with rosy cheeks in priest robes appeared from one of the doors. He beamed at us and came forward to greet us. He had a thick Italian accent. Luca introduced him as Luigi Sabella.

A little while later we were standing facing each other. People I didn't know stood next to us as our witnesses.

"Do you, Luca Messana, take Skye Morrison, to be your lawfully wedded wife, to have and to hold, from this day forward, for better, for worse, for richer, for poorer, in sickness and in health, to love and to cherish, till death do you part?"

"I do," Luca said, his voice strong and filled with conviction.

"And do you, Skye Morrison, take Luca Messana as your lawfully wedded husband to have and to hold, from this day forward, for better, for worse, for richer, for poorer, in sickness and in health, to love and to cherish, till death do you part?"

"I do," I whispered.

He beamed happily at us. "By the power vested in me by God and man, I pronounce you husband and wife. What God has joined together, let no man put asunder. You may now kiss the bride."

Luca's hand settled on the side of my chin and I returned my attention back to him. Then, slanting his head he leaned down and placed his warm mouth against mine. I had to force my hands from snaking around his neck and deepening the kiss. The moment was so special to me. I wanted to make it last and last.

But I didn't and his lips left mine. The priest congratulated us and we began to move towards the entrance. Outside Luca or someone who worked for him had arranged for little girls to throw rice at us. I stood there in a daze of happiness. If only this was real. But a little voice said, *it is real. Enjoy it. It will never come back.*

We rode back to the house in silence.

I was now officially his wife.

When we arrived back at the house, Madam was waiting at the front door. "Congratulations, to both of you," she said softly.

Luca nodded his thanks.

"Thank you, Madam," I said.

"You are now the mistress of this house. Please, call me Melania."

I smiled at her. "Only if you call me Skye."

Her eyes widened, but she nodded and stepped back.

Luca led me to his den. A fire was roaring in the fireplace and the room was wonderfully warm. As soon as he closed the door behind me, he lifted me up into his arms and carried me over to the fur rug. Laying me on it gently, he pulled my panties off... and devoured me. There was no other way to describe the way he ate me out.

Afterwards, he entered me. It was the best sex I'd ever had. I could tell by the awed expression on his face that it was the same for him. All those emotions, all the excitement rolled into a great wave of sensation that tore through us.

"I have to leave for China in an hour, and I will be gone for a week, but you'll stay here and wait for me, won't you?"

I nodded. I would always be here for him, for as long as he needed me.

CHAPTER 46

SKYE

https://www.youtube.com/watch?v=VJKm0KxQ2L4
-Heaven Can Wait-

The nights dragged without Luca. I was happy in the greenhouse with John and I spoke to my father every day, but as the day turned into night I found myself alone and missing Luca. I invited Katie to come and stay a night with me and she did. She still couldn't believe I was married to Luca, but once she had got over the shock of Torrington Hall, we settled down to a girly night, ordered pizza, and sat watching rom coms with masks on our faces. But the next day she was gone.

On the third night I was sitting reading a book in the Blue room, when Melania walked in.

"Would you like anything else before I retire, Madam?" No matter how many times I reminded her, she always went back to calling me Madam and now I was resigned to the fact that it was what felt most comfortable to her. She couldn't see me as anything else but the mistress of the house and her superior.

I shook my head. "No. I think I'm fine."

"Goodnight then. I'll see you in the morning."

"Actually, don't go yet, Melania. Come and have a little drink with me."

Her eyes widened. "Oh."

"Please. I could do with the company."

She ran her hands down her black dress and came forward. "All right. I suppose one little drink won't hurt."

I was so pleased she had accepted my invitation. I jumped to my feet. "What would you like?"

"Just a glass of white wine would be fine."

"Sit, please sit, Melania,'" I invited as she stood awkwardly by the sofa. She perched at the end of the sofa opposite where I had been sitting while I filled two glasses with straw-colored liquid.

I held a glass out to her and sat down.

"Thank you, Madam," she said, taking a dainty sip.

"I'm not really the mistress of this house, you know."

She frowned. "What do you mean?"

"Luca only married me because the FBI were going to force me to spy on him and if he married me they wouldn't be able to make me testify against my husband. So I'm not really the mistress of this house." I smiled to hide my pain. "Now will you please call me Skye."

She stared at me for a few moments, then she calmly took a sip of her drink before she spoke. "I do not know why the master married you, but I do know it is not because he was afraid you would testify against him."

"Why do you say that?"

She shrugged one shoulder, an elegant gesture. "Well, does the master ever discuss business in your presence?"

"No."

"Exactly," she said simply. "Besides, I assume you found some method to let him know the FBI wanted you to betray him."

I nodded.

"So there was never any need to marry you. He could simply have asked you to leave the house," she finished logically.

I sighed. "It's a bit more complicated than that. I owe money to the IRS and they were threatening to throw me in prison if I didn't cooperate."

She took another sip. "Did you owe many millions?"

"No, of course not. I don't know exactly how much, because I haven't calculated, but most probably less than a hundred thousand."

"That's pocket change for a man like him. He could easily have paid your taxes for you and walked away free."

I put my glass down on the low table and looked up at her. "So why do you think he married me?"

She smiled at me. "That I do not know. He is an unknowable man. In all the years I have worked for him I have found him to be deep and clever. Often he thinks way ahead and only years later do I understand why he has done something. I'll even admit the first night he brought you here, I thought he had made a mistake. I thought you were a little golddigger, but I was completely wrong. He had picked a kind-hearted girl of great character and soul."

I blushed at her words. It really meant something coming from a woman like her. "Thank you for saying that."

"It's the truth." She put her half-finished glass down. "Now I must go. I have an early morning."

I stood with her. "Thank you, Melania."

"Thank you for inviting me to have a drink with you, Madam. It was very kind of you."

"The pleasure was all mine," I said with a smile.

Then we wished each other goodnight and she walked out of the room. I wandered over to the fireplace and stared at the dancing flames. I was caught up with my own drama. I had not looked at the situation with the calm logic that Madam had. Why had Luca married me? He was not in love with me. That much was clear. If he simply wanted to keep me here longer all he had to do was ask. Surely it was crystal clear I loved being in this splendid house.

What was there not to love?

Even now when it was winter and the days drew to a close too quickly it was like living in a fairytale, but once spring came I could spend longer in the greenhouse and the outdoors, it would be my definition of heaven on earth.

Besides I was so appreciative of what he was doing for my father I would have stayed with him forever in a hut if he'd only asked. And that's not even taking into consideration what he didn't know... that I was deeply and irrevocably in love with him.

The phone rang. I ran toward it. It was him.

"Hello," I whispered.

"Everything okay?" he asked.

I closed my eyes to savor his voice. "Yes. Everything is okay."

"I'll be back tomorrow, then I'm taking you with me to Italy the next day. So prepare yourself to go away for a few weeks."

My eyes flew open. "A few weeks? Italy?"

"Yes. A few weeks. Italy." He sounded amused. "Have you got a passport?"

"I have," I answered automatically.

"Good," he said crisply.

My brain felt scrambled. "Why are we going to Italy?"

"So you can meet my parents."

CHAPTER 47

LUCA

*S*he was quiet, quieter than I had ever known her to be.

We were on my private plane on our way to Sicily. At first she had seemed stunned by how easy and pleasant it was to fly without the normal constraints imposed on commercial flights. Without the long queues, humiliating pat downs by burly TSA staff, having to walk through radiation emitting metal detector machines.

As we took our seats opposite each other one of the crew members came up to us.

"Can I get you something to drink?"

"Any kind of juice is fine," Skye responded quietly.

"I'll have a whiskey," I said.

"Great. Here are your menus," she said, putting two cards down on the table in front of us.

Another hostess came and placed a plate of fruit in front of us with two small forks. Skye picked up a fork and speared a piece of watermelon.

I didn't know why but she looked sad, as if weighed down. I had forced her to marry me and maybe she just wasn't ready for it.

"We don't have to stay married for too long," I said softly. "After this whole situation with the FBI blows over, you'll be free to go."

She stilled, but didn't turn to look at me. "Okay," she said and placed the fruit in her mouth.

"Anyway, this marriage has to look real so I got this for you." I pulled out the ring box from my pocket and leaning forward, placed it on her table. She stared at it, and then turned to me with her eyes wide. "You got me another ring?"

I nodded. "The one you're wearing is a wedding ring. You need to have an engagement ring too."

"Oh? Is it… is that necessary?"

"It is. My parents will expect it."

Her gaze fixed on the velvety black box. Then she put the fork down and reached for it. She opened it and gasped. "Wow!" She looked up at me. "My God. Is this real?"

"Of course."

I took the box from her, extracted the ring, and slid the ring onto her slender finger. For a second she did nothing, just stared at her finger in shock. It was a beautiful ring. I chose it from a selection offered from the best jewelers in Beijing and Shanghai, but I did not expect her to be this overwhelmed.

She moved her hand and the sparkle from the main diamond was blinding. She looked up at me. "It's really, really beautiful, Luca. It must have cost a lot."

"It did."

She nodded a few times. "Did you buy it in China?"

"Yes, I had the best jewelers in Beijing and Shanghai send their wares to my hotel room, and I decided on this one. It is designed by an Italian designer called Aldo Morro."

"Well, it's beyond beautiful. I'll take good care of it and return it before I leave."

I frowned. "It's yours."

Her eyes widened. "This is mine to keep?"

"Of course. What would I do with it?"

"Wow. I don't know what to say... or how to thank you."

I smiled slowly. "I know exactly how you can thank me..."

She smiled back. "I hear these kinds of planes always have beds in them."

"This one certainly does," I replied, my voice suddenly throaty.

Her teeth sank into her bottom lip. "Can I see your bed?"

And my cock ached for her. Since we were already in the air and the seatbelt signs were turned off... "I thought you'd never ask," I said, as I rose to my feet and held my hand out to her. She put hers in mine and I took her to the bedroom.

I let her precede me into the room, then shut the door and leaned against it.

"That's a big bed," she murmured before she turned around to face me.

There were no words in my head. I hooked my hand into the band of her jeans, my gaze on her beautiful face. All I wanted was to be inside of her once again, and to feel her so completely attached to me.

Her hands came to the top button of my shirt and began to slip it out. Impatiently, I waited for her to finish unbuttoning. She took her time, bending her head to kiss and suck at the skin she was exposing. As the last button was undone I pulled it off and tossed it to a corner.

Then I began to move her towards the bed. When she was settled under me, I released the button of her jeans and yanked the zip down. I kissed her through the lace of her underwear and her back arched off the bed.

"Luca," she shivered.

I relished the sound of my name on her tongue. It felt as if I hadn't had her in months, even though it was only last night I had been inside her.

I ripped her panties off and flung them aside. I needed her, quickly, and urgently.

Her mouth opened into a gasp. Covering her mouth with mine I plunged all the way into her hard, and her surprised cry was lost in my mouth. She grabbed my forearms as I thrust into her. Again and again. Until we became one.

WE ARRIVED past midnight in Sicily, and were immediately driven to my father's large villa by the coast.

Staff were waiting to take us upstairs to our bedroom. Skye was so tired she went to sleep almost immediately. I stood over her and watched her for a while. It was incredible how vulnerable and young she looked when she slept. I could hear the restless sea from one of the windows left slightly ajar and I wished Skye was awake. I wanted to take her down to the beach. Where we could walk barefoot in the cold sand.

Unable to rest I went downstairs in search of my father. I knew I would find him in his polished oak study. He was an insomniac who hardly ever slept. He was seated in his usual place, on a dark green sofa, a goblet of cognac in one hand, and magnifying glass in the other. He was reading the newspapers. He was multilingual and had newspapers from all over the world delivered to him. He liked to read them at night when everyone else was asleep. He turned to look at me. I knew he was happy to see me, but there was no smile or welcome on his face.

"I heard you arrive," he said in Italian, putting the magnifying glass down and leaning back.

I walked to the bar and poured myself a drink before I went and sat opposite him. "Mama is asleep?' I asked.

He made a sound of dismissal. "She tried to stay awake to wait for you and your new bride, but she fell asleep. Wait till tomorrow morning."

"I will," I replied.

"Where did you meet her?" he asked.

"At a party," I replied.

He frowned. "I heard you bought her from the useless frog, Salvatore. Doesn't this make you question her character?"

"I know her character," I replied coldly.

"Hmmm. Time will tell."

"Time will tell," I echoed softly.

He accepted my words and moved on to a different topic.

CHAPTER 48

SKYE

I slept much better than I expected and by the time I woke up the following day, it was already late morning. I couldn't believe how tired I was. I was never usually this tired. Ever. Luca was no longer around.

But when I tried to get up the world spun around me and I fell back onto the bed. The worrying moment passed quickly, but why did I feel so weak and unbalanced? Perhaps it was hunger? I could only remember eating small bites and portions over the last several days, so the first thing on my agenda was a huge breakfast.

Now that I realized it, I was so wiped out I couldn't even properly recall how I'd been brought up to this room. I looked at my ring. I took my phone out and took a picture of it, then I sent the picture to Katie.

Her reply was instantaneous and full of emojis and gifs of shocked cats falling over.

WOW!!!!!!!!!!!!!!! Half asleep but will call you in a few hours. Get ready to tell all.

I calculated the time difference and realized it was four in the morning in Boston. With a sigh I rose and headed into the bathroom. After a steamy shower, I felt a hundred times better and refreshed so I tightened the tie of my robe and went towards the balcony. It was quite cold so I didn't bother stepping out, but through the glass doors, the view beyond took my breath away. We were right by the ocean, and in the distance, were mountains and cliffs with houses built into them. It was like a painting and as I stared, I could feel my whole body relax and calm down.

My stomach grumbled then so I turned around and went to my suitcase where I found a pale green sweater and a pair of dark blue jeans. Then I tied my hair up in a ponytail. I knew I would be meeting Luca's parents at some point today so I put a little bit more effort in my makeup. I was nervous about meeting them and wanted to try and look presentable. When I was ready I headed over to the door.

I pulled it open and peeked out into the lavishly decorated corridor. I didn't want to just go wandering off in someone else's home, but at the same time I didn't want to remain in the room. At that moment a message pinged in my phone. My heart lurched when I saw it was from Luca.

Awake?

I sent back my reply.

Awake and very hungry.

His reply warmed my heart.

I'll come get you. We'll have breakfast together.

A few minutes later, he arrived at the door and I pulled it open for him. He looked dashing. Dressed in all black and with his hair in thick waves and a slight facial growth he looked nothing short of a regal Italian Prince.

"Ready?" he asked softly.

I nodded shyly and went with him. He led me through the beautiful villa to the ground floor dining room where a lavish buffet was laid out. A servant waiting by the table wished us both good morning in Italian.

"Would you like a cooked breakfast?" Luca asked me.

I shook my head. Even the thought made me feel slightly nauseous. Luca spoke to the man in Italian. He explained to me that he had opted for a slice of toast and some poached eggs. I immediately gravitated towards the fruit and fiber cereal. Everything on the table looked delicious but I only had the appetite for something sweet.

We sat at a round dining table overlooking the pool.

"My parents wanted to meet you earlier," he said.

I nearly choked on my mouthful of milk and cereal.

He handed me a napkin that I eagerly accepted and quickly dabbed my mouth with.

"They'll be back later for lunch," he continued calmly. "So perhaps they can meet you then."

"Alright," I said.

"I also have twin sisters, but they're currently at boarding school in New York. No doubt, you'll meet them sometime in the future."

I was quite surprised at that. That he had twin sisters and he mentioned a future where I was part of it. "Really? How old are they?

"Sixteen," he replied.

I nodded.

I continued on with my meal. Then the waiter came to the table with a plate decked with golden yellow scrambled eggs and slices of buttered toast.

It looked delicious, but when the smell of the eggs reached my nostrils, my stomach suddenly lurched. I turned away and stood so fast I nearly threw my chair to the ground.

"Skye," Luca called anxiously, as he too stood.

I held out a hand to hold him at bay as I dry heaved. "Sorry," I muttered. "It's okay. I'm fine."

When I was calm again I faced him. His eyes raked my face while I tried to settle the bout of nausea that had suddenly attacked me. I found I couldn't even return to my seat. The smell was that horrible to me.

"I think… I think I'm not really hungry," I said, with a frown.

I looked at him and he was staring at me with a strange expression on his face. As if he had seen a ghost. He looked like a stranger. I froze. Then he asked the most dreadful of all questions.

"Are you pregnant?"

CHAPTER 49

SKYE

*B*efore I could answer him and tell him there was no way I was pregnant, a man walked into the room. I tore my eyes away from Luca's strangely stunned face. The man who had entered the room didn't look like Luca, but I knew instantly that he was Luca's father. He had cold, dead eyes, which he trained on me.

I felt the blood drain from my face. There could be no worse way to meet my new father-in-law than this. I took a deep breath and tried to smile at him, but he didn't smile back. He then turned his gaze to his son.

Slowly, as if he was moving in a dream, Luca stood. "This is Skye, father," he said robotically. "Skye, meet my father."

His father came forward and stood in front of me. Even though he was no longer young there was something dangerous about him. I had an instinctive fear of him and I had to resist the urge to move backward. I heard him exhale softly. "Now I see why my eldest son was so bewitched."

"Father," I heard Luca warn.

His father did not turn to him, he kept his cold eyes on me. "Take it easy, Luca. It was a compliment. If I was thirty years younger who knows… I might have done the same."

I swallowed hard. I couldn't understand the undercurrents of their conversation. I clasped my hands together. "I… I was just going for a walk so I'll leave you both to talk. Please excuse me."

"Really? It looks as if you've hardly touched your meal," he murmured.

I was shocked by how keen his powers of observation were. I forced a smile. "I realized I wasn't hungry after all. It was really nice to meet you."

"Yes, it was nice meeting you too." His smile didn't reach his eyes. "All right then, enjoy your walk around the grounds while I have a quick word with my son."

"See you both later," I called out, and without looking at Luca I escaped from that sunny room.

I walked down a corridor that led to the front door. Once outside I realized I had no coat on and it was cold. Not as cold as Boston, but windy. The salt filled air blew at me as I walked towards the beach.

Luca was wrong. I wasn't pregnant. Of course, I wasn't. The very thought was ludicrous. I was on the pill and more importantly, I was almost paranoid about accidentally forgetting to take it so I was meticulous in my habit. I hadn't missed a night since the day I went on it.

So I wasn't upset because I could be pregnant, I *knew* I wasn't. I was probably just sickening for something. I was upset because of the way Luca had responded to the idea that

I might be pregnant. He looked as if it was the worst news he could ever have heard. The thought clearly horrified him. I could lie as much as I wanted to myself, but it was now undeniable that my only value to him was as a body in bed.

All he wanted from me was sex.

It distressed me greatly and I felt as if I wanted to cry my eyes out, but I hardened my heart. I was just being a fool. What did I expect? He never promised me love. In fact, he made it obvious that he would tire of me quickly.

I could see men in dark suits hanging around the periphery of the grounds. When I reached the sand I walked blindly towards the beach. Once on the sand I took my shoes off and began towards the water's edge. I was shivering, but I carried on walking until I was walking on wet sand. Seagulls flew overhead as freezing cold waves started to froth around my toes.

I felt so lost. So utterly unhappy. I wanted to scream at the sea.

Suddenly, I felt my skin begin to prickle. I turned around and saw Luca walking towards me. The wind whipped my hair into my face, and I pulled the strands away and held them down.

He came and stood next to me. Taking his jacket off he draped it around my shoulders. His face was veiled and he looked like the unknowable stranger I'd first met at the party.

"You don't look well," he said, his voice mixed with the sound of the waves.

"I'm not pregnant." I told the sea. "I've been taking my pills."

"I've sent someone into town to get a pregnancy kit. It is not foolproof at this stage, but I believe it can give a reading even at three weeks."

I nodded. "Sure, I'll take the test."

We walked back to the house together in silence. I wanted to say something, but the words wouldn't come. At the front door he said, "I have work to do, I'll see you when the kits come."

Then he walked down the corridor and disappeared into the depths of the house. I went up to our bedroom and lay on the bed staring at the ceiling. Katie called, but I couldn't answer the phone. Very soon, there was a soft knock on the door. I went to open it. A dark haired girl in a uniform stood holding a tray.

"Breakfast," she said simply in a strong accent.

Luca must have sent it. I thanked her and relieved her of the tray. There was a bowl filled with cereal and fruit and a jug of milk. I tried to eat some, but the sensation of wanting to be sick returned. I abandoned trying to eat, and lay on the bed. Thirty minutes later, the door opened and Luca walked in. He held two packets in his hands. Wordlessly he came to the bed and held them out for me.

I took them from him and went to the bathroom. My heart was pounding so viciously against my chest that I could barely breathe. I tore the stick out of the packet and sat on the toilet bowl. I was ready to march out of that bathroom and show him I wasn't pregnant and he could go back to just fucking me day and night. But I knew in my heart something had changed. I could no longer pretend to myself that he felt something for me. There was something special between us. Something he couldn't talk about, but it was there.

A few minutes later I stared at the result in shock. I felt as if I had gone completely numb. It was impossible. It must be a mistake.

"Skye," Luca called and my hands went over my mouth.

I rose to my feet and pulled my panties up. Then I went to open the door. I handed the stick over to him and went to sit on the bed. I actually needed to sit down. I never ever in my wildest dreams ever thought I'd be pregnant. How could it be?

A deathly silence filled the room. I then heard him as he came around to me. I couldn't face him.

"You're pregnant."

"So it seems." I think I was in such shock that my voice came out flippant and nonchalant. As if I didn't care either way. Nothing could be further from the truth. I cleared my throat and tried again. "I didn't do this on purpose. I'm just as shocked as you are."

He stared at me as if he was seeing me for the first time and what he saw disgusted him.

"Don't worry. I won't ask you to take care of it, or anything like that. I'll sort everything out myself."

"Is 'sort everything out' a euphemism for get rid of it?" His voice was so cold a bone chilling fear overwhelmed me.

"I didn't mea—"

"That's my child you're carrying," he snarled. "And you're my wife. And I will never allow you to get rid of it, do you understand me?"

I stopped breathing. "I wasn't going to."

"Spare me," he said coldly. "If you don't want the child, you can hand it over to me after it is born."

Bewildered, I stared at him. I couldn't even believe we were having this conversation. "Why would I hand over my child to you?"

"I am leaving for Boston tonight. My visit here is over. You can either stay here and finish your vacation, or you can travel back with me."

I jumped to my feet. "I'll come with you."

"Fine. Be ready to leave at seven." Then he turned on his heel and left.

I stared at the closed door, my strength starting to crumble. The tears I had been fighting so hard to keep at bay poured down my face.

CHAPTER 50

I did it again.

I walked out of our bedroom wanting to smash everything in sight. All kinds of emotions churned in my gut. I trusted her. I let my guard down and trusted her. I actually believed the fantasy she had weaved. What a fool I was. Once was not enough for me.

I have to go and make the same damn mistake again. I trusted another of her species. Heartless liars all of them. They are beautiful to look at but they are poison. They use their bodies to lure hapless men into their snares.

Beautiful liar.

I strode down the corridor and ran quickly down the stairs. I could feel my blood roaring in my ears as I went into the library. My father was sitting on an armchair smoking his pipe and playing a game of chess with himself. His old dog, Punto, was curled up in his lap. The dog was almost twenty now. When I was growing up, I sometimes thought he loved the dog more than he did his own family.

He looked up at me curiously.

"Something has come up. I'm leaving tonight," I said.

For a second he said nothing, then he took his pipe out of his mouth. "I read a story once in a Russian newspaper. It was about a man who picked a beautiful flower growing in the wild and brought it home. His beloved cat ate it and died. Some flowers are to be admired from afar, never brought home."

I swallowed hard. For the first time in my life I wanted to punch my father really hard. Yes, she was a poisonous flower, but she was *my* poisonous flower and I couldn't bear for anyone to say anything bad about her.

"She's pregnant," I said coldly.

He looked at me expressionlessly and I knew what he was thinking, but even he dared not say those words. I turned away from him and walked out of his presence.

I found my mother in the music room. She was on the telephone. She ended her call abruptly and called to me to sit next to her. I stood over her.

"I'm leaving tonight, Mama. Something has come up."

"Oh," she exclaimed surprised. "Will you be coming back?"

"No, I will see you in Boston when you return in spring."

"But I have not even met Skye," she protested.

"She is in the bedroom now. You can go up and meet her if you want."

She seemed astonished. "Without you?"

"Yes, I have to go out now."

"What is going on, Luca?"

"Nothing is going on. I'm just rushed for time."

"I see. I arranged a dinner party in your honor and to welcome Skye into the family."

"I'm sorry to spoil your plans."

She stood. "What's wrong, Luca?"

"Nothing is wrong. Anyway, you should know Skye is pregnant."

She frowned. "That is great news, but why do you not seem happy about it?"

"I am happy," I said, and to my shock I realized that was the truth. Despite everything I wanted that child. I wanted a child I could call mine again. It was too long since I saw a little face look up to me and a little voice call me Papa.

CHAPTER 51

SKYE

https://www.youtube.com/watch?v=1y6smkh6c-0
-Don't You Worry Child-

*T*he flight back was unbearable. I stayed alone in the bedroom for most of the flight and Luca remained in the main cabin and worked on his laptop. When I ventured out once I saw he had fallen asleep in his chair. My heart bled to see him sleep in that uncomfortable position because he did not want to come to the bedroom and share the bed with me.

The journey back to Torrington Hall was accomplished in total silence. I lay my head back and kept my eyes closed. I loved this place and yet I could feel no joy to see the big gates open to let us in. When we reached the house, Melania was standing at the doorway to welcome us back.

Luca nodded at her curtly and walked into the house.

"What's wrong?" she asked me gently.

And that was my undoing. I threw my arms around her and sobbed like a child.

"There, there," she consoled. "Nothing is as bad as it first seems. Come with me. What you need is a big mug of hot chocolate, but not just any hot chocolate, but my secret recipe."

Feeling utterly miserable I followed her into the servants' quarters until we came to a small door. She unlocked it and I followed her into a small living room. It was simply decorated in shades of cream and sage green and was surprisingly classy. She led the way through to a small kitchen.

"Have a seat," she invited as she rummaged around her cupboards for the ingredients needed to make her special hot chocolate.

Sniffing I pulled myself onto a stool at the small square island. She didn't speak while she boiled the milk and chocolate. Afterwards she dropped in a few marshmallows and came to sit with me.

"What about you? Aren't you going to have some too?"

She smiled. "Nope. I only have this on my birthday and special occasions."

I blew the surface and took a sip. She was right, it was easily the best hot chocolate I'd ever tasted. "This is delicious," I said.

She smiled again. "I know. Now, tell me what happened."

I took a deep breath. "I'm pregnant."

"Ah."

"I think Luca thinks I did it on purpose, but I swear I didn't. When I tried to explain to him that I hadn't planned it and he didn't need to think I would ask him for support and financial help because I would take care of the situation myself, he got the entirely wrong impression and thought I wanted to get rid of the baby."

"Oh dear," she murmured sympathetically.

"He was absolutely furious, Melania. I've never seen him in such a rage. He even said, if I didn't want the baby, I should hand it over to him when it is born. It is all such a mess. The thing I can't understand is how I could possibly get pregnant when I am on the pill and I have never missed a day or changed the times I take it."

She looked at me curiously. "Have you ever been sick or vomited? Because that can stop the pill from being effective too."

I frowned as I tried to think. "No, I don't think so," I began, only to stop and stare at Melania in horror. "Oh my God," I whispered.

Yes, I remembered clearly that I had been sick, the night before I met Luca. I'd just taken the pill, then Salvatore had asked me to take him into my mouth. I was so disgusted I had gagged, and then been actually sick in the toilet. Since I had skipped dinner, only liquid had come out. And it never even crossed my mind that my pill could have come out too.

"Oh my God, Melania. I was sick the night before I met Luca. Should I tell Luca about it? Explain to him how it happened?"

She shook her head. "No, that's not a good idea. He's not ready to hear that. He's heard it before."

"What do you mean?"

Through the window, I saw Luca's car on the driveway. It was traveling away from the house. I jumped off the stool, ran to the window and watched it until it disappeared out of sight.

"Luca," I breathed. It felt as if he was gone forever.

"Come here, Madam. I have something to tell you."

I walked back slowly to the counter and sat down. I felt dead inside.

"Before the master bought this house, he lived in a big mansion in the heart of Boston. He had many admirers who used to come to the house. Sometimes they would even stay a few nights with him. One of them was a woman called Alessa. I have to admit I was completely fooled by her. She was the warmest friendliest woman who he had ever brought to the house. She had dark hair and she laughed easily."

She turned her head away from me and looked out of the window.

"I actually hoped he would settle down with her, but he didn't and after two weeks it was over for him. Even though she was gone she used to call me and treat me as if she truly cared about me. About a month later she came back to see the master. She was pregnant. I heard the argument they had. She pretended one of the condoms must have been torn, but I remembered something. I once saw a used condom stuffed under her pillow. Somehow, she had taken the used condoms and impregnated herself.

"I didn't tell anyone what I saw and that was my mistake. If I had he would have been forewarned and known not to trust her. He married her. Once he married her she changed. All the warmth was gone. She treated me coldly, as if I was nothing more than her servant. I think she thought the master would come to love her, but as time passed he moved further and further away from her. In his heart he knew that somehow she had tricked him."

I inhaled sharply. Now I knew why he had looked at me as if he was seeing me for the first time. He thought I had tricked him too!

Melania continued with her story. "But when the baby was born was when things really took a turn for the worse. She had mistakenly thought that it was her pregnant body that he did not want and once she had given birth to the baby he would start to want her again. The opposite happened. He completely lost interest in her and fell in love with the baby instead. I had never before and never since seen a man love a child the way he did. He loved that child more than he loved himself. He would have walked into fire for his son. Actually, there is nothing he would not have done for that boy.

"And Alessa, she simply grew more and more bitter. She was jealous of her own son. He was such a good child, but one time I came into his room and I saw her pinching him for no reason at all. I was so shocked I didn't know what to do. I didn't want to tell on her, but I knew the child had to be protected and most of its care entrusted to another person so I advised the master to get a nanny.

"Once the nanny arrived she would only see the child when the master was in the house. Then she would pretend to love him, and touch him, and coo at him. By this time, the master had moved out of her bedroom.

"He was two when it happened. The nanny had called in sick and I had already planned to keep the baby with me for the morning, but I had an urgent order to make for the kitchen. I thought I would make it first so they could deliver it later that evening, then go to his room, but before I could even finish the order I heard her wailing and screaming. When I ran out she was at the bottom of the steps curled over his dead body.

"The coroner said he died from a broken neck. He did not suffer. He died on the spot. He ruled it an accident. But I knew. And the master knew. It was no accident. I don't know why she did it. It was not as if it would make the master stop loving the boy and love her instead. It was just so completely senseless. So inhuman. So heartless. So unforgivable.

"The coffin was white. I'd never seen a coffin so small. She wore a black designer dress and a black veil to the funeral. In her hand she held a white handkerchief with a lace border which she used to dab at her dry eyes. For the first time since I'd been with the master I saw him sobbing. He fell on his knees next to the coffin and sobbed. Once the funeral was over we all came back to the house. I couldn't even look at her.

"That night she called me and asked me to bring her a glass of warm milk. I remember that night well. She was lying on her bed wearing a soft pink negligee and her matching fluffy pink high-heeled slippers. She did not look sad or unhappy. In fact, she was watching a rerun of *Pretty Woman* on her iPad. She had already taken her make-up off, and I could see that her eyes were not red or swollen from crying. She had killed the only ray of light and laughter in that house and she looked completely unperturbed. As if nothing had happened. I thought then that I hated her and I wished I didn't have to work for her.

"My wish came true. That was the last time I saw her. The next morning, she was nowhere to be found. A few days later her body was fished out of a river. She was wearing a full face of make-up, the black dress she had worn to the funeral and a bit of the black veil she had worn was still stuck to her hair. She had lost her shoes in the river, but in her closet the black Jimmy Choo shoes she had worn to the funeral were missing."

I gasped in shock and Melania nodded.

"Yes, it was revenge. An eye for an eye. A life for a life. It is their way and for once I cannot condemn it. The story that ran in the paper was she was so distraught by her son' death she had committed suicide. Everybody in the house knew it was not true, but no one spoke about it. No one mourned for her. But ever since then the master changed. He became unrecognizable. He sold that house, bought this place and installed all his old staff here, but he hardly ever came to stay, and he never brought women here... until you."

I took a deep breath. It was a shocking story. "Oh my God. What a terrible, terrible story."

"Yes, it is a terrible story. Now do you understand why he reacted the way he did?"

"My God, he thought I wanted to kill his unborn child. No wonder he wanted me to hand the baby over when it was born."

"Yes, the scar has never healed. I honestly think he was falling for you, but unfortunately this happened."

"What should I do?" I whispered.

"Nothing. Do nothing. He must defeat his own demons and find his way to you. Stay here and be yourself. One day he will realize you are not her. You are an angel who has come to save his life."

My eyes filled with tears. "I love him so much, Melania."

"I know," she said and covered my hand with hers. "But you are strong and you can do this. Only you can save him."

CHAPTER 52

SKYE

https://www.youtube.com/watch?v=t99KH0TR-J4
-The Show Must Go On-

*L*uca did not come back in one day or two, or three, or four, or five. The days became a week and then two weeks. My heart ached with his loss. Then my father came back from Switzerland. I sent a message to Luca's phone to ask if I could bring my father to stay for a while at Torrington Hall. It would be good for him, I explained. The fresh air, the clean, wholesome food, the beauty of the land. After an hour he sent his reply.

Yes.

I stared at the one-word message for a long time. It felt as if a knife had pierced my heart. Eventually, I found the strength to answer him.

Thank you. It really means a lot to me.

Then I put my phone away and I went for a walk. I knew me being depressed and unhappy was bad for the tiny life growing inside me so deliberately I turned my thoughts away from Luca and thought of how lucky I was to be living in such splendor. And better still my father and Laura could come here and benefit from all this beauty too. The snow was beginning to melt and I began to look forward to spring.

When I started to tire I went back to the house. Madam was waiting for me with a cup of her special hot chocolate. I didn't know how she knew I was hurt, but she always did.

"It's okay," she said softly. "Have faith. He will come around."

I sat by the fireplace and drank the chocolate. When my father came back from his stay abroad, Sergio went to pick him and Laura up and bring them over. I was so happy to see him. He looked bright and alive. His skin had lost its papery feel. As for them they couldn't believe how beautiful Torrington Hall was. They went around in a stunned daze. I installed them in the east wing where they could have some privacy. Also I knew Laura would want to have Diana over and I figured this way she could come in through the east entrance and go straight to their suite of rooms. I would not need to see her.

My father and I walked the grounds together. We talked and laughed. One day, he put his hand on my belly and with tears in his eyes told me, he was so proud of me sometimes it felt as if his heart would burst out of his chest.

The weeks turned into a month.

One night, I was fast asleep when I felt him come to me.

Instantly, I opened my arms and he slipped my clothes over my head, pulled my panties down my legs, and entered me. I could smell the alcohol on his breath as I held on tightly to him while he thrust into me like a man possessed. A man who could take it no more and snapped.

When I climaxed it was suddenly over very quickly.

He pulled away from me then and sat at the edge of the bed with his hands clawed in his hair. I knew he had not come yet. He looked so tormented that my heart bled for him. When I reached out to touch him, he jerked away and looked at my naked body the way a man who despises his weakness looks at the object of his addiction. With a groan of self-loathing, he stood, zipped up his trousers and left.

I had taken to talking to my child so I put my hand on my stomach and told my little seed that everything would be fine. He just needed to find his way home again. Valentine's Day came and went. Luca never came or even called. Madam bought me a little cupcake with a red heart on it and a card. The message on the card said, One day. One day.

I slipped into his bedroom one morning. He had not been there for weeks, but the faint smell of his cologne lingered in the air. I walked to his bed and lay on it. Obviously, the pillowcases had been changed a long time ago, but I still buried my face in his pillows. When I turned my head and looked at the bedside table, I found myself looking into the laughing eyes of a small, dark-haired child. I reached out a hand and touched the innocent face. He seemed so alive, so vital.

God, how could she? How could she?

One month rolled into another and another. I went for my scan. "Oh, look at his little willie, the nurse," joked.

I went back home. "It's a boy," I told Melania, with tears in my eyes.

"Time for some hot chocolate," she said with a sad smile.

I sat by the fireplace and drank my hot chocolate quietly. I was preparing myself to call Luca. When even the last dregs of chocolate were gone, I picked up my phone and called him. He answered on the third ring.

"I went for a scan today. It's a boy," I whispered.

He made a sound. It was a cross between a sob and grunt of pain. Then the line went dead in my hand. I put the phone down and gently laid both my hands on my swelling belly.

"See, your daddy loves you so much, he can't even speak," I told my unborn son.

Then I went to find Melania. She had become like a mother to me. Laura could never really be my mother because Diana was so possessive of her. Now Melania had become that figure I'd always craved. I lay on her bed and must have fallen asleep, because when I woke up it was morning and Melania was gone. I could see by the dent in her pillow that she had slept next me.

Spring came and it was beautiful. There were fields of daffodils on the grounds. The morning sickness and the tiredness were all gone and I walked the beautiful grounds for hours. My father went for his operation. I hoped I would see Luca at the hospital or that he would at least call, but he never did. I ran in to Diana once at the hospital and I could see that she was heading my way, her eyes on my belly, but I turned around and walked away from her. I was not letting her poisonous eyes touch my child.

He was my gift to Luca. The most precious thing I could give him.

Two nurses came to live at the house. They cared for my father day and night and he became strong quickly. It might have been Torrington Hall. It might have been all the love Laura and I poured into him, but his recovery surprised even his doctors.

My flowers began to bloom. John stood beside me.

"Wow! They are amazing. You have green fingers," he said.

"Thank you, John." I was proud of myself.

"Shall I cut them and take them up to the house for you?"

I turned to him with a smile. "No, let them stay here. They'll brighten up the place for us."

He smiled back. "You know you're right. They really brighten up the place. I think we should plant more flowers."

"I think so too," I said. In a way, I think I had become the daughter he lost. Quite often I invited him up to the house to eat dinner with my father, Laura, and me. On those days, he would drink too much ale, and sleep over in one of the spare rooms.

A wedding invitation arrived from Sienna. My heart began to beat like a drum. I knew Luca would be there. I carefully detached the reply and sent it off. An unworthy part of me said, maybe he was already with another woman. Maybe he would even bring someone else, but I refused to listen to it. He will find his way back to me.

One day. One day.

My stomach was getting bigger and bigger. It was the beginning of summer and I was six months pregnant when a woman came to the house. She told me she had been hired as a nanny for my child. It hurt like crazy, but I understood instantly. Luca didn't trust me with his child. I gave her a room in the house. It was good that this big cold house was filling up with people, and voices, and laughter.

Not mine. Not yet.

CHAPTER 53

SKYE

The Wedding.
https://www.youtube.com/watch?v=CfihYWRWRTQ
-Love Me Again-

*T*he wedding was held in an abbey in the old town of Portofino.

I sat in my lavender dress with my father and stepmother. My stomach felt tight with nerves. A door to the side of the altar opened and Angelo came out. He was wearing a morning suit and he looked like the happiest man on earth. Luca, who was Angelo's best man, followed behind.

I couldn't stop staring, I simply couldn't stop drinking him in hungrily. He was wearing a cream jacket, a white dress shirt, a burgundy waistcoat, and black trousers. He was still as stunning as ever, but he seemed thinner. The scar on his face looked more prominent, which made him appear even more unapproachable and hostile. Oh, how I yearned for him. My heart felt as if it would burst out of my chest. He did not look at the guests seated on the pews.

He did not look for me.

My father reached out and squeezed my hand. I looked at him and his expression said, chin up, you can do this. I nodded and smiled at him. Today, I was determined, would be all sunshine and rainbows. At that moment the music changed and there was a noise at the back of the abbey. We all turned to watch the incoming train of almost twenty bridesmaids and groomsmen, dressed in baby pink floaty chiffon dresses and pristine white suits.

As Sienna came closer, I could not help but be amazed by how fabulous she looked. The new mother and blushing bride was dressed in a beautiful lace and pearl embroidered wedding dress that made her look like a fairytale princess. She was so petite no one would have ever been able to guess she'd had a baby only two months earlier. I wondered if I'd be able to snap back as quickly as she had. Unconsciously, I rubbed my belly.

"Two months to go. Come out safely, my sweet angel. Mommy and Daddy are waiting for you," I whispered to my bump, then realized I must appear mad to civilized society, and quickly looked up.

But no one was looking at me, only my father, and he smiled reassuringly. I flashed him a brilliant smile back. My father didn't know the details of my relationship with Luca and neither had he ever asked, but sometimes he would look at me with sadness in his eyes. Of course, Laura and him knew something was wrong. Luca never came to visit me and yet we were all living in luxury in his estate.

I watched him as Sienna eventually arrived by her groom's side. I couldn't keep my eyes on the happy couple, my eyes had only one focus, on the man standing tall and handsome by their side.

Strange, but as if guided by the primitive instinct to protect what my body considered mine, my eyes found a bridesmaid sneaking glances at him. It took everything I had to push down that green-eyed monster of pure jealousy. Still, I couldn't blame her. He was a catch. A real catch. Everything a woman dreamed of. Sometimes, during the short time I was with him, I had to pinch myself to make sure I was not in a dream.

The ceremony began and then it was completed. They were pronounced man and wife. Angelo grabbed his wife and kissed her passionately. The entire audience applauded and hollered. Even I had to smile at such a wonderful display of love.

Then it was time for the reception. It was being held in the gardens of the Abbey. We melted into the crowd and moved with them towards the great marquee.

Sienna's wedding planner had done a wonderful job. In the golden light of the sunset everything was breathtakingly stunning. I took in the spectacular Abbey flanked by sheer cliffs on either side, and its beautiful renaissance gardens connected by pergolas of blooming wisteria. The terraces were alive with colorful gardenias.

John and I had already begun the task of planning the flower beds at Torrington Hall. Next year, if we worked hard, we could have a truly splendid show of color. I could hardly wait to see our efforts. I caught myself when I realized I had absolutely no idea what next year held. I turned quickly away from the thought as today was about joy and a wonderful occasion.

There was laughter, champagne was flowing, and a seemingly endless table of all kinds of food, but my eyes searched for only one person. Angelo and Sienna made a reappearance and everyone clapped and cheered. I saw him then. Just behind them. Suddenly, our eyes met. So he was looking for me too! I stopped breathing. All noises came to an end. The world stood still. There was nothing. No one else. Just us. My heart cried out for him. My lungs began to burn and I could feel my mouth opening to take in a breath.

Then he turned his eyes away.

I gasped for breath as I watched Matteo whisper something in his ear. I saw him frown and look around. There was a troubled expression in his eyes.

Someone called. "Time for photos, everybody."

I thought I was well hidden, but I saw his father walking toward me. I saw his eyes drop to my belly, then he stood in front of me. "Come and join the family for a picture."

I was dumbfounded. He'd given me the impression he didn't want me to be part of his family when we went to stay at his house in Sicily.

"This is my father, Pete, and my stepmother, Laura" I said. I turned to my father. "This is," I realized I didn't even know his name, "Luca's father."

He nodded politely at my father, but it was absolutely clear he had no interest in him at all.

"Come with me," he invited again.

"Be back soon," I told my father and Laura.

"Yes, yes, go. We'll be waiting here," they both said.

I went with his father. To my surprise I saw Luca running towards us. His face was contorted with terror. He was shouting something. It was the last thing I saw before his father grabbed my hand and pulled it so hard, I lost my footing and started to fall forward. I heard a shot. A scream of shock tore out of my throat as my hands rushed forward to break my fall and protect my baby.

The entire place descended into chaos as chairs and tables and ceramic flew in the air and shattered. The shout continued for another second and then there was another shot. It sounded too close to my ears and I screamed again.

Everything happened so fast, that I couldn't make up a reasonable sequence for the disaster unfolding around us.

The bullet had sounded too close for comfort, but I didn't feel any pain so I knew I hadn't been shot. Next to me I could see that Luca's father was unhurt. I turned my head to look for my father and Laura as I heard two more gunshots but I could see that they were on the ground cowering with all the others.

"Skye!" I heard Luca call sharply.

CHAPTER 54

LUCA

https://www.youtube.com/watch?v=ByfFurjQDb0
-You Are The Reason-

*I*t felt as if I was losing my mind. I could not believe what I was seeing. It could not be. It just could not be. I dropped to my knees next to her. My hands were shaking. Jesus, God, no. Not her. Not her. Not my miracle.

She was looking up at me, with a strange expression on her face, as if she was surprised to see me, as if it was me that was hurt, as blood was oozing out of her wound and spreading into her stomach area of her lavender dress. The assassin had been aiming for my father, but he had hit her instead. Despite my father no longer being in the head of a Mafia family this was his fault. His past. You can leave the family but the past can find you anytime. It is the son of an old enemy out for revenge.

One more shot rang out and I heard the shrill announcement. "It's clear! We have him!"

"Hey you," she said softly. Then she frowned, her hands were still cradling her stomach. "What happened?"

I shuddered as my hand went to touch her face. I was so terrified I was almost paralyzed. "It's okay," I whispered. "Everything is going to be alright?"

She shook her head in a confused daze. Then her hand left her belly and she raised it up to a place where she could see it. She saw that it was covered in blood. "No no, has my baby been shot?" she asked as reality dawned.

Immense panic gripped me at her words. In the distance, I heard my name called, but I did not turn away from her shocked, desperate eyes.

She gripped the front of my shirt, and cried tragically, "My baby... Luca. My baby."

"Lorenzo!" I roared, as the first paralyzing shock of seeing her blood flow out of her wore off. He was our family medic and I knew he was present at the venue. "Where is Lorenzo?"

He was already rushing to my side. I quickly made room for him so that he could examine her. As he moved his hands over her quickly, Skye's father and stepmother dropped to the ground a few feet from us. They looked stunned. No one said a word. My father shouted for everybody to move back. Angelo and Sienna rushed over and stood looking down helplessly at Skye.

Lorenzo turned toward me. Lorenzo was so afraid of me he was visibly shaking. Then he began to speak to me, not in English or Italian, but in Sicilian dialect. I understood immediately that he did not want anyone else to understand what he was saying. "It looks like the bullet has not hit any vital organs and the baby is still alive… but if you take her to the hospital, the doctors there might have to make a choice between saving the life of the child or the mother. They will always save the mother and let the child die. I am able to deliver the baby for you, but I cannot promise I can save her."

Burning fury flared in my chest. I wanted to strangle him with my bare hands. What was the matter with him? Did he really think I was such a monster I would let her die? In a flash I remembered Alessa's face as she begged me to let her live. How could I blame him? Everyone knew what I had done to her. And even today, I felt no regret. I was a monster.

"Stem her blood flow. I'm taking her to hospital," I said through gritted teeth.

Someone had brought a first aid kit and he quickly and expertly bandaged the wound tightly.

I immediately went into action. "Can I lift her?"

"Maybe it's better if we—"

"I'm not waiting for a fucking ambulance. We're in Italy. It could come in an hour."

"I was going to say that it would be better if two people carried her."

"No! I'll do it myself."

I could tell the shock was now wearing off and Skye was trying hard to bear the pain. "It'll be alright my angel. Everything will be all right. I'll make sure of it. We're taking you to the hospital now."

I lifted her carefully into my arms and headed straight out to the waiting SUV.

"I'll take you," I heard Angelo say as he snatched the key from Matteo. "We'll come with. you."

"No!" I said. "This is your big day. There is nothing you can do for Skye. Everything will be fine. I'll call you later."

My father spoke up then. "Your brother is right. Stay and calm your guests down."

"No," he said stubbornly, "I want to support Luca," but when he saw the look I gave him, he understood that I didn't want him to come with me. I didn't want to spoil his wedding any more than it had already been. He handed the keys back to Matteo and stepped back.

"She will be fine," he tried to assure me with a squeeze to my shoulder.

Lorenzo got into the front seat while I carefully got into the back with Skye lying across my lap. Someone closed the door behind me and the car sped away. I stroked her gold hair. She opened her eyes and looked into mine. "If there is a choice to be made. Save my baby. He is my gift to you," she whispered.

My eyes filled with tears for the first time in years. God, how wrong I was. How completely wrong I had been about her. I had let the past cloud my eyes over. She was indeed an angel. All the emotion I had forced myself not to feel bubbled over. My tears fell on her fair cheek. "Don't cry, Luca. I love you."

"Oh, my darling, darling Skye. Please forgive me for abandoning you all these months."

"There is nothing to forgive," she whispered.

"I love you, my brave angel, with all of my twisted, bitter heart."

She smiled through her pain. "You do?"

"Oh, you will never believe how much."

"You can show me later."

"Yes, I damn well will. You're going to be fine. Just fine. Everything is going to be fine. I promise."

The car went over a bump too fast and jolted us. She cried out in pain.

"For fucks sake, be careful," I roared furiously.

The moment we arrived, she was taken straight to the emergency room. I stood by her side as another doctor examined her. Lorenzo gave him the rundown of his initial examination and verdict.

She was moaning in pain, her body and face twisted in agony. I held her hand tightly. I had never felt so vulnerable or defenseless in my life.

"Her contractions are getting too close together ..."

The room began to flood with nurses.

"Where's the OB?" the doctor snapped.

"She's on her way," someone else said calmly.

"What's going on, Lorenzo!" I asked in a panic.

"The baby's heart rate is dropping dangerously low with each contraction and she's too weak to push, so they're going to have to do a C-section right now," he explained anxiously.

"Get her prepped and into the OR," the doctor commanded.

"We have to take her now," a nurse said.

I kissed her lips. "You'll be fine. I swear it. You'll be fine. It'll be over soon. I'll be here waiting for you."

Then I let go of her hand.

It broke my heart when she made a small frightened noise. They began to roll her out of the room. The swing door shut on my face. I could go no further.

Everything had moved so fast and for the first time in years, I realized what being powerless and out of control felt like. I clenched my fists tightly. No. The outcome this time would be different, and I was going to protect what was mine. My wife and child and nothing was going to take them away from me. Nothing.

CHAPTER 55

SKYE

https://www.youtube.com/watch?v=YrLk4vdY28Q

The round lights in the ceiling as they rolled me into the OR barely registered. The only thing in my mind was the brutality of my contractions. Waves of pain coursed through my body and my fingers dug into my palms to help relieve some of the pressure.

I had never in my life been in so much pain.

But then I remembered his promise. Everything will be fine. I believed him, and that more than anything gave me the strength to hope for a time beyond this pain that seemed as though it would never end.

The Anesthesiologist put a mask over my face. "Count backwards from ten," she said kindly.

10, 9, 8, 7... 6... then everything went dark.

I WOKE UP SLOWLY. My whole body felt heavy. Even moving my fingers was an effort. I knew I was in a hospital. I felt fear. My lips moved.

"My baby," I called weakly. "Where's my baby?"

It was only then I realized I was not alone. There was an arm and a head on my thighs. The arm lifted and he straightened. I stared at him in shock.

He looked haggard. More unkempt than I had ever seen him or thought was even possible. His eyes seemed to be full of pain, red and strained.

I panicked. "Where is my baby?" I cried desperately.

"It's okay, It's okay, he's alive, but he's too tiny. They put him in an incubator, Skye," he said brokenly.

I sighed with relief. "He'll grow," I said with a small smile.

I raised my hand and rested it against the side of his face and he shut his eyes as if to savor the feel of my hand. I thought of the ride in the car when he said he loved me. Did I dream it?

"You care about me?" I asked, my voice hesitant.

His eyes immediately came open. "I love you, Skye. I love you."

My fingers slid into his hair as I grew desperate to hold him close.

He responded to my silent request and moved his head till my lips could touch his cheek. "I waited so long to hear that."

I felt him shudder as he turned, and his lips moved across my face till they found mine, and the kiss was the sweetest thing I'd ever tasted. He lifted his head. "I have a confession to make."

I knew he was no saint and I knew how sexual he was. Sometimes we would have sex five or six times a night. And that all these months without me, I knew he would have been with other women. In fact, I didn't want to know. I put my finger on his lips.

"Don't tell me. It doesn't matter. It's the past. I love you and nothing else matters."

"You don't even know what I'm going to say, do you?" ·

"You were going to tell me you were with other women, weren't you?"

He shook his head in wonder. "You thought I was sleeping with other women in the last few months?'

My heart started to flutter. "You didn't?"

"Of course not. I was in hell."

"That's good, because so was I. I missed you like crazy."

"Me too," he said with a smile. "Don't you want to hear my confession then?"

I laughed, which actually hurt my stomach. "Ouch."

He looked concerned. "What is it?"

"It hurts when I laugh," I said with a happy smile. "So tell me. What's the big confession all about?"

"You know when the FBI contacted you and asked you to spy on me?"

"Yeah?" I said carefully.

He cleared his throat. "They were not the FBI. They were just some actors I had my PA hire working from a script."

"What?"

He looked a bit sheepish. "Yeah, sorry."

I stared at him in astonishment. "Why would you do something so horrible?"

His eyes were remorseful. "Many reasons. Because I knew our time together was coming to an end and I wanted to keep you longer. Because it was a good way to test you and see what kind of loyalty you would show. Past experiences had taught me to trust no one. Also because I had to go away and I was afraid someone else would take you away from me. And because I really wanted to marry you, but I knew I had my inner demons to sort out and I was just buying myself some time."

I blinked with astonishment. The idea that anybody, let alone a man like him, would go to such elaborate lengths to keep me in his life and marry me, was overwhelming to say the least.

"You could have just asked me to stay with you, Luca."

"No. I was not ready to accept what my heart knew. I needed time."

"So the FBI were not really after you?" I asked, still bewildered.

"No. They have no reason to want me. I run a clean business. It's true that when I first took over from my father, the business was a criminal enterprise, and I still have acquaintances, links, and favors owed to me from that world, but Mafia bosses end up in jail eventually or an early violent end. I didn't want that for myself. It took years but slowly, bit by bit I turned the business around into something totally legitimate and above board."

My mind had gone blank. All the things I thought about him were completely untrue.

"Say something," he murmured.

"Okay," I said slowly. "I forgive you for the deception. While we're talking about deceptions, I want to tell you how I got pregnant. I was taking the pill, but one day before I met you, I was sick right after taking the pill and Melania said it must be that time that the pill was rendered ineffective."

"I know you would never deceive me. You're not that kind of person. I was just blinded by the past that I couldn't see it then."

"Hey, what does our son look like?"

He grinned. "I got a photo for you." He took his phone out and showed it to me.

My heart hurt as I saw his unbelievably small frame and flushed skin. How I wished I could keep him inside my body a little longer, until he was bigger, stronger. Luca heard my intake of breath and lowered his head leaning against mine to render support.

"I know. I know. It hurt me too."

I choked back my tears but they still filled my eyes and came pouring down my face. I held on tightly to his hands while he cradled me in his arms.

"Thank you," I said to him. "For saving me. For giving me him. It is the best gift ever."

EPILOGUE

SKYE

One year later.
https://www.youtube.com/watch?v=an4ySOlsUMY
-How Long Will I love You?-

𝒯he entire family was gathered in the living room of Luca's father's residence in Boston to celebrate Dante, our son's first birthday. There were balloons everywhere and a table full of gifts. We were all gathered around the long dinner table where Angelo and Sienna's son Fabio and Dante were sitting in front of a big birthday cake. The toddlers were incorrigible when they got together, but I never expected them to do what they did.

We were all singing Happy Birthday when both boys suddenly, and without any warning entered into a competition of seeing how much of the cake's icing they could lick off.

Luca lunged forward, grabbed Dante and pulled him off the destroyed cake, while Sienna rushed to pull Fabio off the cake too, but it was already too late, their faces were covered with icing. To the amusement of Luca's mother. She was terrible for letting the boys do anything they wanted.

The other day, she let Dante play with an old Roman artifact that cost many thousands of dollars. Of course, he broke it. I was horrified when I saw what he had done while I was in the bathroom, but she laughed and almost proudly pronounced that the antiquity had survived great wars and hundreds of years until it met Luca's son.

When we finished laughing and singing, Luca held Dante over the cake and he blew ineffectively at the candle until Luca surreptitiously blew it out. We all clapped and Dante looked pleased with himself. Luca put him down and he immediately ran towards Fabio. They banged into each other and fell on their butts. For a moment they looked surprised then, Dante began to cry. I picked him up.

"Aw baby," I said as I tried to comfort him. But he didn't want me. He wanted his dad. I raised my eyebrow at Luca and he came over and took Dante from me. Immediately, Dante stopped crying. Luca looked so proud and happy my heart swelled in my chest.

"If you keep looking at me like that things are not going to end well for you tonight," Luca whispered in my ear.

Even after all this time I felt my cheeks begin to flush.

Luca laughed.

His mom came over. "We need the boys for the pictures," she said and plucked Dante out of Luca's arms. We watched our son try to rip her expensive pearl chain as she carried him away.

"Do you think she is going to turn him into a spoilt brat?" I wondered.

"No. We'll set him straight when the time comes, but it's right that all grandmother's thoroughly and utterly and completely spoil their grandchildren."

His arms locked around my waist as we watched the cousins, born only two months apart. "They really are inseparable, aren't they?" Luca commented.

"Do you know what would be really funny?" I asked.

He turned to look at me. "No, what?"

"If either Sienna or me were to get pregnant and they got to add another baby to their gang."

"Don't do that," he laughed. "Sienna won't forgive you. I think she thinks Dante is a bad influence on her son."

I didn't say anything and he turned to me suddenly, his expression disbelieving. We spoke with our eyes. "Are you serious?" he asked, his voice full of hope.

I nodded. "Yup. We're having another monster."

With his arms hooked around my waist, he lifted me up into the air, and spun me around.

"What's happening?" Someone asked and I hit his shoulder gently to put me down. However, he was so happy he refused to put me down, spinning me round and round. The rest of the party passed in a daze of happiness. Every time I turned to look at Luca, he was staring at me.

"Mama," he said, "Will you take care of Dante for a while?"

"Of course. Let the boy stay the night here if you want."

Luca looked at me. "Shall we?"

As if in a trance, I nodded. It had been a long time since it was just the two of us. We even took Dante with us on our honeymoon. He didn't take me home. He took me straight to a hotel. We didn't speak as the bellboy showed us to our suite. When the bellboy left, he pressed me against the door and kissed me deeply. The effect on my brain cells was devastating.

"THANK YOU," he said. "For the colors you have brought into my life."

"You're welcome," I told him, and kissed him right back.

His hands began to work at the buttons and zips on my pant suit. Once he got rid of that, he went for the lacy bra and matching thong I wore underneath.

He pulled it away and let his gaze linger on my breasts, down to my hips and pussy, before returning to my eyes. The intensity in his gaze made my knees buckle.

He walked me backwards until the backs of my legs hit the bed. Then he flung me backwards and watched me bounce on the bed. Taking his clothes off he moved on top of me.

My eyes were on his lips, moistened and pink and oh so soft. I could almost feel his tongue in my mouth, the memory vivid from all the other times he had kissed me senseless. Our lips drew together as though pulled by invisible magnets, but he stopped just short of kissing me, preferring instead to tease me out of my mind. Frustration tied me up in knots.

We were somewhat pressed against each other, his head lowered towards mine. The tip of his nose would graze up my neck, and then across my cheek and then he would pull back to stare at me. One time his tongue slid out to lightly graze my bottom lip.

"Have I ever told you how beautiful you are?" he asked.

"It won't hurt to hear it again," I teased.

"You, Skye Messana, are the most beautiful woman in the universe," he breathed.

"For God's sake, kiss me, man," I pleaded, "before I lose my mind."

And he did...

The End

COMING SOON...

THE OTHER SIDE OF MIDNIGHT

(Unedited)

Chapter 1

Autumn

It's just struck midnight, but I've no intention of leaving the backroom of the art shop where I double as Larry's shop assistant and cleaner and going home. I sneaked back in here after dinner to finish my little painting, but I've become so totally engrossed in it, I could be here for hours more.

I know most artists prefer working in daylight. Not me. I love creating things long after everyone else is tucked up in their beds and the air is pregnant with all their dreams.

My brush, loaded with precious oil paints that take up a great proportion of my wages, glides effortlessly across the canvass, as I move it quickly and instinctively. I'm a still student with much to learn, but I have to admit my painting is starting to look really good. Maybe it's because this painting is special... important. Well, it is to me, anyway.

I take a few steps back to gaze critically at my canvass. It's a strange scene. An old, crumbling, ivy grown castle built into the side of a snow-capped mountain. A road, so narrow only a horse driven carriage could fit, leads up to the fortress. I'm tempted to add a carriage and snorting black horses onto the road, but I'm afraid I'll spoil the painting.

It's important that I don't ruin it, for I have attempted to paint this scene countless times before, but always had to give up after a few strokes. I knew I couldn't capture the vivid images in my mind, and something deep inside me demanded I replicate it exactly as it lived in my mind. I couldn't understand why I had to, I just knew I did.

I start moving forward to add more color to the castle, when I stop suddenly. The skin at the back of my neck is prickling. The silence is undisturbed, but the air is different.

My heart slams into my rib cage as I swing my head around and look through the half-open door into the small show-room beyond. All the lamps are turned off, but from the light of the streetlamps I can see right through to the rusty little bells attached to the door. I've been so lost in my work I'd not heard them ring, but I know.

Someone has entered the shop!

It can't be a customer at this time of the night, and I know it is not Larry. He would have called out. It is either one of the wild kids in town up to no good, or a robber. Dad sent me for karate classes when I was in high-school and I know some good moves. I can definitely handle any kid, and probably even a robber, if he isn't carrying a gun.

But I have an even better idea.

I reach for a stained rag on the wooden trolley next to me and hurriedly wipe off as much paint from my hands so it won't be slippery and tip toe over to the cupboard. I throw the cloth on the floor and pick up the baseball bat next to the cupboard. Gripping the smooth solid wood tightly with both hands, I start to move stealthily towards the door. I'll be damned if I'm going to be cowed by any intruder.

My heart is beating so fast, my blood roars in my ears. I'm ready to swing the bat hard at the slightest provocation... until I trip on the temporary plastic covering Larry placed over some wires he ran across the room just until the electrician came on Tuesday.

I've bumped my foot against the plastic a few times, but always managed to regain my balance. Not this time. This time the damn thing finally gets me. I feel myself pitch forward. My hands instinctively let go of the bat and fling out to try and grab on to anything that would break my fall, but I only connect with the trolley full of paint tubes and a jar of turpentine filled brushes.

Grasping for the trolley is a big mistake. Not only does it not stop my fall, it accelerates it. The trolley shoots a few feet forward, until it collides with an immovable object, then both the trolley and I crash to the concrete floor in an almighty racket.

The breath is knocked out of me as my back slams onto the floor and paint tubes bounce off me and the jar hit my chest and spills out its contents. I can feel the pungent turpentine seeping into my clothes and reaching my skin.

"Shit," I curse, as I lie there a winded, bruised, stained mess.

Then, I became aware there is someone else in the room with me. I turn my head and see a pair of highly polished black shoes a few feet away from me. My shocked eyes travel upwards and my brain notes how immaculate the creases in his black trousers are. The material is smooth, expensive. He is wearing a long black coat that looks luxuriously soft, the way good cashmere does.

A belt with a custom insignia on the buckle. A two-headed eagle or a phoenix perhaps.

My gaze travels further upwards. Flat stomach. Black turtle neck sweater. Pale skin, blonde hair, sensual mouth, strong jaw, narrow nose and...

Suddenly, my eyes locks with the stranger's, and something shifts inside of me.

I hold my breath without even realizing it. As I stare into those translucent icy blue irises full of mysteries, time stops. It isn't the way romance books describe it. The rest of the world doesn't drop away. Instead those eyes reach into my soul and whirl me away into another world. It's like a sense of déjà vu as if I've once danced in the snow with this man while a full orchestra played just for us.

I think of steel hardened by fire and feel strong sexual desire for him flower in my belly, but I just can't explain why I would feel that. He is sooooo not my type. I'm contemptuous of arrogant rich men who believe they can buy anything with their money. And there is no doubt he is such a man. I can tell by the curve of his mouth. Nothing has been denied this man. Ever.

For he is like a marvelous piece of art. His pale beauty and gold hair have a strange... darkness to them that immediately makes you wary, but is at the same time so magnetic, so fascinating, you can't look away, you want in. And all you can do is stand there, or in my case, lie there and stare stupidly.

"Are you alright?" he asks. His voice has a hypnotic quality, smooth as honey dripping from a spoon, but laced with a powerful note of authority.

I want to hear him speak again.

He takes another step towards me and bends slightly from his great height to hold a hand out to me. At the moment, I realize something else about him. He is clean. Immaculately clean. Not a blonde hair out of place, not a speck of dust on his expensive clothes, his nails are beautifully manicured, and his skin is so clear and blemish free it is as if he is one of those Gods from Mount Olympus who used to occasionally step down to earth to mate with human women.

I feel my hackles rise.

I do not like this man at all.

I know wholeheartedly, instinctively, definitely.

He is dangerous to me.

Chapter 2
Rocco

The smell of turpentine is overpowering, but I can still smell her. She wears no perfume. Just the clean, honest scent of her sweat. I don't let it show on my face, but being this close to her actually makes the blood course through my veins with a deafening force. And the mixture of lust and excitement is almost crippling. All that I thought was dead has come alive again.

I see all kinds of emotions rush across her face. Shock, confusion, surprise, sexual attraction, and finally dislike. Dislike so intense it is closer to hate. I can see she is going to run with that emotion.

Ignoring my outstretched hand, she scrambles to her feet. I retract my hand and watch her put as much space between us as the cluttered area will allow.

"How did you get in here?" she demands aggressively.

I stroll away from her. "You left the door unlocked."

"There's a CLOSED sign on the door," she snaps.

"Is there?" I ask mildly.

"Yes, there is. We're closed. If you want to buy anything you must come back tomorrow. We open again at 10.00 a.m."

She stares at me uneasily. She has convinced herself she hates my guts, but she is trembling, trembling with the same irrational lust I throbbing in my body. I understand her perfectly. Hate is easy. All the other options terrify her.

"I have to go away in the morning, but I've seen something in the shop I want. Would you be so kind as to put it away for me? Tell Larry to charge it to my account, and I'll send someone around to pick it up on Thursday."

She frowns, immediately suspicious. "Which painting is it?"

"Miranda Taking A Bath."

"Oh," she says covering her hand over her mouth. The action serves only to smear more paint on her cheek. My eyes linger on the soft curve.

She drops her hand in confusion. "Of course, I'll put it away for you."

Now that I've established I'm a valuable customer willing to buy the most expensive painting in the premises, I start to walk towards the painting on the easel. But she rushes quickly to stand in front of it and block it from my gaze.

"Ignore this," she mutters uncomfortably. "It's just something I'm working on. Uh, please come out to the shop floor with me. This area is Staff Only."

"What are you creating?" I ask softly.

"Oh… uh. It's nothing. I'm just a student… playing around."

"Let me see it," I say softly as I stare into her warm hazel eyes. They are full of golden flecks. I let her drown in my gaze until, unable to resist, she moves aside.

The raw beauty of her work takes my breath away. I take in the white squiggles that are supposed to be seagulls flying high over the abandoned castle, the pieces of rock that are falling from the castle rampart. I feel such a sense of loss I want to reach out and touch the wet paint, but I don't. I'm careful to keep my expression neutral and totally veiled, as I drink in her creation. Seconds pass. The air is so quiet I can hear her heart hammering fast and loud in her chest.

I tear my gaze away from the painting and turn to her. "I want it."

Her eyes widen with astonishment. "What?"

"I'd like to buy your painting."

She shakes her head. "It's... it's not for sale."

"I'll give you one hundred thousand for it."

This time her jaw drops with disbelief. "What?"

"Or... name your price."

The shock is replaced by white hot temper. It makes her eyes turn a luminous green. The gold flecks become sparks of bright light. Entranced by her wild beauty, I wait for her passionate outburst eagerly, but she takes a shuddering breath and takes control of herself. I bought the most expensive item in the shop, after all.

"How do I explain this? The paintings for sale are all out on the floor. This piece is not even finished."

I take my wallet out of my coat pocket, count out ten bills, and put it on the old wooden bench. "Here's a thousand. The rest when you finish it."

I can see she is hopelessly poor and cannot help being drawn to the money, but her throat moves as she swallows hard, and stop herself from saying something rude.

"The painting is not for sale," she says through gritted teeth.

"Then take it as the deposit if you change your mind."

Her eyes flash. "I won't change my mind?"

I smile slowly. "Keep it, anyway."

She folds her hands in front of her body defiantly. "Why would I want to keep your money?"

"Consider it a tip for a fabulous service rendered," I murmur.

She inhales sharply. Even in her great anger she cannot fail to pick up on the sexual tension.

"Tell Larry, Rocco Rossetti called. And don't forget to lock the front door." Then I turn and walk away from her. There is a small smile on my face. You *will* be mine, Autumn DeLaney. Nothing and no one, not even you, will stop me.

Chapter 3
Autumn

I watch his back disappear into the gloom of the shop, then I hear the sound of the rusty bells twinkle as he pulls the door open. Then the door shuts quietly. Only then, can I jerk out of the trancelike state I am in. I run to the door and lock it. Then I lean my back against it and take deep gasping breaths.

What on earth is the matter with me?

The attraction is not mental. I feel hot and bothered and there is a strange fluttering in my stomach. I place my hand on my belly as I feel the wetness seeping out of me. I cannot believe the visceral reaction my body is displaying. My whole body is craving him. I stand there in the darkness, leaning against the door, breathing in and out until my body calms down.

Then I pull away from the door and walk back to the small back room. I feel strangely restless. Frowning, I pace the floor like a caged animal. Back and forth. Back and forth. I am aware something has happened to me, but I don't know what it is. All I know is I was a different person before the stranger walked into this shop.

I glance at the money lying on the ledge. Then I walk up to it. I pick up one bill and smell it. The scent of new leather fills my nostrils. Then underneath it, another scent floats up... him. Instantly, my heart starts racing. Who is he? Why does my body react to him in this way? I jerk the money away from me and put it back on the pile. I move away from it as if it is tainted or dangerous.

I turn away from the money, walk to my painting, and look at it with new eyes. Yes, it's good. I know that, but it's not worth one hundred thousand dollars. Only a fool would pay that much for an unfinished work by a totally an unknown artist, and there is no way in hell he is one. I clasp my hands tightly together.

What does he want with me?

Who are you Rocco Rosetti?

I am no longer able to paint so I switch off the lights, lock up, and go out through the back door. I get on the purple bargain bicycle that I found on Craig's List for $35.00, and ride back to the trailer park where I live. Almost all the caravans are in darkness, except for Mirabella's. She is an old gypsy and I think she makes portions late into the night. Once or twice I've run into her selling little good luck charms in the supermarket carpark. Once she winked at me and said, "There's a Prince waiting for ya, little one." I was afraid she was going to ask me to buy one of her good luck charms so I smiled politely and hurried away.

I chain my bicycle to the metal railing outside my caravan and unlock my door. I switch on the lamp and everything feels strange. My cozy little home feels claustrophobic and cramped. I go into the bathroom and look in the mirror.

There is paint on my face and hair, and I look a terrible mess, but it is my eyes I am drawn to. I can't hardly recognize them as mine. They are very bright and my pupils are much larger than I've ever seen them. Shocked and confused, I quickly undress and shower. Under the cascade of warm water my hand strays between my thighs.

I cannot stop myself.

I close my eyes and circle my clit. I think of him, those magnetic blue eyes staring into mine as his fingers slip into me. "Autumn," that commanding voice calls, and I climax quickly and with a hoarse grunt.

I pour shampoo on my palm and rub it into my hair. Then I bow my head and let the water pour over me. How strange. The throbbing need for him is still not gone. My body remains as unfulfilled and unsatisfied as it was before I masturbated. I know doing it again will not do the trick either. The only way to quench this... this intense hunger is to allow him into my body.

Something I'm never going to do.

I switch off the tap and get into my toweling robe. I should dry my hair, but I can't be bothered. A few steps later I'm in my tiny kitchen. I have no appetite, but I boil some water and make myself a bowl of ramen noodles. Then I settle on the battered couch and quietly slurp it down.

Afterwards, I pull my crane blanket over me, and think of him. Those eyes. As if he could look right though me and into my soul. I find my hand straying once more between my legs, but I stop myself. I should go to sleep, but I know I won't be able to. Not until I get him out of my mind.

I force myself to think of my painting, of my father, my mother, my brother, my to-do list, my laundry...

Half an hour later, I still cannot stop thinking of him or repeatedly replaying our bizarre encounter in my head. Nothing made sense. His appearance in the shop. His insane offer for my painting. My reaction to him.

I grab my phone and call my best friend, Sam. We studied together, but I came here to paint and she went on to Atlanta to study something technical and to do with computers. What exactly my turpentine soaked brain has never quite been able to grasp.

As soon as she picks up I launch into my story. I tell her everything that happened at the store. For a few seconds, there is only silence from her side.

"Sam?" I call.

"Yeah, yeah, I'm here. I'm just thinking." Sam is the opposite of me. She doesn't rush in where angels fear to tread. She thinks about her every move carefully.

"Okay, have you finished thinking?"

"Maybe you're a better artist than you think," she says.

Sam is a total sweetheart, but I can't help rolling my eyes at her naivety. "Oh please. He offered a hundred thousand bucks for a painting that is not even finished yet."

She laughs. "Perhaps he has so much money he can afford to throw lots of it at anything he fancies." She pauses, then adds dramatically. "Or maybe you're what he fancies."

"What man do you know offers a hundred thousand to sleep with a paint-splattered woman?"

"Maybe he's kinky?"

"Can you please be serious?"

"I am being serious. If I was a man with lots of money, I'd pay that for you."

"Thanks Sam. I feel incredibly valued right now, but can we please step back into the real world for a minute."

She laughs. "Fine. Have it your way. Personally, I think very rich people are mad. Who knows? Maybe, he really liked your painting, but how could he possibly hang it up next to his Van Gogh and Monet if it was only a thousand dollars. His friends would laugh over their caviar and cocaine when they came over to dinner. This way he can boast that clever him found this unknown artist in a tiny little artist town who is really hot right now and he found her first."

"Hmmm... I wonder if you are in the wrong career path. Don't you think you'd do better as a novelist?"

"Well, if I was a novelist, I would say, be careful. He sounds like a dark one."

"What's that supposed to mean?"

"Just the vibes I get from you. I get the feeling he's disturbed you, and not just about the money. There's something else bothering you, isn't there?"

"Yes," I admitted. "I can't get him out of my mind and I really, really, really want to go to bed with him, but at the same time I'm scared to. There is an air of danger about him, something unknowable about him."

"When you say unknowable, I'm hoping you don't mean rapist/serial killer unknowable."

"No, no, nothing like that. He is too beautiful, mysterious, and magnetic. I can't imagine a woman saying no to him."

"Here's what I would do if I was you. When you see Larry tomorrow ask him all about this guy. Get all the details. If he is legit and he asks you to then go out with him to a very public place. I'll call you while you're out and you can loudly say you're having dinner with him. That way he will understand that if anything happens to you, the police will be on to him immediately. If he turns out to be dodgy in anyway at all just walk away."

My stomach churns as I say the words. "No, I won't go out with him."

"Why not?"

"I cannot explain it in words, but there is something about him that scares me. That I could fall too deep and never recover."

"Wow! I've never heard you talk like this before."

"I've never felt this way before."

"I'm the one who is more reserved and cautious of the two of us, but you know what. If such a man appeared in my life, I would go for it. I would risk a broken heart because otherwise I would spend the rest of my life thinking what if..."

Preorder the book here:
The Other Side Of Midnight

ACKNOWLEDGMENTS

ABOUT THE AUTHOR

Thank you so much for reading my book. Might you be
thinking of leaving a review? :-)
Please do it here:

Beauty & The Beast

Please click on this link to receive news of my latest releases
and great giveaways.
http://bit.ly/10e9WdE

and remember
I **LOVE** hearing from readers so by all means come and say
hello here:

ALSO BY GEORGIA LE CARRE

Owned

42 Days

Besotted

Seduce Me

Love's Sacrifice

Masquerade

Pretty Wicked (novella)

Disfigured Love

Hypnotized

Crystal Jake 1,2&3

Sexy Beast

Wounded Beast

Beautiful Beast

Dirty Aristocrat

You Don't Own Me 1 & 2

You Don't Know Me

Blind Reader Wanted

Redemption

The Heir

Blackmailed By The Beast

Submitting To The Billionaire

The Bad Boy Wants Me

Nanny & The Beast

His Frozen Heart